Sweeper

Paul Cockburn

Virgin

Many thanks to CeGe for all the US research.
Of course, if anyone complains, that means
it's her fault.

First published in Great Britain in 1996 by
Virgin Books
an imprint of Virgin Publishing Ltd
332 Ladbroke Grove
London W10 5AH

A catalogue record for this book is available from the
British Library.

ISBN 0 7535 0056 6

Typeset by Galleon Typesetting, Ipswich
Printed and bound by
BPC Paperbacks Ltd, Aylesbury

One

'I don't want to die; I don't want to die!!!'

The phrase was getting on Chris's nerves. None of us do, he thought to himself, but if you don't shut up, your odds of surviving are going to be zero.

He opened his eyes. The seatbelt light was still on, as it had been since their plane wandered into the storm. Chris took a long, hard look to his right, where the large boy with the sweaty face and the baby moustache that Chris could count the hairs in was clutching his hand luggage in his lap. He had his eyes closed and was rocking backwards and forwards while he repeated his prayer over and over again.

'I don't want to die; I don't want to die!!!'

Chris was about to dig his elbow into the guy's ribs when the plane lurched again. For a moment, Chris felt quite weightless, but then the seat came up and whacked him in the behind like a good, solid boot. Several of the other passengers were screaming.

This did not look good.

One of the cabin crew walked past, her face betraying the fact that she wasn't happy either. This didn't make Chris feel any more comfortable. Then the attendant leant forward and rested her hand on the fat boy's wrist.

'It'll be all right, son,' she said.

Amazingly, that actually silenced him (Chris wanted to give the woman a medal). The boy nodded his head at her furiously, mopped his brow with a handkerchief and rested his head back against the seat. Although he still gripped his fists tighter each time the plane lurched, he was no longer repeating the same prayer and his whimpering was much quieter.

Now all Chris had to cope with was the sound of the plane shuddering and shaking.

1

Chris took a look out of the window. He was seated just over the rear edge of the left wing (was that port or starboard? – he couldn't remember). The DC10's engines were visible underneath. They looked like they were shaking on their mountings, and Chris could see the wings bending as the aircraft fought the fierce winds outside. At the moment, the aircraft was in a patch of clear sky, but the windows were streaked with rain, and they were surrounded by rolling black clouds.

In the distance Chris could see lightning.

Perhaps looking through the window wasn't such a hot idea. Chris looked around the cabin. Several passengers were holding their sick bags, their valuables or each other. The rest of his neighbour's family were just across the aisle, each one telling all the others at high volume that they should keep quiet. The whole family was as well proportioned as the son, and every one of them looked sick with fear. Unkindly, Chris imagined the plane would fly a lot better if they weren't aboard.

As if to punish him for being so mean, the plane bucked, again, as if it had run into something solid. The clouds outside did look rather tough . . .

'I can't believe this is happening,' the fat boy whispered. Chris looked up, but the guy was talking to himself, not to anyone else. 'My stars said this was a good day for travelling!' Chris smirked, hiding it behind his hand. The fat boy didn't notice, he just kept whispering to himself. 'I've got my whole life in front of me,' he said. That was almost the final straw as far as Chris was concerned.

Look, he thought, rehearsing the speech in his mind. You think you've got problems? This is only the second time I've flown in my life. I'm zillions of miles from home, on my own. My dad will be back in England, eating dinner, with no idea that my plane is about to lose its wings somewhere over the USA. This was supposed to be the best summer holiday of my life; a free trip to America, playing in a soccer exchange for a week and then flying over to meet a mate in San Francisco. Two weeks ago, I took part in a trial at Oldcester United and won a place in their youth team. In two terms' time, I start at the first ever soccer school in the UK, a specially built academy of excellence for young players. If anyone has their whole life in front of them, it's me.

2

No, too long, he decided.

'Hey, keep calm will you,' he said, this time out loud. 'We're not going to crash.' That was better.

The boy was utterly amazed to be spoken to like that. He looked at Chris for the first time since he had levered himself into his seat just before take-off. Other than ask when the in-flight meal was served, the kid hadn't said a word to Chris all flight.

'Excuse me?' he said, in a high-pitched wail. 'Aren't you frightened?'

'The only thing that's freaking me out is you,' said Chris. It was only when he said it that he realised how true that was. He actually wasn't that frightened by the way the plane was shaking and ducking and diving. It was less frantic than some of the rides at Alton Towers (even if the special effects out of the window were better).

Chris just didn't feel like dying, not today. There was too much going on; too much to do.

The aircraft lurched again. The fat boy whimpered.

If I died now, Chris thought, would I come back as a ghost? The idea made him giggle. After some of the things that had happened to him recently, Chris wasn't sure if he believed in ghosts or not. But if they did exist, and if they came back to wander the earth because of something they hadn't finished, Chris knew what his thing would be.

Football.

To say that Chris Stephens was crazy about football was an understatement. Except for a few days a year when he was forced to pay attention to school work, family visits or some other activity, Chris lived and breathed football. Nothing else in his life came close to being that important.

He'd been bitten by the bug going to see his local team, Oldcester United, in a close-fought FA Cup game. It was a few years before the Premier League was started, and Oldcester were languishing in the old Third Division, entertaining Cambridge Utd and Fulham. Chris had never been bothered about going, but his father was offered two tickets for the third round of the Cup, on a cold, windy January afternoon. Oldcester had drawn First Division strugglers

Coventry. United went 2–0 down quickly, then come back to go level with a stunning free kick and a desperate, scrambled goal.

In the last few minutes, Oldcester had laid siege to City's goal. It was the most exciting thing Chris had ever seen. There were eight or nine goalmouth scrambles, and one scorching volley was headed off the line by a defender who was knocked into the back of the net as a result. It was unbearably exciting. It was brilliant.

By the following season, Chris and his father were season ticket holders, going to every home game and as many away games as work, school and transport expenses allowed. It hadn't mattered that Coventry had smashed United 4–1 in the replay a week after that magical first game, or that promotion had been missed by two points. Chris had caught the Oldcester United disease, and there was no cure.

The symptoms were the same for all United followers. Sometimes, things went brilliantly. United won the Autoglass Trophy not long after Chris started going, then they won promotion twice to get themselves into the top flight. Chris had a lingering memory of the day United beat Liverpool 3–0 at Star Park in their first season at the top.

More usually, though, supporting Oldcester meant agonising last-minute defeats by Wimbledon, Swindon, Bolton and Norwich. Not to mention early-season humiliation by lower division outfits in the Coca-Cola Cup. But that was the price you paid to be an Oldcester supporter, and it was worth it just for those rare days when the reds and blues swept away a much more glamorous team without running short of breath.

In addition to watching football, Chris was also afflicted with an even worse illness – he loved playing it. There was no one day when it all began, nor could Chris remember kicking a ball around from the first day he could walk. Sometime around his sixth or seventh birthday, though, Chris had started playing football almost as much as he talked about football.

And Chris talked about football all the time, even back then.

Over the next few years, everyone around Chris noticed that he was actually pretty good at it. He was strong, quick for his age, and he could play off either foot with equal skill and power. He got picked for his junior school team.

Shortly after that, mucking around with his father in the garden, Chris learnt to head a ball. He also discovered that although going in goal and tackling were fun, what he liked best was scoring goals. He tried to change position in the school team, but they kept him in defence.

When Chris went up to Spirebrook Comprehensive, it was obvious that he was going to walk into the school team. But in which position? Chris told nobody about playing as a defender. When Mr Lea, the PE teacher, was working out who to play where, Chris formed a partnership with Nicky Fiorentini, a quicksilver winger with an explosive temperament and bucketloads of skill.

The two together were lethal, destroying defences in the Schools league. They were a natural partnership. It was quite spooky watching how Chris would time his run into the box, angling to find space, and how Nicky would then deliver a perfect cross for Chris to slot away. They didn't need to look sometimes. It was instinctive, like being able to see inside the other guy's head.

Just a couple of weeks before, that partnership had been lifted to a new, higher level. Chris and Nicky had both been accepted on to the Oldcester United youth scheme, something they had spent years dreaming about and planning for. When United opened their brand new, state-of-the-art School of Excellence, Chris and Nicky were going to be in poll position, ready to take their places in the first scheme of its kind the UK had ever seen. A school for gifted players.

And from there, what next? A contract with United? A first team place? Premierships, FA Cups, European glory? International honours? Lifting the World Cup?

Who knew? It might all come true, or it might all come to nothing. Anything could be hidden round the corner, but – for now – he was still firmly on the road towards becoming a professional footballer for Oldcester United. He could still dream of running out on to Star Park's green pitch, dressed in red and blue, with thousands of fans applauding his every move.

A plane crash would definitely put the dampeners on that dream.

It just couldn't happen.

'You've got some mouth on you, you know?' the fat boy said.

Chris came back from his daydream, and realised that the plane was still bobbing up and down inside the aircraft. Lightning flashed somewhere close by outside. Occasionally, the lights in the aeroplane flickered, which wasn't good for anyone's peace of mind.

'Come again?' he asked.

'You do realise what's happening, don't you?' the lad went on, mopping at his sweaty face. 'We're five miles up in the air, in the middle of a storm. Any minute now, the wings could fall off or –'

Chris wasn't prepared to listen to any of the other possibilities. 'You worry too much,' he said. 'I bet planes fly through worse than this all the time. The pilot knows what he's doing. Try thinking of something else other than crashing and you'll feel a lot better.'

The fat boy looked at Chris as if the Englishman was green skinned. He leant closer, looking into Chris's eyes. All Chris could focus on was that poor excuse for a moustache above his mouth. It looked like a caterpillar.

'You're Australian, right?'

'What? No – I'm English.'

'Yeah? So this is all stiff upper lip, tally-ho stuff to you, right? Well, this isn't the Blitz or the Battle of Britain, pal, this is the USA – and we don't mind showing a little emotion when we're about to meet our maker.'

Chris wasn't sure he understood what point the fat boy was trying to make. Did people die differently in different countries?

Long before he could have thought of anything to say himself, Chris heard the fat boy speak again. 'You don't sound like an Englishman,' he whimpered.

'What are we supposed to sound like?'

The boy laughed once. 'Well, I thought you all sounded like this – "I say, chaps, jolly good show, let's shoot some foxes." ' Chris winced at the attempted upper-class accent. 'Except for cockneys, of course, they all talk like Michael Caine, right? The actor?' Chris knew who Michael Caine was. 'Like this – "Strike a light, guv'nor. Apples and pears. Dog and toad." '

Chris looked past his neighbour, hoping that no-one else was listening. Unfortunately, several other passengers were using the conversation to distract themselves from the bumpy ride. All of his neighbour's family were paying very close attention.

'That's the worst Michael Caine impression I've ever heard,' said Chris, honestly. He was an expert. There was a kid in his class called Glyn who did nothing but Michael Caine imper-sonations. Even when he tried to do someone else, it sounded like Michael Caine. Chris told this to the fat boy, who laughed with a bit more feeling than before.

'So where do you come from?' he asked.

'Oldcester. It's kind of in the middle.'

'Near Scotland?'

Chris decided against a geography lesson at this point. 'Right next door,' he agreed.

'So, do you play golf?' the guy asked.

'No, football.' Then he remembered where he was and who he was talking to. 'Soccer,' he corrected himself.

'You play soccer?' said the boy. 'It's really taking off here in the States, you know, with kids. Of course, they grow out of it by the time they go to college.' He stopped, as if he'd realised what he'd just said, and how Chris might be offended. 'It's different in England, I guess.'

'Yeah, we never grow up,' admitted Chris.

His neighbour laughed, his face slowly recovering a little colour.

'My dad took me to one of the games when we had the World Cup here in '94,' he said. 'Ireland vs Norway.'

The scoreline flashed into Chris's mind. 'Nil-nil. Norway packed ten men in defence. They didn't even leave their own half when the final whistle blew. You couldn't have been to a worse game in that tournament.'

'The final was pretty tedious, too,' the boy agreed, adding that he had watched it on TV. 'I mean, don't you guys ever get bored of all those nil-nil ties?'

Chris recalled some of the better games he had seen in that tournament. Brazil vs Holland in the quarter-final (come to

7

that, just about any of the quarter-finals); Germany vs Belgium in the round before. Plenty of goals.

'Some one-nil or nil-nil results are the most exciting games,' he said instead. 'What about the USA against Brazil in the second round? You guys gave them a hell of a scare, and they went on to win the World Cup.'

That was the kind of thing Americans liked to hear, Chris knew.

'Ask him what he was doing in New Jersey,' asked the boy's mother from across the aisle. Perhaps she was having trouble with the language. Chris saved his neighbour the trouble of repeating the request.

'The team I play for –' Used to play for, he corrected himself in his mind, but he decided they didn't need to know that '– was on an exchange trip with a school from Newark.'

'That's where we live!' the boy said, grinning. Chris didn't remark that he might have guessed they had some connection with the area, having just flown out of the airport, but he decided against it. 'Do you know Mount Graham High School?' he asked.

The boy's face twisted unpleasantly. 'That's some kind of posh, rich man's school, isn't it? I think I heard of it.'

Chris started to think that telling the boy about the exchange visit wasn't going to be such a good idea. Chris had quickly discovered that Mount Graham wasn't a typical New Jersey school. Most of the kids Chris played against thought Mount Graham's students were all snobs. His neighbour obviously felt the same.

Just as he was searching for an alternative subject to talk about, the aircraft shuddered even more violently than before. His neighbour began to whimper.

Chris took a look out of the window. They were actually flying through the cloud now, so everything was pitch black beyond the small area of light cast by the aircraft's lights. He could hear the engines straining as they struggled to keep the aircraft on course in the teeth of a violent head wind.

For the first time, Chris felt a small twinge of fear in his stomach.

The aircraft took another heavy swat, and he felt that twinge jump into his throat. His heart was beating fast, and he sensed that he had become lighter, as if the plane was falling. It had slid sideways a little too, making Chris lean closer to his neighbour. The boy was back to being as pale as a sheet, his mouth wide as if he was practising to break the world screaming record. Plenty of other people made a contest out of it as the lights went out again. Everyone knew the aircraft was dropping rapidly.

How soon would they hit the ground, Chris wondered?

The plane seemed to fall for several minutes, but perhaps it was only seconds. Suddenly the aircraft levelled out. Chris was dumped back into the depths of his seat. His travelling companion wasn't thrown about quite so much, but then he was probably wedged tight.

'OK,' came a voice over the intercom. It was the pilot, sounding calm and laid back. Chris had seen his picture in the in-flight magazine – he looked about sixteen, with softly tanned skin, blond hair and gleaming white teeth. It had come as no surprise to Chris to read that he was from California.

'I think we've had enough excitement for one trip. The weather doesn't get any better than this further west, so we're going to divert this flight to the nearest available airport and set down there for a spell until it clears. It's still going to be a bit bumpy for a while, but I think we'll be on the ground in less than thirty minutes.'

As opposed to thirty seconds. It was an improvement as far as Chris was concerned.

The cabin staff were quickly bombarded with questions about what this meant. They didn't have much of an idea where the plane might land, but suggested it might be Chicago. Everyone would be put up in a hotel overnight and continue their journey to the west coast when the weather cleared up.

Chris sighed. How long would that take?

Before he could get round to feeling too sorry for himself, he heard the large boy whining again. Chris turned to look at him.

'What now?' he snapped.

'I hate landings.'

Chris was on the verge of pointing out that, in that case, perhaps he should avoid the taking off part of flying as well, but then he was struck by a wave of sympathy. He'd been pretty frightened himself for a while.

'Listen, you know you said you don't like Mount Graham High? Well, I can tell you a story that you might like. It's to do with the exchange trip I was on. You see, the reason Mount Graham were able to run the swap was because they won a state soccer tournament in New Jersey last summer . . .'

TWO

The Parchmont Panthers' left back was keeping his distance, having been made to look pretty stupid by Chris once before. Their midfield players were getting tired, and were slow coming back to support the defence. That left a huge, wide space for Chris to run into as he saw Polly slip the ball to Jazz, and the Asian midfielder look around for options up front. Seeing Chris tracking across in front of him, Jazz knocked the ball forward and ran right, looking for a possible return.

The switch left the defence wondering just who was going where. The central defenders decided they'd stick close to Rory Blackstone, whose solid, big-hearted presence up front was drawing them in like magnets. That left Chris and Jazz one on one against the two full backs, having switched so that the Americans were facing new threats racing towards them.

Chris turned mid-run, meeting Jazz's pass and feeding it back across the pitch for his team mate to pick up. Jazz played it back to Stamp, who hit it first time beyond the left back. After an afternoon of chasing Chris's elusive shadow around, the full back was blown. Jazz skipped past him, collected the pass and made for the goal-line. He had to cut back on to his left foot before he could make the cross, but that only increased the uncertainty in central defence. The ball swung in, looping slowly towards the near post.

The Americans hated near-post crosses; that much had been obvious earlier. This time two defenders and the keeper raced to intercept the ball, only Rory got there first, nicking the ball off the corner of his brow. At the far post, Chris was slowing to a walk when the ball arrived. He tapped the chance into the empty net while the defenders and keeper looked around at each other wondering who was to blame.

Several of those watching the game winced. It was obvious that the Parchmont Panthers, said to be one of the best school teams in the state of New Jersey, couldn't begin to live with their English opponents.

There was a polite ripple of applause from parents, students and teachers as Chris ran back to the halfway line. A tall girl working the scoreboard spent the next ten minutes trying to find an eight among the metal tags in her bag.

Waiting for the weary defenders to pick the ball out of the net, Rory got chatting with his opposite number on the American team, an Irish-American named Sean O'Flynn.

'Keep this up and the whole state of New Jersey will give up the game for good,' O'Flynn said, grinning. He clearly wasn't suffering quite as badly as his colleagues.

'We've been lucky,' said Rory, worried in case their opponents were starting to think Riverside were rubbing it in. 'It was only two-nil until five minutes before half-time.'

'And five-nil not three minutes after it. I've been warning this lot all this semester that having you lot in the tournament would be a big shock.'

Chris was surprised himself. When Mount Graham had visited Britain, he'd been impressed by their fitness and determination, and by the speed with which they had responded to the excellent coaching at Oldcester United. However, the general standard in this tournament had been awful.

Over the seven days of their stay, the Colts had a competitive match every day after the first. The first four days had seen them compete in a round robin group against schools and colleges all over New Jersey. They'd travelled a lot, but at least they had the mornings free to explore different places. They had managed to lose the first game, but decided this was just because of a little jet lag. They had then won 2–0, 4–1 and 6–2 in their remaining games, winning the group.

The last game had been against a team from Jersey City, and they had spent the morning touring New York, which was just over the Hudson River. It was a day to remember.

Starting on the Friday, they pitched up at Mount Graham High, who were hosting the finals of the tournament on Friday, Saturday and Sunday. This too was a round robin competition, against the winners of the other preliminary groups and Mount Graham, as defending champions and hosts.

On Friday, the Colts had thumped a team from Atlantic City. That had been quite a match. The Americans had come on to the pitch while a set of speakers had been blaring out Bruce Springsteen's 'Born In The USA'. Chris was sure that the Americans had come into the game a little too pumped up. Aided by an amazing start in which their opponents had given away two penalties in the first five minutes, the Colts had won 5–1.

Now they were 8–0 up against Parchmont, who had driven upstate from a place called New Brunswick. They weren't anywhere near as bad a team as an 8–0 scoreline suggested, but they were being outclassed on the day. People were wondering how Mount Graham had been able to come second in the mini-tournament in which they had played in the UK. On the other hand, other teams from Europe who had been invited to the USA in previous years had never done so well.

Chris listened as O'Flynn put it down to the new formation the Colts were trying out. 'That's the most attacking line-up I think we've ever faced,' he said. 'Three full backs, one of them attacking as a sweeper, then five men across midfield. You guys are controlling the park.'

O'Flynn had a good eye – that was just the formation the Colts' manager, Iain Walsh, had invented for this tour.

'We don't normally play like this,' Rory was confessing to O'Flynn. They were standing side by side, looking upfield towards the Americans' goal, more like team mates than opponents.

'It's working, though,' O'Flynn replied. 'And our lads are playing right into your hands. You've run all of us ragged – look at the state of us! The lads are fit enough, but they run when they should pass and they wind up chasing after disasters because they don't have any positional sense. It's a lack of experience.'

That seemed about right to Chris as well. However, he knew too that the Colts were playing out of their skins. They would have beaten experienced teams from Italy and Holland just as easily.

Exactly why this was, Chris didn't know. But there was one factor giving them a desire to perform this well. The game against Mount Graham on Sunday would be the last time the Riverside Colts played together.

Chris had not been the only one to get through the trials OK. Their captain, Zak, Rory and Russell Jones, the goalkeeper, had all been selected. Zak would have been moving up into the Colts' senior squad after the summer anyway, as would Stamp and Tollie. That meant half the side were playing their last game as a unit.

They were a good, tight team. It was well known in Oldcester youth football that the Colts had been formed with Oldcester United's blessing to provide an extra outlet for talented players, those who weren't quite ready for the full United youth team. They had an excellent coach in Iain Walsh, who played for Riverside's senior team, plus occasional tuition from Sean Priest, the youth development manager at United.

They'd won the District League handsomely. Chris had scored a lot of goals, and several others had played some great football. If it was all coming to an end, they were determined to go out on a final, winning note.

'You could try playing with a sweeper,' Rory was advising O'Flynn. 'It'd give your defence that little bit of security, and if you find someone who can play a few passes, it's a grand attacking platform as well. Your wing backs can push up when the chance arrives and your midfield gets more support.'

'What do we do about someone like him?' O'Flynn asked, with a nod in Chris's direction.

'Is there not an Indian witch doctor you could ask to put a spell on him?' asked Rory. The two exiled Irish lads laughed at this idea.

Later on, Chris would often wonder if someone hadn't been listening.

After the semi-final, there had been an unexpected treat for the Colts. A van arrived, bringing a camera crew, a beady-eyed man with a loud voice, a woman with a clipboard and three others. The beady-eyed man started braying directions to his staff while the three men wandered over towards the Colts, looking around in a slightly dazed and confused manner.

'Strewth . . .' gasped Zak. 'That's . . .'

No-one dared say the names in case they broke the spell. But there they were, large as life. Chris had no idea what possible link could have brought Alan Shearer, John Motson and Uri Geller to this school playing field in the USA, but there they were – walking towards him.

'Hi!' said Shearer. 'Are you the team from England?'

They might just as well have been from Mars for all the sense they made when they mumbled their replies. Chris managed to get his brain into gear first.

'We're from Oldcester. It's an exchange trip . . .'

'So I hear,' the Blackburn and England striker said. 'Doing pretty well, too, right?'

Chris didn't like to brag, but he was prepared to make an exception in this case. He told the trio about the game they had just played.

'Quite remarkable!' commented Motty, in a way that suggested he was about to hand over to Trevor Brooking.

'We're over here shooting a video,' Shearer explained. 'It's to encourage more American kids to take up the game. It's all Uri's idea.'

Chris remembered that the magician had some kind of connection with Reading. There'd been a TV programme about it.

'So, what, you want us to be in this video?' asked Zak.

'Good heavens, no!' cried Geller. 'If they see you thrashing their countrymen like this, no American kid will ever want to take up the game.'

'We were going to film Mount Graham,' Shearer went on. 'But I think there's some kind of problem.'

'So what will you do?' asked Chris.

'Oh, it's no big deal,' the (other) striker replied. 'We're going all over the country. We'll just do some more somewhere else, I guess. We were supposed to fly out of here on Tuesday; maybe they'll bring that forward.'

'We're leaving after the final . . .' sighed Jazz.

'Oh, well, never mind. Good luck anyway,' said Shearer. The loud-voiced director was calling them back. 'Maybe we'll get to see you play another time.'

'So, what happened in the final game?' asked the fat boy.

Chris smiled. He had been enjoying remembering that brief encounter with one of his idols. He was only sorry that he'd forgotten to ask Alan if he'd think about a transfer to United.

He wondered where the strange threesome were now. Oh well.

Chris returned to the real world. He had promised his fellow passenger a good end to the story, and wasn't about to let him down.

'Mount Graham cried off. Said the team had come down with food poisoning.'

'They never even played?' the boy asked, utterly amazed.

'No,' said Chris with a single shake of his head.

'That's disgraceful!'

Plenty of other people had thought so at the time, not least Mason Williams, the Americans' captain. He had the unpleasant job of informing his house guest and opposite number, Zak, that Mount Graham couldn't field a team for the Sunday game and would have to scratch. Zak had the impression that Williams would have fielded a team of mums and babies rather than pull out, but it wasn't his call.

'They did have eight players sick in bed,' Chris explained, 'and another three or four who were pretty poorly.' What else could Mount Graham's principal have done? At the same time, there was the feeling that Benford Carter, who Chris had met when he brought the American team to the UK, had decided not to put out a string of second-team players to get slaughtered by the Brits.

'It's un-American,' his neighbour announced, his brow in a deep frown and his lip curling. Chris bit his lip before he could remark that it was un-British, un-Swahili and un-Mongolian yak-herder too. He knew what his travelling companion meant. 'I'd have played!' the boy added, and Chris had to bite his lip even harder. Even so, the mental picture of this guy thundering up the field wouldn't go away easily.

'So, what happened?' the boy asked, after a minute of working through the situation in his head. 'You Brits won the tournament, right? What did they do about the rest of it?'

'Well,' Chris replied, 'there was a bit of a stink about it.' The winners of the competition won a cash prize — money which Mount Graham had used after their win the year before to finance the exchange. The rules of the competition had been designed to ensure that the overseas guests couldn't win the cash, even though they took the trophy. Stamp and Tollie had been outraged. They had planned to buy stereo equipment with their share of the winnings.

The rules also stated that the cash part of the prize couldn't be won by the host team either – a rule designed to stop the same team winning two years in a row. Parchmont and the Atlantic City team had put in a complaint saying that Mount Graham shouldn't even be placed second in the championship table. The row was still blazing when the Colts left Mount Graham to head for Newark Airport.

There had been talk of getting lawyers involved. As they boarded the bus which would take them to catch their plane, the Colts had watched their hosts and the coaches and players from the other two teams still arguing about just who should have the honour of being the highest-placed American team.

It had been a strange way to say goodbye.

But, Chris was starting to realise, that was how things were in the USA – strange. Apparently, the rivalry between Mount Graham and Parchmont went back a long way. Chris could understand that – back home, Spirebrook Comprehensive had a similar feud running with the morons at Blackmoor. No-one knew how it started – it was a sure bet that anyone who had been around at either school when it did was now long gone – but there were plenty of new rows to fan the flames. Chris had been involved in a few run-ins with the guys from the other school himself.

The key difference between what he saw in the UK and what he saw in the USA, though, was the attitude of the teachers. After the last rumble with Blackmoor, the guilty parties on the Spirebrook side had been lectured for an hour by 'Andy' Cole, the head teacher, and several other teachers had made Chris and his mates suffer for some time after. Chris remembered some of the homework assignments they had been set with a shiver of horror.

The American teachers, on the other hand, seemed to be as much a part of the grudge as the students. Benford Carter had always appeared to Chris to be a nervous, edgy little man. Put nose to nose in a shouting match with the principal of Parchmont, though, he was a wild tiger. The pair of them had been about ready to take off their coats and set about each other as the coach left.

Definitely a strange way to say goodbye!

For Chris, there was the added strangeness of knowing that, although he was travelling to the airport with the rest of the team, he wasn't flying back with them. They had an 8.30pm flight back to Heathrow. Chris had a 9.15pm plane to San Francisco. The others had reached the end of their trip – but Chris had a week with his mate Jace Goodman to look forward to.

Dropping him off in the departure lounge used for domestic flights, Walsh had asked Chris to keep out of trouble in the 45 minutes between the two flights. After all, he would be left alone in a busy international airport for all that time – who knew how much trouble he could get into?

Chris had promised to avoid being abducted, to ignore any terrorist hijackers and to leave defusing any atomic bombs to the experts. That covered most of the possibilities. He had a book, a few Marvel comics he had bought in a store in New York and an American soccer magazine. That should keep him occupied.

Meanwhile, outside, the weather had been growing steadily wilder, with strong winds coming from the west. Walsh had joked about how the Colts' plane would get blown quickly back across the Atlantic, while Chris would be stuck in the same place for hours.

Sitting in the plane during a howling storm, it didn't seem like a very good joke any more.

Three

-------- ⚽ --------

'Well, that wasn't so bad, was it?' asked the captain. Chris barely heard him over the cheering of the other passengers. The fat boy at his side had jumped to his feet and was hugging his mother. Chris found himself terrified at the prospect that his fellow flyer might want to hug him too.

'We've set down at Indianapolis International Airport,' the captain was continuing. 'We'll be arriving at the terminal in a few minutes. When you leave the plane, you'll be met by airline representatives, who are arranging to bus you to hotels in the city. It looks like the weather will start clearing some time tomorrow, so get a good night's sleep and we'll continue your journey in the morning.'

Chris looked at his watch. It was just after midnight. Even so, he felt wide awake. It was hard to imagine being able to sleep much.

'On behalf of Delta Airlines, I'd like to apologise for the problems with your flight . . .'

No-one was listening to the pilot any more. Thirty seconds ago, he'd been the hero who had brought them safely down to earth after the white-knuckle ride they had endured in the air. Right now, all everyone wanted to do was to get off the plane and as far away from flying as they could.

Chris didn't feel in such a rush. Besides, being in a window seat and separated from the exits by the largest family (pound for pound) in the universe, he decided he wasn't going to be getting off in a hurry.

He looked out of the window at the lights of the terminal building and the other aircraft parked along from theirs. Rain was lashing down by the bucketload, and scraps of paper and other pieces of litter were being chased across the concrete by the gusting wind.

He took the time to check the map in the in-flight magazine, trying to work out where he was. He found Indianapolis fairly quickly, pretty well on a straight line between New York and San Francisco. Chicago was off to the north with the Great Lakes above, St Louis was to the west, Cincinnati to the east, and there were other NFL teams dotted around pretty close by. Then Chris found the scale, and realised that Chicago was about 150 miles away. The flight had covered perhaps 700 of the 2500 miles the journey was supposed to take.

So, after all the excitement of their aborted flight, they were only a third of the way across America. Chris knew now they would be dragged across to a hotel, having probably spent several hours at the airport waiting for things to get sorted out. Then tomorrow, they would get to start the process all over again.

Chris sighed, and watched the rain pouring down outside.

Welcome to Indianapolis.

The airline almost had a riot on its hands when a smart-suited young woman from their office at the airport suggested that the passengers spend an hour or so in baggage claim collecting their luggage. It was the middle of the night and no-one was in the mood to watch for suitcases. They wanted to get to the hotel and get some sleep; some were worried about people who were waiting for the plane in San Francisco.

The woman said full information on the delay was being relayed to the west coast.

Her second attempt to get on to the Christmas card lists of the 300 or so passengers of Delta Flight 715 was to suggest that they went without their luggage altogether, leaving it on the plane. There were protests all over again. No-one wanted to climb back into the same clothes tomorrow.

A sharp-faced man with a nasty tone in his voice said he was some kind of important politician in California, after which the woman promised to get their cases delivered to the hotels where they were staying by first thing in the morning.

Chris watched the excitement from the safety of the sidelines. The events of the day were catching up with him, and he really just wanted to get some sleep. Those people who thought a 50-minute row at the airport was helping to get things sorted were fooling themselves . . .

Finally, the smart young woman led the weary passengers to a fleet of buses. The airline had found them beds for the night in about six different hotels and motels. She started reading names from long lists, shuffling pieces of paper, trying to cope with relatives who had been separated and various other demands from her rebellious passengers.

After about two more hours, Chris was finally on a bus, watching as it drew away from the main building of the airport and headed towards the city.

He had never been so tired in all his life. Within seconds, his head was nodding and he was drifting off to sleep.

About half a second later, or so it seemed, he was awake again. Now that they were out from the shelter of the airport, the weather outside was rattling against the windows like a hail of stones. Chris blinked as he looked out into the neon-lit night, watching rain falling in almost continuous sheets. To make it worse, the wind was buffeting the bus, wailing like a ghost. If it hadn't been so warm, Chris would have believed he was at home in November, not in the middle of the USA in July.

He wondered how far they would have to travel. They were on a road called Executive Drive, which seemed lined with swank hotels. The idea of a night in one of those appealed to Chris, but the bus didn't slow down at all. In fact, it gathered speed as it approached a highway.

The signs suggested they were actually heading for the city itself, eight miles distant. Now that the coach had changed direction, the rain wasn't lashing on the window at Chris's side, so he decided he might as well try and get whatever sleep he could.

At the second attempt, he snatched a luxurious five seconds of sleep before the coach rocked as if it had struck a small mountain. Chris jolted upright. What had caused the bus to shake like that?

Thump! The coach lurched again. There was no sign of any explosions or landslides and the driver was steering them on through the night, seemingly unconcerned. Chris looked out of the window, wondering if they were on some kind of dirt track, but no, it was a main highway. Three lanes of traffic each way – just like the M1.

'I'd forgotten how bad the roads were in Indiana,' he heard a voice up front somewhere comment The woman's neighbour agreed.

'Worse than New York.'

'Have you ever been to Ohio?' the woman asked. 'Now that's what I call bad roads.'

Chris turned away from the discussion, remembering that there were 50 states in the USA. The woman probably knew how bad the highways were in at least 30 of them.

Still, at least he knew what was going on. The bumpy ride was being caused by the highway! He stared down at the surface of the lane below his window. It was as pitted and ridged as the surface of the moon.

Crazy. Americans drove just about everywhere, but their roads were diabolical. Chris wondered why he hadn't noticed it while the Colts had been travelling round New Jersey. It was probably because he'd never tried sleeping on the highway before.

He decided he might as well wait until they got to the hotel. The coach was eating up the miles to the city centre How far could it be?

There wasn't much to see outside. The dark clouds hovered overhead like a blanket, throwing down rain, and there was lightning way off in the distance somewhere.

Road signs swept past, announcing turn-offs to different parts of the city. The highway was lined with diners, gas stations, auto repair stores and big warehouse sized stores selling shoes or furniture. Some of them were open, even though it was the middle of the night and there was a hurricane beating at their doors.

Lights burnt, turning the highway into a broad ribbon of daytime. They went past some houses – single-storey wooden homes with big yards. The factories, shops, houses and offices got larger. Even the road was smoother. Chris guessed they must be close to the city centre.

Chris wondered if the hotel they were heading for would be in the centre of town. The city's bright lights were reflecting off vast pools of water in every street. It looked pretty cool.

Still, one city was much like any other, and Chris couldn't call to mind any famous landmarks that he should be looking

22

for in Indianapolis, so maybe this was his chance to snatch a little sleep . . .

'Ladies and gentlemen, since I see most of you are awake, let me just take this opportunity to point out some of the landmarks of the fine city of Indianapolis as we pass through the downtown area . . .'

Here's the place where all the bus drivers get murdered, thought Chris, who didn't feel like looking out for any lesser sights.

'Of course, you will all know of the Indianapolis Speedway, home of Indy racing. That's off to the west of the city, so I'm afraid we won't be seeing that.' Chris tried hard to contain his disappointment. 'However,' the driver continued, 'over there on the left is the RCA Dome, home of the Indianapolis Colts.'

Hearing that last word jerked Chris completely back from his state of heavy-eyed drowsiness. The Colts? What were they doing here?

Then he remembered that Indianapolis had an NFL team called the Colts. He looked out of the window towards the vast stadium, with its bright signs promoting the new season which was only two months away. Curiously, it made Chris nostalgic for home. The Riverside Colts played on a small pitch at Oldcester University. There had been a small, wooden pavilion with tiny changing rooms close at hand until a fire had wrecked it before Easter. For the last few games of the season, Riverside had used two portacabins plonked down on the cinder car park for changing rooms.

There was a car park around the RCA Dome too. Empty, it looked bigger than some English counties. You could get a lot of portacabins in a space like that.

'It used to be named the Hoosier Dome, of course; Hoosier being the nickname for someone from the state of Indiana. Don't ask me why! You're better off asking someone from New York or Alaska what that name means than asking an actual Hoosier!'

Chris could see the driver's smiling face in the large rearview mirror. His best guess was that Hoosier was an American word for someone who felt unnaturally jolly at 2am.

'The Colts used to be a bit of a joke team, but the last two seasons have been real good for us. This year, we'll go all the way! Now, up ahead you can see the AUL building, which is the tallest building in Indianapolis. We'll soon be passing Market Square Arena, the home of the Indianapolis Pacers . . .'

Baseball? Basketball? Chris really didn't care.

'This here is called the Circle. That statue there is the Soldiers and Sailors Monument. Every Christmas, it gets covered with lights and decorations – we call it the world's biggest Christmas tree.'

So it went on. Union Station. Department stores. The TV station. Chris even got to see the street where the bus driver lived. Did Indiana have the death penalty, he wondered?

Mercifully, Indianapolis didn't have a huge, sprawling downtown area, and soon they were coasting out towards the eastern suburbs. At once, he began to slow down, heading over towards the edge of the highway, following signs to a place called Lawrence. They slid down a ramp, met a broad street lined with shops, then found another street filled with hotels named Ramada, Marriott or Travel Break. They pulled up at Ramada. The tour was over.

'Here we are, folks.' The driver beamed back at them, rising to his feet. 'I hope you didn't mind that little detour. Maybe, now you've seen how beautiful the city of Indianapolis is, you'll come here on purpose real soon.'

Exhausted and giddy with lack of sleep, Chris stepped off the bus and into the brightly lit lobby. Even then the ordeal wasn't over. They had to check in. Chris, being unfamiliar with the ways of hotels, managed to be the last one to get a key to his room.

'I'll let everyone know when I hear from Delta in the morning,' the hotel receptionist said. 'In the meantime, you all get a good night's sleep. We'll have breakfast ready from 7am.'

Chris checked his watch. It was 3.30.

He stumbled into the lift and managed to find his room. At last, he opened the door and found himself in a comfortable though compact space, with a bed and TV and a tiny bathroom. The bed looked wonderfully comfortable. Chris fell on it, stretching out without bothering to get undressed.

'Damn,' he muttered a minute later.

He was wide awake.

Four

Back home in Britain, on the other hand, his father had managed to get to sleep OK. He sounded as if he was yawning with each breath when Chris finally managed to get him to answer the phone. It had taken Chris a couple of attempts to get the right number – dialling from the USA just added an extra level of complexity. When the phone was answered with little more than a 'Huhgh?', Chris knew he'd managed to get it right at last.

'Where are you?' his father asked.

'The plane had to put down in Indianapolis,' Chris explained. He sketched out the rest of the story (without mentioning anyone being afraid of crashing). He got the impression his father was trying to break into the flow a couple of times, so he shut up.

'I know all that,' his father said. 'Robert Goodman called from San Francisco airport. I just wondered where you were staying.' Of course. Mr Goodman wasn't a scatterbrain who would forget to let Chris's father know about the problems with the flight. When the arrangements for Chris's extended stay in the USA had been worked out, Bob Goodman had gone to great lengths to explain that he would call Chris's father immediately in the event of anything unforeseen.

Chris had laughed about all the fuss, but his father had given him one of those looks that was supposed to remind his son of all the times he had ended up on some wild adventure. Not least the time when Bob Goodman's son, Jace, had flown to the UK pretending to be one of the Mount Graham team; had been kidnapped by a sub-Mafia hood who had followed him over; and how Chris had dived into the middle, making sure Jace was rescued, Mr Goodman saved from a double-cross and the bad guy chased from the country to face prison back home.

That probably qualified as unforeseen. Or not, in Chris's case.

'So what's happening?' Mr Stephens asked.

'Nothing, really,' Chris replied. 'We may hear something in the morning. I think the weather's easing up,' he added, looking out of the window. Certainly the rain wasn't crashing against the glass quite so hard any more.

'Good. Maybe they'll fly you out tomorrow. Either way, be sure to ring Jace's dad as soon as the airline tells you anything. You have his mobile, right?'

'Of course,' Chris sighed.

'Good.' There was a long pause. Chris could imagine his father trying to get his brain to work. 'Good,' Mr Stephens said again. After another moment, an idea must have popped into his head. 'The airline is paying for the hotel, right?'

'That's what they told us.'

'What about this call?'

Ah. Now that he wasn't so sure about. The woman at the airport had suggested they could call home, but had she realised Chris wasn't an American?

'We'd better cut this short then. Listen, if there's any trouble with money, spend it first, we'll worry about it after. Don't go hungry or feel you can't call somebody just for the sake of the cash, OK?'

'OK.'

After a few more words of comfort, his father rang off.

Chris replaced the receiver in the cradle and looked round the narrow confines of his room. Having pretty well taken in everything there was to see in a microsecond, he slid across the bed to the window. He had to rub the glass with the back of his sleeve to get rid of the condensation. Even then, there wasn't a lot to see. The window looked out over a small yard with a fence at the bottom; beyond that there was what he guessed was a park. It was hard to make out details in the darkness, but a light on the outside of the hotel building did provide a little illumination. He could see trees and what might have been a lake in the distance. The howling, ghostly wind was making the trees thrash dementedly.

Between the lake and the fence, there was a broad sweep

of flat ground. Chris found himself imagining what a good football pitch it would make. He sighed deeply.

For the first time, he started thinking about how he had played his last game for the Colts. Even though he would still be teamed up with Rory and Russell when he started playing for Oldcester (plus he and Nicky would be team mates again), it was still odd remembering that he would no longer take the field on a Sunday afternoon against the likes of Cathedral or East Sheils. Nor would he ever pull on Riverside's almost-but-not-quite version of the United strip again. Come September, Chris would be wearing the real thing.

What had been really strange, though, was the way it had come to an end. That match against Parchmont had been their last game together; cheated of a final outing against Mount Graham, the Colts had stood around the empty pitch while the Americans argued. It was a terrible anti-climax.

Now here Chris was, separated from the others even more quickly thanks to his planned holiday in California – and even that had gone wrong. Now he was stuck in a room the size of a matchbox, staring out of the window at a stretch of grass, and wishing he could get a game tomorrow.

At least the weather really was letting up. The rain fizzled out quickly, as if someone had finally found the stopcock. It was still very windy, though. Chris wondered if he would be flying out tomorrow.

The view from the window having finally lost its appeal, Chris sat on the bed and tried the TV. One thing he had got used to since his arrival in the USA was non-stop, round-the-clock TV. Some of the guys had got into trouble with Iain Walsh for staying up until 2am watching cable; Rory had sat goggle eyed in front of one station that showed round-the-clock *Dr Who*.

Right now, something like that would be just what the doctor ordered. Chris found the remote and started surfing the channels. It was quite funny that the first thing he found was an all-nite (he was getting used to American spelling . . .) weather station It seemed it was about to stop raining in the Indianapolis area.

'No kidding,' sighed Chris, zapping the smiling blonde woman in the tailored blue suit.

He found a terrible sitcom about some guy who was a

retired secret agent looking for a new job, or at least that was what Chris thought was going on in the four or five minutes he gave it. There was a moment (well, three minutes) of hope when he found an episode of *Voyager*, but it was a repeat that he had seen twice at home. He discovered a station broadcasting heavy metal music (two minutes), another showing a country and western singalong show (a nanosecond) and then a wildlife documentary (four minutes, but the first two and a half minutes were commercials), followed by cartoons dubbed into Spanish (kind of funny for the first three minutes).

A dodgy black and white movie (no!), a Court TV channel (get real!), a low-budget version of *The X-Files* (arrgh!) . . . the list went on and on.

Not so much surfing as drowning, Chris finally gave up when he hit Channel 57, his thumb getting sore from hitting the 'next channel' key. The local news was on. He decided to watch and see if they said anything about the airport.

They did, but first he sat through an odd little story about a prominent businessman from Indianapolis who was trying to build a holiday resort for hikers and hunters somewhere 'upstate'. It seemed the place he had chosen, overlooking a lake and surrounded by forest, was technically the property of a Native American tribe called the Wabash Iroquois, but that the last few members of the tribe were living somewhere else. Apparently, the businessman had found a way to buy the land for next to nothing, because of a forgotten clause in a peace treaty signed with the Indians in the 1880s.

The Wabash were protesting, but the reporter said that their chances of defeating the plan were slim; something to do with a legal hearing due to take place on Wednesday for which they needed to deposit a $500,000 bond. The Native Americans' spokesperson said they just didn't have that kind of money, but were going to do all they could to raise it.

The spokesman looked very old, very calm, but very assured. 'We know help is coming,' he said.

One of the ways they were hoping to raise the money, the reporter said, was through a schools soccer tournament being held at a place called Indy Sports. There was a $50,000 first prize, donated by a unnamed millionaire. The Wabash were taking part.

It sounded a bit like the New Jersey championship Chris and

the Colts had just romped through. $50,000. Chris wondered if he shouldn't call the guys and have them come back to the States. If there were other competitions like that during the summer, they could really clean up.

The local news programme moved on to the story from the airport, talking about the dozens of flights that had been diverted to Indianapolis because of storms to the west. The worst of the high winds were expected to clear by mid-afternoon, and the flights would all be gone before nightfall.

Good, thought Chris. He was quite happy with the idea that he would soon be on his way to join Jace and his father for a week (well, six days now) in sunny California. As he recalled the way Jace had described how hot San Francisco would be at this time of year, Chris heard the local news station switch to the weather report.

It was the same blonde girl, he was sure of it. No-one else could have that much hair and those glistening white teeth! She was wearing a green outfit now instead of the blue but it had to be the same woman . . .

'In the next hour,' she chimed, 'the rain will start clearing away from the Indianapolis metropolitan area –'

Zap.

29

Five

—— ⚽ ——

Battered back into being sleepy by the endless stream of channels showing 'reruns', badly dubbed drama and self-improvement programmes, Chris felt his eyelids growing heavy. He lay sprawled out on the bed, working his way through more snatches of late nite entertainment before he gradually slipped into sleep.

The TV was hissing at him when he woke up again.

Even Channel 57 had finally gone to bed. His brain was still swimming with images from the hundreds of commercials he had sped through in just an hour's viewing. A Guy Called Bob (spelt B-A-H-B, Chris was sure) had been selling his used cars on at least 56 of those channels.

'If you're looking for a good deal, just ask for A Guy Called Bahb!' Chris muttered, sitting upright.

He was still pretty heavy eyed, but he was sure that a few hours' sleep would have done him no end of good.

Which was why it was such a pity he'd had less than an hour or so.

'I don't believe this,' Chris said out loud. The words echoed back off the walls. He realised he could hear someone snoring in the neighbouring bedroom Was that what had woken him up? He didn't think it likely (after all, his father wasn't what you'd call a silent sleeper). Then he realised that another noise had actually lessened in the few minutes he had been asleep.

He crossed to the window and peered outside. The wind had died down, so that the trees were now just swaying gently, as opposed to the manic dance they had been celebrating earlier. The ghostly wailing of the gale against his window was also a lot less determined, more of a poltergeisty moan.

The sky was lightening to the west, even through the dark blanket of storm clouds that was still sitting off that way It was almost 6am. Perhaps the slight hum of early morning traffic from the other side of the hotel had made him stir, or maybe it was just that he was still operating on a strange mix of UK and USA time, his body unable to tell when to sleep and when to wake up in strange bedrooms.

He blinked.

Now he knew what had woken him. The noise, which must have been there all the time in the last few minutes, throbbing away under his consciousness, was the dull, distant beat of a drum. The beat was regular, quite fast, like a thudding bass line from a dance track, the kind of thing that comes booming out from open-top Fords. Chris imagined some pale-faced guy in sunglasses, hands resting on the top of the wheel.

This beat, though, wasn't coming from any speakers. It was a real drum, pulsing out through the hand of a real person. Chris could just about make him out. He was sitting on the stretch of grass Chris had seen earlier, huddled under the spreading branches of a tree. His arm was rising and falling with the driving energy of the sound, slightly out of sync because of the distance. There was a faint rattling noise as well.

Chris couldn't see the drummer's face or much of his shape. He looked quite large; tall, but not fat. He was wearing dark clothes, including some kind of rain cape draped over his head, protecting the surface of the drum as much as himself.

Something else was moving a little further off, on the other side of the strip of grass. The drummer was not alone.

Chris blinked again. What was this?

Another man was . . . was . . . actually, Chris couldn't think of a word that adequately described what the guy was doing. It was a skipping kind of walk, as if he was hopping and dancing along an imaginary line, whirling his arms around. Chris peered out into the gloom, trying to see if he could make out any details, but he couldn't. It was hard enough to make out even what the guy was wearing – some kind of loose-fitting, light-coloured suit, it seemed. Chris also thought he might have his hair in dreadlocks or plaits or something.

As he watched, the guy stopped abruptly, gave a kind of circular shuffle, then continued along a new line, at right angles to the first.

Obviously a nutter.

He was moving towards the hotel now, but Chris couldn't see his face even then because of the way he kept his head bowed down to the ground.

Chris had to wipe the window again; his breath was fogging the glass. When he looked again, the guy had turned another right angle, and was moving across Chris's line of vision, not that far from the fence. The drummer was behind him now, still banging out his regular beat. Chris thought he caught the edge of some kind of song, but it was very faint.

The line-shuffling man turned another corner, away from Chris.

Chris continued to watch. The guy went away from him, about halfway to the trees beside the lake, then turned left again, heading towards the drummer. When he next stopped, he turned around completely, tracing the same line he had just followed, even making the turn in the same place, heading towards the fence.

He covered ten or fifteen metres and then the drumming stopped.

The shuffling man faced the drummer, then took four or five long paces towards him. He stood stock still on the spot where he finished up. The drummer started up again, faster than before. Once again, Chris thought he might have heard someone chanting or singing. The glass was muffling the sound, though.

He decided to open the window. It would improve the view and his hearing. There was a bar across the bottom of the window, and he leant on it and felt it snap back against the frame. As he did so, the window swung outward, pivoting on a point about two-thirds of the way towards the top. It made a deep, creaking noise.

The wind crashed into his face, but Chris heard a very short snatch of the drummer's beat and the strange, piping singing. Then both stopped. He tried to open his eyes, but the gusting storm was still throwing a lot of force across the landscape. He had to squint between his fingers.

The shuffling man was gone. Only the drummer remained.

And he was looking right at Chris.

He had an old, old face, lined and worn. His forehead was high, grey hair a long way back on his scalp, swept towards the back. His eyes were in shadow, but Chris knew they were looking back at him. The mouth was set firm, the corners down.

The man sat cross-legged under his dark rain cape, his drum in his lap. Chris stared at him and the man stared back. The wind howled around them both, rustling the cape and throwing dust into Chris's eyes.

In the end, Chris had to admit defeat. There was nothing to hear out there now but the gale anyhow. By the time he had pulled the window closed and snapped the bar back into place, wiped the moisture from the inside of the window and pressed his forehead against the glass, the man was gone.

Chris wasn't completely freaked by what he'd seen. After all, he'd spent a lot of time with Nicky over the last few years, so he thought he knew what weird meant. All the same, he couldn't get back to sleep.

He went down to breakfast spot on 7am, while the rest of the other stranded passengers were still in bed.

No-one from the airline had arrived. Chris didn't recognise any of the hotel staff from last night either. Feeling very out of place, he slunk into breakfast, finding himself a table at the back, near a window that overlooked the same yard that lay below his bedroom.

The dining room staff fussed around some non-airline guests, but no-one went near Chris. He watched the other tables, trying to get the hang of how the hotel operated. There was a bar over by the far wall where the guests fetched their own cereals and fruit juices. Maybe he should just wander over and –

'Hi! I've not seen you here before!'

The voice came from slightly behind him. Chris turned, and nearly fell off his seat in surprise.

'Nicky?'

'What?'

'Nicky?'

'Who?'

They could have kept that sparkling conversation up for a while, Chris realised, but he'd worked out now that this couldn't be – wasn't – Nicky Fiorentini. But it was close.

The longer you looked, the more you saw the differences.

This guy had the same black hair, but it was much shorter. He also was maybe an inch or two taller and much heavier. All the same, though, when Chris looked into the laughing, bright eyes with their intense, dark centres, and saw the thin mouth and the angled chin, all he could think of was that Nicky must have been cloned at some secret Fiorentini factory back in Italy, and one of the doubles sent out here to wait tables.

'Sorry,' said Chris at last. 'You really look like someone else.'

The guy struck a pose. 'The other guy's a lucky man, then, am I right?'

'He thinks so,' said Chris, grinning back.

The Nicky lookalike came closer to the table, a small pad in one hand and a cheap pen in the other. He had black trousers and a crisp white shirt on.

'You work here?' Chris asked.

'You some kind of detective?' the guy joshed in return.

'No, I . . .'

'It's OK, I figured that out for myself. You're one of our stranded guys, right? Came in last night from the airport?'

'Right. How could you tell?'

The boy pointed the end of the pen at the room key Chris had dropped on the table.

'That's one of the worst rooms in the hotel. They'd never give it to a real guest.'

'Thanks . . .' muttered Chris.

'No problem. Hey – looks like I make a better detective than you, huh?'

Chris grinned back at him and tried to think of a snappy comeback. Something the boy had said earlier came back to him. 'One of *our* stranded guys?'

'Yeah, right,' came the reply, with a short, mocking laugh. 'My family own this place. What, you think I'd work here by choice? I mean, look at these threads!'

'That's what I figured,' Chris fibbed. 'OK, your turn, detective. Guess where I'm from.'

The guy stuck the end of the pen between his lips. He sucked on it as he thought. 'Hmmm. The flight was Newark to 'Frisco, right? Well, that ain't no New Jersey accent, that's for sure. And you're too pale to be a Californian. Foreign, right?'

34

'Too easy.'

'OK – Australian.'

'Wrong!' laughed Chris. 'My shot for the match. My guess is that that's your mum over there, wondering how long it can take for you to take one table's order.'

The waiter looked nervously back over his shoulder to a woman standing at the end of the counter, topping up the orange juice. Her face was stern enough to scare people to an Olympic standard.

'Good call! Guess I'd better let you be the detective after all.'

'If it's any consolation, you'll never look like a waiter in trainers like those,' remarked Chris.

The guy looked down at his feet, turning up the toes of his brilliant white Jordans.

'Brand new. I'm breakin' 'em in.'

Chris was envious. They were at least 100 quid's worth of footwear.

'Listen,' the guy said. 'I'm having fun and all, but can you tell me something I can write down? I need to at least look busy.'

Chris touched his key, turning the disk so that it was easier to read. Then he stuck out his hand.

'Chris Stephens, Room 414. I'm a Brit, by the way.'

The waiter stuck the pen between his teeth and shook Chris's hand.

'C. G. Amantani,' he said. 'Welcome to the Lawrence Ramada Inn. You want tea, coffee . . . or can I get you a Pepsi Free?'

Chris laughed. A week ago, Zak had thought that he was being offered a free Pepsi and had been really offended when the guy in the store demanded money for the can of sugar-free coke.

'Tea would be fine,' he replied.

'Man, you are English,' laughed Amantani. 'Now, what can I get you to eat?'

Chris was feeling more English than ever. 'Lots of bacon, lots of toast.' A toasted bacon sandwich sounded about as delicious as he could imagine.

'You got it,' said CG, shaking his head as if he didn't believe it. 'Help yourself to stuff from the bar; cereal and stuff. I'll be back in a minute.'

35

He wandered off, walking in that way only young Americans are designed to do. He hadn't written anything down.

Thirty minutes later, Chris dropped his napkin on the table, completely stuffed. The bacon had been scalding hot, and each rasher had been the size of a steak. The toast had been cooked on just one side for some reason, but it was great bread and there was plenty of butter. A single sandwich like that would have kept Chris fed for a week at home, and he'd had three. Even Nicky's mum, who always cooked enough for a busload of people, would have thought they'd pushed the boat out.

'Brilliant . . .' he sighed, stretching out to give his stomach more room.

'I'll say,' CG replied through a partly filled mouth. He picked up a cup and slurped down some of the tea. 'Maybe I'll start eating like an Englishman from now on.'

Chris laughed, but not too hard in case he burst. 'Aren't you going to get into trouble for this?' he asked. CG had matched him, sandwich for sandwich.

'What are they going to do, fire me? Besides, we won't be that busy until your fellow passengers come down. You want more tea?'

'No,' admitted Chris. What he really wanted was help getting up. 'So, what does the C. G. stand for, CG?'

His new friend wrinkled his nose and turned his lip up in a sneer. Now that really did look like Nicky.

'You work it out, Mr Detective. They're just handles my family uses. All my friends call me CG.'

'Fair enough,' said Chris, not sure whether that yet applied to him. He noticed that the airline rep had arrived and was sipping coffee at a corner table, looking as if she hadn't managed to get a lot of sleep. Did she have good news about their flight, Chris wondered? Obviously nothing was happening in any great rush, judging by the way she was finding time to read the paper and wait for the other passengers to surface.

His thoughts travelled back to the strange events of the night before.

'What's behind the hotel?' he asked, and then added, in case CG thought he was having trouble seeing through the glass, 'On the other side of the fence.'

'It's called Indy Sports – a kind of year-round sports facility. It's got indoor courts for basketball and volleyball,

36

then outdoors you got baseball, soccer and stuff. It's OK. A lot of our guests go for a walk out there.' Chris nodded. 'I'll be over there myself later,' CG added.

'For the soccer tournament, right?' asked Chris, grinning.

'Wow! Right!' gasped CG, quite amazed. All the same, there was a gleam in his eye and a wicked confidence in his voice that really was Fiorentini territory. Perhaps the two families came from the same part of Italy?

'It's OK, I don't know much more than that,' Chris admitted.

'Oh. OK, it's the Indiana State Schools Championship. My team got through the prelims last semester. Now the best sixteen teams take part in a knockout tournament over the next two days. And guess what –'

'A millionaire has put up fifty thousand dollars prize money for the winning school.'

CG almost choked on his last piece of toast. 'Man, you're good!'

'I watch a lot of TV,' Chris half-explained. 'But surely you won't be able to play today? All that rain?'

CG shrugged. 'Should be OK. It's been a dry summer, so a lot of it will drain away. The park seldom gets waterlogged, especially after a little storm like last night's . . .'

'That was a little storm?' Chris spluttered.

'You should have been here in '95.' CG smirked and tapped the side of his nose, telling Chris nothing whatsoever.

'That wind will have helped too,' said CG in conclusion. 'It'll be a little greasy on top, sure, but I bet we can play.'

Chris found that very hard to believe. Where Riverside played, on the university campus, if it rained in a nearby town the ground got wet. Going back a few years, the nearby river had burst its banks once and the Colts' home pitch had become better suited to water polo than football.

'So, what's the opposition like?' asked Chris, the New Jersey Invitational event uppermost in his mind.

CG shrugged. 'Who knows? First time my school's qualified. There's only one other team from Indianapolis. The rest are from Gary, East Chicago, Lafayette, Peru . . .'

'Peru?' laughed Chris.

'Yeah,' said CG, who took a moment to see what had tickled Chris. 'Not the country, stupid. Peru, Indiana. It's about sixty, seventy miles north of here.'

'Sorry,' Chris replied, gradually getting himself back under control.

'We got a Brazil too,' said CG, and Chris lost it again.

'You're weird,' CG sighed. 'Most of the rest are from up north too. But there's an outfit from Vincennes, and – get this – we've even got a team of –'

'Red Indians,' said Chris, partly to himself. Small tumblers were turning in his mind, unlocking the answer to at least one of last night's puzzles.

'You are spooky!' said CG, grinning. 'Only you ought to know the correct term is "Native Americans". Tell me you heard about them on the local news. I mean, we didn't make TV in England, right?'

'I couldn't sleep,' admitted Chris. He considered telling CG about the drummer and his strange partner out in the park, but held on to it for now.

'So, who's favourite?' Chris asked. Once again, CG shrugged. If it had really been Nicky, he would have known the strengths and weaknesses of all the other teams, but CG was clearly more of a turn up and play sort of guy. Perhaps the Fiorentinis and Amantanis were from different parts of Italy after all.

'The other team from Indianapolis,' CG said after a while, 'they'll be tough to beat. Walked through the prelims. It's a rich old school called The Orchards. Fat cats' sons, that kind of thing. Heated pool, sauna, private clinic, the works. They won the whole thing last year; went on to some kind of national championships in Tampa Bay.'

'They sound like they're pretty good.'

'For sure,' said CG, sounding very serious. 'Last time we played them, they won five-one. Man, that was a tough game!'

Chris nodded. He'd been on the wrong end of a few hammerings himself. On the whole, he preferred to dish them out . . .

'Do you play?' asked CG, suddenly.

'Well, actually . . .'

'Get out of town! Really?' CG leapt to his feet. 'You want to come take a look?'

Chris almost followed, but he knew he shouldn't leave the hotel. 'I can't. That lady from the airline is going to want to talk to us soon.'

'Oh, right!' said CG. He looked at his watch. 'I guess it's a little early anyhow. Tell you what, though. If you've got some time after you're done listening to her, ask for me at reception. I'll be going over Indy Sports at ten.'

'Fine,' said Chris. CG snapped his fingers, as if that confirmed the arrangement, then went off to clear tables. Chris saw his mother pull him to one side and lecture him about not spending all morning chatting to guests and eating toast instead of working. Chris listened hard, but he only got half the information he needed.

Six

⚬

The luggage had arrived from the airport. Chris's bag was at
the top of the pile. Later on, he found out he'd been lucky. Half
the other guests were given the wrong cases. There were
similar piles in hotels all over Indianapolis. Nothing was going
to get sorted before it all had to be dragged back to the
airport again.

His luck ran out there, though. He went up to his room to
shower and change, but the only way to get the water above
freezing was to have it running at a drip every ten seconds or
so.

Perhaps he didn't smell so bad.

He put on some fresh clothes and went back downstairs.
He had to sit and wait while all the other guests arrived
downstairs for breakfast in ones and twos. The airline rep kept
checking lists and counting heads. It took at least an hour to
satisfy her that everyone was there.

'OK,' she said. 'The good news is that we've been cleared to
depart at 2.10pm. The bad news is that the bus can't get here
before eleven, so I'm going to have to ask you to wait
around the hotel until it arrives. *Please* –' Her voice sounded
desperate at this point '– *Please* don't wander off. We have to
be at the airport on time. If you're not here when the bus
leaves, we'll have to leave you behind. In such an eventuality,
Delta Airlines . . .'

There followed a short speech she had memorised about
how it wouldn't be the airline's fault, and about how the
airline wouldn't be responsible for them, and about how
they would have to pay for new tickets to continue their
journey. Chris was sure she didn't need to worry, though
no-one looked desperate to revisit the tourist centres of
Indianapolis.

Chris tossed his bag on to the pile in the lobby and went off to find CG.

When the dark haired boy appeared from behind a door marked PRIVATE, he was wearing an all white football strip. It was so clean, the bright lobby lights reflected off it like a mirror.

'You going to dazzle them to defeat, Carlo?' Chris asked.

'Yeah, we –' CG's laugh stopped. 'How do you do that?' he gasped.

'You had a row with your mother,' Chris told him 'Parents usually use Sunday names when you're in trouble.'

CG knew what he meant. 'Lucky she didn't use the whole thing, right?' He walked round from behind the desk, checking his watch. 'How many Italian names are there beginning with G?' Chris wondered out loud. He could only think of one 'Giovanni?'

CG was grinning broadly. 'Not even close.' He looked very confident. 'Tell you what, you get the other name, and lunch is on me.'

'Safe bet,' replied Chris, his hands in his pockets. 'We leave at eleven.'

CG made a face. 'Aw. Still, you're gonna come over Indy Sports, right? Check out the competition for me?'

Chris hesitated. 'Well . . .'

CG checked his watch again. 'Look, it's nine-thirty. It takes five minutes, tops, to get to the park. We'll go now, check it out, and you can be back here for ten-thirty latest.'

What could go wrong with that?

'OK.'

They set off for the main doors. As they slid open, inspiration popped into Chris's mind. 'Giuseppe,' he guessed.

'Way off! Way off!!' laughed CG.

There was a short pathway running up the side of the hotel which connected to a gate that led into the park. There was a lot of activity already. Chris saw men in track suits putting up nets and corner flags, while others carried clipboards and pointed to show that they were in charge.

Yellow school buses were disgorging hordes of players and supporters over by a low, wooden building with red walls

41

near the lake. CG said that was where the changing rooms were. A few of his team mates had already arrived, and were watching the chaotic scrum outside the building with amusement. They were kitted out, ready to go. Home advantage, thought Chris.

There were three pitches side by side in front of the red building. Chris saw that another pitch off to their right was also being prepared. One touchline ran perilously close to the back fence of the Ramada Hotel.

'They'll be fetching the ball out of our kitchen all day,' joked CG. He started to lead the way down to the pitches nearer the lake.

Chris didn't hear him or follow him.

'Which one was my room?' he asked, trying to work it out for himself in the meantime. CG stopped, walked back and performed a quick calculation and pointed up to one of the windows.

Chris had guessed correctly. He looked back out over the grass again, towards the lake and the small stand of trees that curved around one corner of the pitch. In his mind, he could hear the beating of a drum.

He walked towards the lake. CG opened his mouth as if he was going to say something, but kept silent. He watched Chris, curious about what had caught his new friend's eye. Chris was walking along the touchline now, towards the corner. As he reached it, he turned round in a kind of circle, then he followed the goal-line. CG became even more amazed as Chris walked past the goal, then when he reached the edge of the penalty area, he pivoted left and started walking round the box.

The route was as clear to Chris as if he could see the strange, shuffling man in front of him. Around the penalty box to the far side, then retrace your steps back to the middle. He took five long steps to the penalty spot. The goal was directly in front of him.

'So . . . are we all done here?' asked CG.

Chris doubted it, but he'd learnt something. He was sure he had interrupted some weird ritual the drummer and his line dancing friend had been performing. Of course, that wasn't what CG was talking about, he realised.

'Yeah . . . sure . . .' he said.

'Come and meet the others.'

Chris didn't look back as they followed a path around the trees to the red building. By the time they reached the throng, Chris had more or less convinced CG that he wasn't a complete headcase.

'Who are the guys in yellow and black?' he asked.

'Ah!' said CG. He turned to spy on the sharp warm-ups being performed by his competitors, under the watchful eye of a rugged, brawny coach. A tall man with shoulder-length blond hair stood nearby. 'Those guys are from The Orchards, the rich man's school I told you about. See the big guy? That's Mark van Zale, a former running back with the Colts. He's their senior coach.'

'And the guy in the suit?'

'One of the fathers, I guess. Looks too well dressed to be a teacher or principal, even at The Orchards! He looks kinda familiar . . .'

Chris was thinking the same, only that didn't make sense unless . . .

'Would he have been in the news?' he asked.

CG snapped his fingers. 'That's it. It's Gary Lukas, the property guy who's trying to buy Iroquois land upstate. There's been a lot of fuss about it. The Native Americans aren't his favourite people, it seems.'

Chris was sure there were all kinds of questions he should be asking at this point, but he didn't know where to begin. Besides, what did it matter? In just over an hour, he would be on the bus, on the way to the airport, and Indianapolis and its goings-on would be the last thing on his mind.

While these conflicting thoughts were swirling round his mind, Chris saw one of CG's team mates jogging steadily over.

'Hey!' the boy called, smiling. He was tall, slow moving and laid back. Chris wondered what position he played. The guy gave him a good looking over too.

'Hi, Jon,' said CG. He did some quick introductions, presenting Chris as 'a Brit whose plane got sucked down in the storm' and Jon as the left wing back for CG's team (Chris hoped he could move a bit more sharply on the field).

'We've got the Sabres this morning,' Jon announced.

'The team from Lafayette,' CG explained. He searched around quickly, then pointed across to a group of players in blue and white striped shirts. 'That's them.'

Chris nodded and gave CG's opponents the once-over. They looked OK; fit, excited and ready to go. Their coach was making them go through some rudimentary stretching exercises.

CG was building up Chris's description for Jon. 'Chris plays for some team back in England. The real thing – in the Championship and everything.'

Those weren't quite the words Chris had used on the way over, but he didn't bother to correct CG. Jon looked less than impressed.

'Who's that? Manchester United?' He clearly knew enough about English soccer to ask that much.

'No, Oldcester.'

'Never heard of them,' said Jon. It wasn't said with any spite, it was just a simple statement of fact. All the same, Chris could tell that Jon wasn't going to be overawed just because Chris was from England. 'You make 'em up?'

'Keep watching English football on TV,' said Chris. 'You'll see us soon enough.'

'Yeah, losing to Manchester United . . .' Jon grinned as he spoke.

CG attempted to restore the peace before any real trouble broke out.

'See anything?'

Chris almost told him that 30 seconds of watching them warm up was hardly going to make him an expert on the Lafayette Sabres, but decided not to play into Jon's hands.

'They don't have anyone really tall, do they? What's their keeper like?'

'Dunno,' said CG, shrugging. 'Lafayette's just a small college town; the Sabres don't normally get this far. We've certainly never played them before.'

'Well, you could try them out with a few deep crosses early on. Push up on the wings, and hit flat crosses across the box.' He looked at the tops of the tall trees, swaying as the air stirred them. The storm had passed, but there was still plenty of wind left. 'Don't let the ball sit up in the air; with this wind, it'll be impossible to control. If your midfield operate up to the edge of the box, behind the strikers, they might find a few chances dropping their way.'

CG was beaming as if he had been given some guaranteed

plans for success. Jon wrinkled his face. Since he had just given them a plan that required him to chase up the flanks from the first whistle, Chris didn't expect his advice had made him any more popular in that quarter.

'We've got pitch three,' Jon said, indicating the one furthest from where they were standing. 'It's pretty slippy.'

'All the more reason to run at their backs,' Chris remarked. 'It'll be harder for them to turn quickly.'

Jon's eyes flared a quick 'Why don't you shut up?' at Chris.

'We kick off at ten-thirty,' he continued.

'Great,' said CG. 'I was hoping we wouldn't have to wait.'

'What about the Wabash Iroquois team?' asked Chris.

Jon was clearly confused as well as irked with Chris now.

'What you interested in them Indians for?' he asked.

'Native Americans,' Chris and CG corrected him in stereo.

'Whatever.'

'I'm just curious,' said Chris. 'No-one gives them much of a chance, do they?'

'I don't know anything about them!' Jon griped, then he contradicted himself in the next second by adding: 'They're playing on the pitch up at the top, out of the way.'

Chris knew he meant the one at the back of the hotel, the one he had been able to see (or not see, depending on your point of view) from his window.

'Hey look, there they are!' said CG, pointing.

Chris turned, and got his first look at the Native American team. They were spilling from the back of a flatbed truck that had just pulled up on the grass alongside the yellow school buses that had dropped off the other teams. The players were already in their strip – blood-red shirts over a mixture of shorts, cut-down jeans and joggers. Their footwear was equally varied, but none of them had proper boots.

They had a ball, which a couple of them immediately started heading back and forth. Chris noticed it was a basketball and winced.

The rest of the Iroquois team clustered together, eyeing their surroundings carefully. They looked fit enough, as far as Chris could tell. Two of them were very tall, hard-faced young men with proud features. These two gestured for the others to follow, heading off towards the noticeboards which

45

contained the information about who was playing who where and when.

Chris ignored them. He was watching the cab of the truck.

A tall, rugged man with a scarred face stepped from the driver's side. His night-black hair was tied back into the nape of his neck, a short tail hanging to the middle of his shoulders. He was big and powerful. When he moved, it was like watching a tiger. In a few short paces, he caught up with the boys, stooping to whisper something to them.

The lorry's passenger door opened more slowly. Someone was taking a great deal of time to get out of the seat.

It was an old man, Chris realised as the feet swung into view, clad in ankle-length boots and knee-high leggings tied with cord. He reached out carefully, searching for the floor.

Before he allowed his feet to touch the ground, he placed the end of a long staff down first, taking some of his weight on it as he left the cab. The staff was made of some kind of dark wood, with shells, feathers, strings of beads and strange rattles attached to the top.

The old man's hair was white, swept back from a forehead that had more lines than a telephone exchange. Two smears of red paint were daubed on his hollow cheeks. He wore a loose shirt, embroidered with pictures of mountains. There were feathers woven into his hair.

'Now, that's a Red Indian . . .' he whispered to himself.

The old man turned and leant back into the cab. He brought out a small, round drum. The staff made a clattering noise as he turned back.

'That's him!' Chris said, still aiming the comment just at himself. To his amazement, at that moment the old man looked up, turned his head as if he had smelled something on the breeze, and looked directly at Chris.

They held each other's eyes for a moment. The old man seemed to be smiling. Then CG broke the spell.

'You going to come see the first ten minutes of our game?' asked CG.

Chris managed to break eye contact with the old man. 'What was that?' he asked.

'Gonna come see us kick off before you go?' CG repeated.

'I'm not sure . . .' said Chris.

'Go on!' urged the other boy. 'Look, watch ten minutes, then go back through the gate. You'll be back in the lobby by ten forty-five latest.'

Chris looked at his watch. It was close on ten to ten already. The last few minutes seemed to have flown by.

'OK,' he said.

'Go on,' urged the other boy. 'Look, we've ten minutes, then go back through the gate. You'll be back in the lobby by ten forty-five. Blast.'

Chris looked at his watch. It was close on ten to, already. The last few minutes seemed to have flown by.

'OK,' he said.

Seven

⚽

After watching just ten minutes' play, Chris wouldn't have wanted to bet much money on CG's team getting past the first round of the tournament. And that was despite the fact that they were 1-0 up.

Just as Chris had thought, Lafayette were very shaky at the back against anything played in from wide, but the only evidence he had of that was one cross from the right which the keeper flapped at while the defence had stood and watched. A black kid on CG's team had fastened on to the loose ball and snapped in a shot which had cannoned off a defender's legs and gone in.

That was it though. For the rest of the time he had been watching, the Lawrence Phantoms had been penned back in their own half. It made grim watching. The blue and white shirts came forward in numbers, mostly driving up the middle. CG's team mates in midfield tackled well and made a brave attempt to man mark, but every time they won the ball they seemed starved of options. Jon and the other full back seemed mesmerised by their opposite numbers, and remained glued to them no matter which team had the ball. Lawrence chased a few long punts upfield, but the ball always came back at them.

Just before Chris left, the Lafayette Sabres clipped the bar. Chris was sure it would end up somewhere between 6-1 and 10-1 in their favour.

Chris's attention was only half on the game, though. He was thinking about what he had seen before the kick-off.

The sixteen teams had been welcomed and introduced by some local dignitary on the school board. He'd rambled on a bit about pride and honour and then raised a cheer when he mentioned the $50,000 prize money. At this point, he intro- duced a weasly faced guy in a bright blue suit. The guy jumped up on to the makeshift podium, holding up his hand to quiet the imaginary applause.

He introduced himself as a representative of the mysterious millionaire who had put up the prize money. He had a giant cheque in one hand and a small, silver trophy in the other. The sixteen finalists would play a four-round knock-out, winner take all.

Was it Chris's imagination, or had he looked across at Lukas as he said that?

Blue Suit stepped aside. Council Guy thanked the various hotels and individuals who were providing accommodation for the travelling teams (the Ramada where CG worked was one of them), then read out the first-round ties – four to kick off at 10.30am, the others at 12.45pm.

There was a more than respectable crowd of parents and other spectators clustered around the podium. Chris noticed that the local TV station, WISH, was there. The woman journalist and her bored-looking cameraman (who was wearing an NFL shirt and a baseball cap to show where his sympathies lay) cornered Blue Suit as soon as the speeches were over, obviously trying to find out who the mysterious millionaire was. Blue Suit straightened his wispy, light brown hair, fixed his tie and hit the journalist with a dazzling smile. Obviously, he had nothing to say.

The woman came to the same conclusion in a microsecond and switched her attention to the teams. She was on her way over to the blond man standing by the huddled yellow and blacks when she saw the old man with the drum. She threw a body swerve that was better than most displayed on the four pitches all day (despite the fact that her heels kept sinking into the ground) and went towards him. Chris followed.

He missed the introductions. By the time he got to within hearing range, the woman was already signalling at her colleague to start filming.

'Chief Grey Mountain, all week you've been talking to the media about this event, and how the $50,000 prize money was going to make a big difference to your campaign to fight the development of the land at Bitter Lake . . .'

The old man offered her the very slightest of smiles. 'That's right,' he said.

49

The woman looked into the camera lens. 'In case viewers have been on another planet, this story concerns the plans local property developer Gary Lukas has for creating a multi-million dollar leisure facility on land owned by the Wabash Iroquois tribe near Martinsville, Indiana.' She turned back to face Grey Mountain. 'Chief, to fight this project in the courts you need to find $500,000, isn't that right?'

'Yes,' said the old man.

'So this $50,000 would mean a great deal to your people?'

'Yes.'

The journalist allowed one small flash of frustration to cross her face. Clearly she wasn't happy at having to trail out long, complicated questions just to get one-word replies.

'What makes you so confident you'll win?' she asked, with just the barest hint of a mocking smile on her lips. A few onlookers around Chris snickered.

'Our players have skill and spirit. They are fighting for their land,' replied Grey Mountain, his voice even and calm.

'But they don't have a lot of experience . . .'

Grey Mountain's face didn't show the slightest emotion. He was looking at a point halfway between the woman's shoulder and the camera lens, focused on nothing in particular.

'It was the Native Americans who invented soccer,' he said.

It was Chris's turn to laugh.

'Also, this land on which we play today, this too was once Indian land.' He turned to face her, the first movement he had made. There was no change in the tempo or colour of his voice as he added: 'Of course, I could say the same for the whole continent.'

The woman smiled, happy with the soundbite 'Even so,' she said, 'you face some formidable opposition, including a top-rated team from The Orchards school – a team captained by Gary Lukas's son.' The old man didn't comment 'Don't you have something more to rely on than home field advantage?' she added.

'Just a whole load of mumbo jumbo,' came a dark, low voice. The crowd parted as two heavy looking minders swept through, followed by the smart suit, shoulder length hair and bright smile of the very man they had just been talking about 'A lot of hot air and precious little physical fact   much the same as their objections to my project.'

The woman turned on her heels (screwing the left one into the ground), clearly delighted at this bonus for her film.

'Mr Lukas,' she greeted, smiling.

'Good morning, Sally,' the man replied, giving her an equally dazzling display of teeth in return. 'It's good to see you again.'

The woman blushed, flattered that he had remembered her name. Chris admired the way Lukas had taken over the situation with just a few words.

'We were just saying –' the journalist began.

'I heard,' interrupted Lukas, managing to make it look decisive but not impolite. 'I just thought I'd come over to wish the Chief well. May the best team win, eh?' He stuck out his large hand. Chris saw the heavy ring on Lukas's little finger. There was enough gold there to finance the prize money for a dozen soccer championships.

The chief pointedly ignored the gesture.

Chris saw how the people standing around them reacted. There wasn't a lot of sympathy for Grey Mountain in the mixed faces scattered around the group at the centre.

Having left it just long enough to ensure that everyone saw how he had been ignored, Lukas withdrew his hand. 'Well,' he said, with just a little disappointment in his eyes, 'I meant what I said. All the kids here today are striving to do their best for their school and their community. I wish them all luck.' He turned as if to leave.

The reporter wasn't going to let things go that easily.

'What about the Bitter Lake development?' she asked.

Lukas held up his hand. 'Not today, Sally!' he pleaded. 'On Wednesday, you'll have all the time in the world to talk about court cases and legal rights to property. Today is about the great sport of soccer. Let's not allow the undignified squabbling of old men stand in the way of what our boys are here to achieve.'

Given that it would be a hard judge who called the smiling, tanned and tastefully dressed Mr Lukas 'old', it was quite a neat way to turn attention back on to the weathered face of Grey Mountain. The businessman was no stranger to dealing with the media.

He snapped his fingers as if an afterthought had occurred to him. He faced Grey Mountain again, gesturing towards the

51

item the Chief carried (and which had stopped him shaking Lukas's hand, Chris realised).

'Speaking of not getting in the way of the event,' he said, 'I hope you're not going to play that thing during the game.'

Grey Mountain said nothing. Every onlooker (and the video camera) was focused on the drum.

'It's not going to be very fair to the other teams having you thumping away while they play.'

'The music of the drum focuses our team's spirit,' Grey Mountain replied.

Lukas made a mocking face for the benefit of everyone looking.

'Well, maybe that's true,' he said, 'but it also distracts the opposition. There's a rule in this game about unsportsmanlike conduct, and it applies to the people connected with a team as much as it applies to the eleven players. Would you like me to fetch a referee to explain it to you?'

Grey Mountain's face barely moved as he replied: 'That will not be necessary.'

Lukas grinned. 'Good. I need hardly point out that he would have ruled in my favour. And next week another referee is going to rule in my favour about the rules of a different game. Get used to the idea of losing these arguments, Grey Mountain. Get used to losing, period.'

A sharp blast on a whistle brought Chris back to the present. CG had just committed a clumsy foul on the edge of the area. The Lawrence Phantoms came out of it pretty lightly. It could easily have been a penalty, and some refs would have booked CG as well.

Chris watched the wall form up, then checked his watch. It was 10.43. Time to go. He wanted to see if he could catch CG's eye, maybe see if the Phantoms survived this dangerous moment, but it was already getting a little late. He turned away from the game and started to walk briskly along the path towards the red building.

Chris caught sight of the yellow and black shirts of The Orchards team as he went past the end of the pitch. They were already 1–0 up. A large group of supporters, including cheerleaders, was roaring them on.

Chris could see Lukas watching the game. It made him realise that Grey Mountain had disappeared after the interview. The Iroquois would be playing up on the top pitch, he remembered. He wondered how they were getting on. He would also have loved to ask the Chief about his claim that the Indians had invented soccer.

Ten forty-five. There really wasn't time to find out.

A large crowd was milling around in front of the red building, so it was as easy to go round it, down towards the lake. That was what brought Chris into a clear view of the small stand of trees that screened the top pitch from the rest. That was what gave him a clear sight of Grey Mountain, sitting at the edge of the lake alone. The Chief wasn't watching the game. Perhaps things weren't going well.

Chris's detour also meant he was the only one able to see that Grey Mountain wasn't going to be alone for long.

Lukas's two minders were following the edge of the lake, close to the trees. They were glancing around furtively.

This didn't look good.

Chris found himself breaking into a trot, knowing that he had to get involved, knowing that if he didn't do something things could get ugly. At the same time, he could hear the clock ticking . . .

'Hey!' he yelled. 'Hey, no!' It was no use. The wind was blowing briskly into his face. Besides, the way the two minders were moving suggested that their first reaction to hearing 'Hey! Hey, no!' wouldn't be to stop and say 'OK!'

The old man couldn't hear him either. Chris picked up the pace.

The two goons slipped into the trees and vanished. The old man disappeared as Chris ran around the lake shore and the trees moved across to mask him. Chris ran on, blindly.

He hit the edge of the small group of trees 30 or 40 seconds after the two men. There was a small path, worn away by people taking a short cut. Chris followed it at top speed. The old man had been right down on the edge of the lake, and Chris made sure he could see the water at all times as he blasted through the overhanging branches.

Then, suddenly, his view of the lake started to get a lot closer.

One of the branches had proved to be an arm. It had

53

stabbed out and smacked a hand into his shoulder. Chris went flying, arms outstretched, carried on by his own pace. He had an instant where he heard a struggle behind him and voices arguing, then he smacked into the wet ground at the edge of the lake, his arms splashing into the water up to the elbows.

He slithered through wet mud, so that both of his arms were wholly submerged. Some of it splattered up into his face.

Great. Now he'd have to change before he caught the plane.

He pulled himself off the ground, although the mud clung on firmly, as if it was going to be sorry to lose him. As he stood, he held his arms well away from his body, but, frankly, a little water dripping on to his T-shirt would have been an improvement. He was covered from waist to chin in red mud.

Flinging some of the dirt off, he looked around. There was a tree trunk flat on the ground nearby; Chris was pretty sure that was where the old man had been sitting. He wasn't there now.

The edge of the wood was close by, close enough that Chris could see the top pitch and the game between the red-garbed Iroquois and their opponents, who were wearing the most garish football kit Chris could ever remember – a kind of green and orange sash through a yellow shirt. The shorts were orange too.

It was possible that the old man had been sitting facing the water just to avoid getting a migraine. But he wouldn't have left his young charges completely alone, would he?

Which meant . . .

Chris looked back over the lake, towards the red building and the spot from which he had been looking *this* way just a few moments before.

Sure enough, there they were. The two minders were either side of the old man, propelling him along at a speed Chris knew Grey Mountain would never have chosen for himself. The Chief's feathered staff wasn't even touching the ground as they directed him along the shore, using the building to mask them from sight. Directly ahead of them, there was a dark van with a side door.

Grey Mountain didn't have his drum.

54

Chris looked round, and there it was on the ground on the far side of the fallen tree trunk. Chris grabbed the drum. He thought about calling out to the members of the Iroquois team, but they were even further away than he was. He was sure there wasn't much time.

Back the way he had come. Chris tried to sprint, but his clothes were clinging to him and the mud was heavy. So was the drum, surprisingly so. It didn't look like he was going to make it.

Falling back on a plan of action he had abandoned earlier, Chris yelled loudly as he emerged from the trees. 'Hey! Hey, you – stop!!!' Naturally, the only people who didn't stop, turn round or stare were the two goons. Some spectators watched in amazement as the strange clay monster lurched towards them.

No-one did anything constructive to help. After all, this was America.

As the thugs reached the van and bundled their captive inside, Chris skidded on some loose earth on the edge of the lake. He was still twenty metres short. Linford Christie would have been on them in another two seconds, but Chris wasn't quite in Olympic class. Besides, what was he going to do when he caught up with them – drip all over them?

An idea popped into his head. Chris lifted the drum up, drew his arms back over his head and fired it at the two thugs.

A long throw can be as good as a near-post cross if it's done right. The striker has to be ready to flick the ball back over his head, setting up someone else to smash in the close-range chance.

'Never let the ball hit your head – always hit the ball!' How many times had his father said that in their games in the garden. It was just the same with a drum. These guys clearly weren't soccer players.

There was a deep, satisfying WHUMP as the drum bounced off the first guy's oily, black-haired head. He then cracked the front of his skull on the van door.

He wasn't playing any more.

The other guy was pretty surprised by the turn of events. He watched the drum fall to the ground about a half-second before his pal joined it, his small, piggy eyes as wide as they would go. Then his eyebrows lowered angrily and he squared off to face Chris. That was bad enough, but he also dived inside his jacket with his right hand. Chris had seen enough American cop shows to know that the thug wasn't looking for a notebook.

THWACK! Another satisfying noise. A feather floated to the ground as the piggy eyed man swayed on his feet. When he dropped to his knees, Chris saw the Chief inside the van, clutching the staff.

Chris was still running towards the van, which didn't make sense, but which seemed inevitable somehow. Grey Mountain was clambering out of the side door and opening the cab.

'Get in!' he commanded.

Something in his voice made Chris want to obey. The fact that neither of the thugs were out for the count (although they'd probably be fighting for the aspirin bottle before teatime) just made the decision a little easier.

The van's engine roared into life. Chris jumped over the two sprawling minders and fell heavily into the cargo area behind the front seats.

He heard loose earth and twigs flying from under the wheels as they spun, fighting for grip. Grey Mountain had floored the accelerator and the van was sliding to the left and right far more than it was going forward. Slowly, though, the Chief got the vehicle under control. It gathered speed, bouncing across the grass. A corner flag got levelled as they passed the pitches.

'Hang on!' cried Grey Mountain, about 30 seconds too late. Chris was rolling around on the floor of the van like a milk bottle.

'Where are we going?' he yelled over the roaring engine. Then another thought occurred to him. 'Why are we going so fast? They can't follow us – we've got their van!'

'They may have borrowed someone else's,' replied Grey Mountain, heaving the wheel over to the right. The van picked up even more speed and stopped swaying so hard. Chris realised they must have hit some kind of paved road.

There were windows in the back door. Chris slid across the floor and looked out. A small road was spooling out quickly behind them. There were people walking along on either side, some carrying picnic baskets and toys, others walking their dogs; several of them were staring in alarm at the van as it sped past. Nowhere, though, was there any sign of pursuit.

'Ah –' Chris began.

'Trust me, they are coming,' replied the old man at the wheel.

Chris managed to slither to the front of the van as they weaved through the traffic on the right-hand side of a dual carriageway. Clambering over the seats, he fell into the cab beside Grey Mountain. He saw they were doing 60mph.

'Uh . . . what's the speed limit here?' Chris asked.

'I don't know, I've never driven this van before,' Grey Mountain replied mysteriously.

As they avoided a small white Honda by a fraction of a millimetre, Chris wondered how often Grey Mountain had driven at all. The Chief turned right at the next junction, running a red light. Chris's heart was beating faster.

'Look, we have to go back,' he said. 'I'm being picked up at the hotel at eleven!' The dashboard clock was showing five minutes to. OK . . . 'Or you could drop me at the airport.'

'The airport lies the other way,' Grey Mountain said. He drove across the forecourt of a gas station, emerging on the other side having executed another turn. Chris felt his heartbeat speeding up. It was one thing being in a high-speed car chase (even if he couldn't see anyone doing any actual *chasing*), but it was another to watch Grey Mountain drive without using the brake once.

'Yeah, but if we're just running away, couldn't we go in the other direction?' he asked.

Grey Mountain didn't comment. At the next direction, he threw the van in a 180 degree turn. The central reservation along this wide road was filled with trees and flowerbeds, partially masking the traffic going the other way. As they passed a dark red saloon, Grey Mountain's mouth curled in a slight smile.

'Now we can go back,' he said, slowing the van to a legal speed. Chris looked out of the rear window. He hadn't received enough of a glimpse of the red saloon to know who was in it, but the Chief was obviously convinced. Whoever it was, they didn't make the same risky turn. The highway behind the van was filled with normal traffic. They cruised along with the flow, anonymously.

'Is that it?' asked Chris, picking lumps of mud off his jeans.

'For now. They will continue in that direction for a mile or more,' Grey Mountain announced.

'How can you be sure?' asked Chris.

'This is the road they would expect me to follow,' Grey Mountain explained. 'It leads to my home.'

'And . . ?'

'Didn't you see that blue baker's van ahead of us?' Grey Mountain continued, with a slight note of impatience in his voice. 'It was riding high, which means it was empty. The Dutchman's Bakery is about a mile further on along this road. The van is similar enough to our own to confuse our pursuers until it reaches the bakery and turns off.'

Chris was impressed. Either he was being fed the biggest line of hogwash he had ever been told (all with an impressive straight face) or Grey Mountain had managed to take in all that information and formulate a plan while they were playing dodgems with the traffic.

'Are we heading back to the park?' asked Chris.

'Of course. Don't you want to know how we did in the game?'

Chris laughed. Right now, football was the last thing on his mind (and there hadn't been many times in his life when he could have said that).

The clock ticked past eleven Chris prayed that the airline bus might be late or that the airline lady would hang on for a few moments. Some hope. Chris began to formulate plans to cover himself if the airline had left him behind.

'You'll run me to the airport, right, when we get back?'

'I wouldn't want you to miss your flight,' Grey Mountain replied.

That said, they lapsed into silence as the Chief drove back, obeying traffic lights, speed restrictions and other courtesies They tiptoed into Indy Sports, sliding carefully into the space they had left 25 minutes before.

Very carefully indeed.

'Get out of the van!' yelled the police officer, gun levelled at the cab. 'Hands where I can see them!'

Eight

⚽

On TV, there's something quite glamorous and exciting about American cops. Those sharp blue uniforms with the copper-coloured badges, the heavy belts, the holster, the truncheon along one leg. These guys mean business.

Up close, though, Chris realised that they weren't so cuddly. They had the uniforms, but they also had flak jackets with the word POLICE stencilled front and back (in case there was any confusion). The nearest one was making even more sure Chris understood who he was (and who was in charge) by having a large handgun pointed at Chris's head.

His colleagues were being equally stroppy with Grey Mountain. Each of them was yelling strings of words that blurred together. 'Outtathavan! Onthafloor! Handsbehindyerhead!'

Chris's life in a quiet English city with policemen armed with a whistle and a baton the size of a child's toy hadn't prepared him for a situation like this. Foolishly, he believed this was a good time to attempt an explanation.

He managed an 'I –' and a half-step forward.

'DONMOVE! KEEPYOURHANSWHEREICANSEEM!!'

Chris froze on the spot. He was very clearly aware that there were a great many people looking at him. Three police cruisers were parked outside the red building, their flashing lights distracting the players on the three lower pitches. Dozens of spectators had turned to watch the more interesting spectacle of the police dealing with the returning van. Chris noticed Gary Lukas among them, his hands on the shoulders of a player in yellow and black who was his spitting image.

Gary Lukas Snr was smiling. His son looked happy too.

Chris watched him, keeping perfectly still as the police officers moved closer to frisk him. The cops slipped some kind of narrow plastic tape over his wrists, tying his hands behind his back (apparently he didn't rate proper cuffs).

One of them led him towards a cruiser, pressing down on his head as he pushed Chris into the car.

Chris said nothing. He just sat perfectly still, dripping mud all over the back seat.

The police were dealing with Grey Mountain in the same manner as they'd dealt with Chris. His staff and drum (recovered from the floor where they had left it) went into the trunk of one of the cruisers, rattling and thumping as they landed. Grey Mountain smiled at Chris through the window.

It took a few minutes before the police drove them away from the scene. Shortly before they left, the two teams from the top pitch walked down to the red building. The fashion victims looked crestfallen. The Iroquois players were smiling, though they didn't appear overexcited. The tall, muscular guy with the scarred face came as close to the cruisers as the police would allow. He didn't look at all surprised to see Grey Mountain arrested.

'We won,' he said, in a deep, booming voice. Chris heard a few people hiss from among the crowd. Lukas was smiling even more broadly.

Grey Mountain allowed his weathered old face to crease very slightly. Chris started to feel angry. Overhead, he could see the trails of an aircraft heading west.

OK, there was no way it could be *his* plane, but the principle was the same.

'So, kid, where do you live?'

'I told you. Oldcester, England.'

The detective smiled. He had several teeth missing and the ones that were left had a dark brown stain in the gaps between. He smoked an evil-smelling brand of cigarettes, taking the next from the packet before the last was even finished. His lighter was industrial strength.

'England, yeah, right. You said.' Leaning back on his metal-framed chair, the detective smoothed a hand over the large swelling of his belly. There was a half-eaten sandwich beside him. Chris was starting to feel hungry, but the alien mess between those two slices of bread did nothing to make him feel like eating. There were traces of it on the detective's tie and shirt. Both had small burn marks on them, possibly from the cigarettes, but Chris didn't rule out the food.

'You don't sound English,' the detective said. He smiled. Chris thought it was like being face to face with a shark.

'I'm not Australian,' Chris snapped. He caught himself a moment too late, hoping that he hadn't made the cop angry. In fact, the detective looked quite pleased with the answer.

'No-one accused you of being Australian, kid. Though, come to think of it, maybe you do sound a bit that way. That why you denied it, kid? Trying to throw us off the scent?'

Chris sighed. He was already of the opinion that the cop was as bright as *Columbo*, only without all the intelligent bits.

'Look, sir . . .' Chris began, hoping that he would be able to explain things so that the cop would understand.

'Don't get cute with me kid!' the detective exploded. Chris felt his understanding of the situation slipping.

'Sorry?'

'I got nothing to be sorry about, kid. You do.'

This was getting more and more unreal.

'I was just trying to be polite . . .' Chris said.

'Polite? You want to be polite, kid, you call me by my rank and name. Don't get cute, OK? I'm Detective Enzio. You want to speak to me, you call me Detective, or Detective Enzio, you understand?'

Chris didn't, but he decided that nodding would be a good thing to do right now.

'What was that, kid?'

In his head, Chris was saying, 'My name is Chris; Chris Stephens. Not kid. You want to be polite you call me Chris, or maybe Stephens. Mr Stephens maybe. Not kid.'

It came out as 'Yes, Detective Enzio.'

Enzio grinned his hungry smile and took another long drag on his cigarette. He tapped the end of his pencil on the form laid on the desk. It didn't have too many pencilled words just yet.

'Good. So, name?'

Chris started to sigh, but he managed to stifle it. He scratched some mud from his sleeve.

'Chris Stephens.'

'Good,' said Detective Enzio, scribbling in one of the spaces He'd written the name once before, in the same space, but had rubbed it out when he thought Chris was being 'cute'. 'Address?'

'8 Chelmsford Street, Spirebrook, Oldcester,' he replied automatically After a moment's hesitant thought he added· 'England.'

Detective Enzio laid down his pencil once again 'Where's your passport, English boy?'

Chris glanced at the clock on the wall. 'On a Delta Airlines plane at the airport.' Not for much longer, though In twenty minutes, it would be on its way to a holiday in California without him, along with the rest of his gear.

Detective Enzio stabbed at Chris's wallet with the rubber end of the pencil. 'You didn't think to carry it with you?'

'I didn't think I'd need it. I only went to the park to watch a friend play football . soccer.'

Enzio sneered to show how likely that was. Once again, Chris's extensive knowledge of US cop shows came to his aid He knew Enzio wouldn't believe anything he said, unless he confessed to whatever dreadful crime they had hauled him here for (assault with a musical instrument, most probably)

'You got a lot of friends here in Indianapolis, English boy?'

'I met him this morning,' muttered Chris. Even he didn't like the way that sounded 'He works at the hotel.'

Detective Enzio wasn't writing any of this down He lit a new cigarette, then put out the old one Chris felt a warning tickle in his throat, but decided not to cough At the same moment, Chris saw a NO SMOKING sign on the wall of the interview room He kept that to himself as well.

'When did you meet Chief Grey Mountain?' Enzio asked.

'I didn't,' said Chris. 'Not before . . . well, that is, I saw him when I arrived at the park, and then I saw him again sitting by the lake and these two guys were heading towards him . . .'

Enzio wasn't interested in Chris's story. 'You made a big mistake gettin' involved with that crazy old man,' he snarled. 'You seen them rattles on that stick he carries? Them's from rattlesnakes.' Enzio shivered. 'I hate snakes,' he added.

Chris wasn't a big fan of them either, but he was close to preferring them to Detective Enzio He was struggling to see what being in possession of dead rattlesnakes had to do with any of this.

'This flight you's s'posed to be on,' Enzio said, switching the subject yet again. 'Where's your ticket?'

Chris was caught off guard yet again. He grinned back apologetically.

'In your bag, right?' Enzio laughed. 'On its way back to England?'

'California,' Chris corrected him at once. 'I'm going to see a friend –'

'When did you meet him? On the way to the park?'

'Easter,' said Chris, ignoring the sarcasm in Enzio's voice. 'He came to England at Easter. It was an exchange visit. Now I'm supposed to be going to California to stay with him –'

'Name?'

Did he mean Jace's or his, Chris wondered? He really didn't want to guess wrong. Detective Enzio's face started to cloud over as the delay grew longer.

'Jace Goodman . . . his father's name is Bob – Robert.'

He'd guessed right. Enzio scribbled down the name. 'Address?'

'Albany, California. Near San Francisco. I can't remember the street.'

'How are you supposed to get in touch with these Goodmans?'

'I have Mr Goodman's mobile number,' Chris explained, brightening now that he was on safer ground. That moment of triumph lasted for very little time. 'It's in my diary,' he confessed, before Enzio could ask. 'In my bag.'

Enzio leant back even further on the frail metal chair, testing its strength and endurance in a particularly risky way. He studied Chris, and Chris studied him. Chris got the worst of the deal. He'd already noticed the cigarette stains on Enzio's fingers and teeth, the big belly and the blotchy skin. Now he got the chance to study how Enzio's hair was thinning and how there were sweat stains under his armpits. There was a holster under one of those armpits as well. It looked as old, frayed and past it as the detective. He was desperate to break the silence. Chris knew it was only a matter of time before he said something that would land him in even more trouble.

'You could call the airline,' he insisted. 'My name will be on a passenger list.' You could even get them to hold the flight while you whisk me to the airport in a police cruiser with the lights on and the siren wailing.

'You trying to tell me my job?' asked Enzio. Chris bit his lip before the words 'you could use the help' struggled out.

Another cloud of cigarette smoke appeared from between the detective's lips. Chris felt the urge to cough more than ever.

In that same moment, the door opened and the blast of cool(er), fresh(er) air blew the cloud up to the ceiling, where it hung nervously in the shadows above the light.

Chris and Enzio looked to see who had come in. The first through the door was a smart, intelligent-looking detective in a clean, well-cut suit. His hair (he had some) was brushed back neatly and he didn't have a cigarette in his hand. Chris liked him already.

'Enzio,' the newcomer said, 'this is . . .'

A woman in a dark suit and white blouse pushed past him, marching to the desk. She had a briefcase and a visitor's badge hanging from her breast pocket. She couldn't have looked more like a lawyer if she'd had the word LAWYER written in big letters on her jacket the way the uniformed police did on theirs.

Chris stared. She might well be coming to his rescue like the cavalry, but Chris was rather more awestruck by her hair. It was as black as coal and hung in a long, thick plait from the base of her skull to the bottom of her spine. If she had spun her head quickly, she could have killed everyone in the room.

'My name is Waters,' she said crisply. 'Detective Enzio, are you aware that my client is a minor?'

'Your client?' mocked the detective. He looked at his colleague, flicking an eyebrow to both interrogate and condemn the younger cop. 'A minor, you say?' he asked, allowing the chair to fall forward so that the front legs hit the floor with a bang.

'Why haven't you called Child Services?' the woman demanded.

'Who says I haven't?' sneered Enzio, with another glance at the other detective. The younger man was still in the doorway, leaning on the frame. His face expressed nothing at all.

64

'Then why are you questioning my client without them being here?' the woman demanded. She was reaching inside her briefcase, pulling out a very official-looking document.

'I –' began Enzio. He didn't get to say anything else.

'Detective Enzio, I have here a copy of the statement from the two gentlemen who made the complaint about the stolen van. They now state that they consider the matter to have been a 'misunderstanding', and that they are not going to press charges. In those circumstances, I would think you're finished with my client, wouldn't you?'

Enzio bared his brown-yellow teeth. 'Quick work, counsellor.'

The woman didn't register a smile or a returning growl. She snapped her fingers and pointed at Chris's wrists, still bound by the plastic tape.

While she watched Enzio snip the tape with a pair of scissors, she looked at Chris's fingertips.

'Did you fingerprint my client?'

'It's just a matter of routine –' Enzio started.

'Make sure those print records are destroyed immediately, Detective Enzio. My client is a non-US national with no criminal record and no charges pending against him. I'd hate to file charges of wrongful arrest of a minor against this department.'

She took Chris under the arm and pulled him to his feet.

'You should also be aware that we may still bring evidence of an attempted abduction to your notice. I wish you better luck with that case.'

Enzio said nothing. He was lighting up another cigarette. Waters looked at the sign at the wall and tutted.

Enzio was slowly rising to his feet, feeling behind him for the jacket he had draped over the chair. He didn't seem happy to see Chris leave.

'Hey kid,' he called. 'You want to make sure you catch your plane. Leastways, you want to make real sure you and I don't ever meet again.'

'You're right there,' muttered Chris.

He stepped out into the hall, the tall woman right behind him, closing the door. The third person in the rescue squad was standing there, just behind the young detective. Enzio took one look into the hall and shivered.

'Hi, Chris,' said Grey Mountain, shaking his staff so that it rattled. 'This is Detective Moran. A good guy. And you've met my granddaughter? Round here they call her Ms Waters, the lawyer, but you can call her Running Waters.' He winked. 'Or Flood Waters, as I've always called her.'

Nine

According to Detective Moran, the Spaghetti Factory in downtown Indianapolis was famous for its spaghetti. Just as well really Chris got through two platefuls and some pancakes for dessert Getting grilled by Enzio had left him hungrier than he had been for years.

Grey Mountain drank soup from a mug. Running Waters worked her way through a huge burger and three cups of coffee.

Detective Moran arrived back at the booth carrying a tray loaded with a plate of fries, a mineral water, a large coke, a milkshake and a mug of scalding hot coffee He put his mobile phone down on the table. Chris noticed it was switched off.

'OK,' he said 'I don't have long.'

Running Waters dived into her briefcase and threw a pad of lined yellow paper on to the formica tabletop As she turned to the right page, Moran handed over the drinks Chris took his coke and drained half the glass at one go.

'One,' Running Waters said, tapping an expensive fountain pen on the first of the notes she had written on the pad. 'Lukas is behind all of this. He –'

'Stop right there, Ms Waters,' the young cop sighed. 'That allegation isn't going anywhere, and you know it.'

Running Waters looked up at him with a flash of anger in her eyes 'Why? The dispute between Lukas and my people is a matter of record. The Bitter Lake dispute gives him a motive. By abducting my grandfather, he –'

'There's your problem, right there Lukas didn't abduct anyone; his goons did. First, you'd have to convince a jury that there was an abduction – after all, in the end, your grandfather drove the van away himself –'

'*After* he had been dragged into the van from beside the

67

lake!' She gestured angrily in Grey Mountain's direction. He was struggling to get the cap off the bottle of mineral water. Without really looking at him, Running Waters took the bottle, slipped the top into the grip of her left fist and tore off the cap with a sharp twist.

Moran watched this with evident respect. He paused for a moment, then counted on to the second of his fingers. 'Two, you'd have to prove that Fehnman and Spanish Johnny were following Lukas's orders and not acting off some idea of their own.'

'Those two? An idea of their own? Give me a break . . .'

Detective Moran smiled, but continued to tick off his points on his thumb. 'Three, that motive cuts both ways. Your people are prepared to do almost anything to keep the land at Bitter Lake. A jury might think that included framing Lukas for a so-called abduction.'

Running Waters controlled her obvious unhappiness with the way Moran had shot down her case by sipping at the mug of coffee. The fact that she didn't argue, though, made Chris think Moran was probably right. He watched them both thinking through their replies.

'If you're not prepared to help, why are we here?' Running Waters snapped.

'I'm prepared to help, but you're not giving me anything I can use,' said Moran. He sat back in his seat with the tall glass of milkshake perched on his chest. 'And none of it is new.'

Running Waters put her mug down on the table and steepled her fingers under her chin as she leant forward. 'The abduction is new,' she smiled. 'And we have a witness.'

Chris found himself at the centre of attention from three pairs of eyes; Running Waters looking very pleased with herself; Moran clearly trying to make up his mind; Grey Mountain as unreadable as ever. Chris felt very self-conscious. He brushed crumbs off the new clothes Grey Mountain had bought for him and wondered if he was supposed to say anything.

Moran beat him to it. 'Ms Waters –' he began.

'What? Are you going to say that this boy has a vested interest in seeing my people keep their land?'

'No,' conceded Moran, 'but let's be realistic. He's a minor and a non-national. Our priority for Chris has to be to get him on a plane home, not to try to find ways to keep him here so that he can be a witness in a criminal case. It could take a year to get to court.'

Home? Chris wondered if he ought to make the point that he was due in San Francisco, not Oldcester.

Running Waters didn't give him a chance to speak. Chris could see now why Grey Mountain liked to call her Flood Waters. Tidal Wave would have been another good name.

'We can get a deposition from him,' she said briskly. 'That would be enough to press charges and to bring us through pre-trial . . .'

'Ms Waters,' said Detective Moran, his voice calm and even. Once again the lawyer's eyes flashed. 'You and I both know that this has nothing to do with any criminal abduction charges. The only hearing you're interested in happens on Wednesday. You're hoping to use today's incident to influence the judge when the hearing takes place about the Bitter Lake project. Maybe drum up a little publicity on the way.'

Running Waters sat back, silent. Chris had noticed that this was her preferred way for dealing with small defeats in the argument. Any second now, she would change the direction of her attack . . .

'So, you're going to do nothing?' she demanded.

'I didn't say that,' Moran replied before slurping the last of his milkshake. 'But Enzio's not going to go after Lukas just because you say so. He thinks this is all some game you guys are playing. We're going to need something more solid.'

Running Waters put the pad back in the briefcase and the pen into her jacket's breast pocket. She didn't look pleased with what she had been told. Her coat was draped over the back of the chair; she picked it up, threw it across her shoulders, and pulled up the long rope of her hair so that it lay outside the coat.

'I have to get back to the office, grandfather,' she said quickly. 'There is still a lot of work to be done before Wednesday.'

She kissed him on the forehead. Grey Mountain wrinkled his nose.

'I'll walk you to your car,' said Moran By the time he finished the sentence, she was already halfway to the door. He put the tall glass down and scampered after the lawyer.

Grey Mountain didn't move until after they were outside

'I wish he'd hurry up and ask her for a date,' he said, pulling the fries and the last part of Running Waters' burger to his side of the table

Chris grinned Grey Mountain had been silent for virtually the whole meal, pretending to be uninterested Chris knew it was all an act.

'You must be proud of her being a lawyer.'

Grey Mountain couldn't reply at first, since he had stuffed his mouth almost full of fries After chewing steadily for a few seconds he managed to mumble· 'It's cheaper than hiring an outsider Pass the ketchup, will you?'

Chris handed the plastic bottle over Through the window, he could see Moran jogging after Running Waters' fast retreating back

'Can I ask you a question?' Chris said.

'You just did,' Grey Mountain came back instantly

Chris sighed He wasn't going to be deflected that easily 'What ' he began

Grey Mountain was looking directly at him, the bottle of ketchup in his hands, tilted over the plate of chips 'You want to know what we were doing on the soccer pitch last night ' He squeezed the bottle, which bled ketchup on to the plate

'That's right,' said Chris 'It was you I saw, wasn't it? Playing the drum while the other guy –'

'Danced,' said Grey Mountain, and he forked another mound of fries into his mouth His eyes closed with evident pleasure

Chris waited patiently while the Chief finished chewing. Grey Mountain opened his eyes to find that Chris had moved the plate over to his corner of the table Chris was prepared to be every bit as awkward as the Chief

'Very well,' Grey Mountain said, sounding a little weary, as if he was tired of explaining everything he did His eyes closed Chris imagined him looking into his mind as if it were a great book, or a well illustrated CD Rom 'Listen carefully Back before the white men came, my people roamed this land freely, from the Great Lakes to the Ohio River We didn't own the land, it owned us. It gave us food and shelter, and in return we cherished it, cared for it

'Then the first settlers came Sometimes we fought them; other times we were at peace' His eyes opened 'Actually, one of my ancestors fought at Quebec. You know of Quebec?'

Chris nodded, though his knowledge was sketchy. There had been a war against the French and part of the fighting had taken place in what would become the USA and Canada. The British, under General Wolfe, had defeated the French at Quebec and taken control of Canada. Wolfe had been killed.

'You fought with General Wolfe?' Chris asked.

'Heck, no,' said Grey Mountain. 'We were with the French. My people always knew you British would be more trouble. It's just a pity we weren't better at picking the winning side.'

Chris laughed. The story was a sidetrack, aimed at distracting him. He also knew Grey Mountain was making fun of his new English friend.

'So?' he said at last. 'Go on.'

Grey Mountain eyed the distant plate, sighed and closed his eyes once more. 'When we were at peace, we agreed to share the land. To us, such things came naturally. As I said, we do not own the land, we are merely its guardians. There was plenty for all to share; water, buffalo, wood, fur . . .

'At least, so we thought. But your people arrived in greater and greater numbers, and there was no longer enough to share. And the white men didn't believe as we did. They thought they could own the land, cut it up into pieces large and small. They built cities on fertile land; poisoned the water; killed all the buffalo. And we gradually became smaller and less significant.

'Many years ago, my people were defeated in battle. We had to sign a peace treaty with a blue-coat general named Wayne.'

John Wayne? Chris wondered, although he kept the thought to himself.

'He made us give up our land to the settlers. We were left only a small part on which to live. The settlers built cities, roads and railways. They came in increasing numbers; millions arrived in just a few short generations. And wherever they drew their property boundaries, they cut into the land, reduced it, wounded it. Once the land was marked and divided, it could never be the same.

'On some of the land that was taken from us, there were holy places. These places were special to us. After our defeat, we feared they would be lost for ever. So, when we made the treaty with General Wayne, we made sure that those holy places would remain whole. We gave the land to the government, but the treaty stated that the holy places would never be built on, never be the white man's to despoil, so long as the Iroquois still lived there.

'Bitter Lake is one of those holy places. My people believe that their ancestors visit the valley, to speak with anyone who comes to visit them, to pass on their wisdom. But for some time now, no-one has lived there. There are so few of us left, and the young ones do not care to live in our villages for long. Bitter Lake has been silent for a long time.'

Chris started to realise what must have happened. Lukas had found out about the treaty somehow, and realised that since no-one was living there, Bitter Lake belonged to the government, and that he could buy it.

'So, why can't you just move back there? Build a few houses?' he asked.

Grey Mountain looked even more tired than before. 'Lukas owns all the land around the lake. He has put up fences. Guards patrol the only routes in and out. We cannot get in. Also, a judge signed a piece of paper, saying that the land was vacant on January 1st, the date Lukas bought it from the government. This means that even if we were to move back, it would be too late.'

Chris nodded. The legal side of things didn't make a lot of sense to him, but he could tell from the tone of Grey Mountain's voice that the Iroquois had been taken to the cleaners.

'So, what does this court hearing on Wednesday do?'

'We must convince a judge that our people have not abandoned Bitter Lake,' Grey Mountain said. 'We are saying that it was not a place where we lived, but a place of worship. "Continuous occupation" only means that we continue to use the site in that way.'

He looked out of the window at his granddaughter, who was holding an animated discussion with Moran by the door of her jeep.

'If we win, it means Lukas can't build. We want him to sell the land back to us.'

Chris thought about that for a moment. He could see where the prospect of the deal falling through would make Lukas desperate.

'So, where does this half million dollars come into it?' he asked.

Grey Mountain's face was starting to get that stubborn streak about it again. 'It's his way of stopping us proceeding. We have to deposit $500,000 with the court by Wednesday, to prove we aren't just making nuisances of ourselves.'

The Chief was looking out of the window. Running Waters was pulling out of the car park, her bright red jeep glistening in some weak sunshine.

'So far, we only have $175,000. We need the prize money from the soccer tournament.' Chris did the sum in his head. Actually, they needed to win another six tournaments as well. 'Running Waters may be a good lawyer, but she can't work miracles.' Chris was thinking the same thing. Grey Mountain looked exceptionally gloomy.

'You think she and Moran will get together?' Chris asked, changing the subject suddenly.

Grey Mountain shrugged. 'Who knows? My son would prefer that she married Joseph Blackdeer.' Chris knew he was talking about the scarred-faced man. 'I worry about her being involved with a policeman.'

'Why?'

'They work long hours, and the pay sucks. I think Moran would make her happy, but could it last?'

'You'd prefer Joseph Blackdeer too?'

Grey Mountain turned quickly, looking quite horrified. 'A football player? Great spirit, no! I want her to marry a dentist. Good money, and the hours aren't so long.'

Chris laughed. He had fallen into the old man's trap, thinking of him as being some kind of inward-looking old native. He wouldn't make that mistake again.

'I can't imagine anyone ever thinking you could be a nuisance,' said Chris, grinning, as he pushed the plate back. Grey Mountain glanced quickly out of the window and saw Moran was on his way back. He took another handful of the fries and filled his mouth quickly.

'Some would say we were masters at it,' the old man replied, and he slid the plate back in front of Chris just as Moran returned.

Ten

—⚽—

Moran looked quite troubled as he drove them away from the diner. For one thing, he couldn't remember having eaten over half his fries before he escorted Running Waters out to her car. Chris guessed the detective was also thinking about whatever he had been discussing with the Iroquois lawyer in the car park.

They were heading back to Indy Sports. Moran had managed to get Chris booked on a flight out of Indianapolis at 8.50pm. He'd squared things with the airline, telling them that Chris had been a witness to a felony. He had also left a message with Bob Goodman's message service (which he had tracked down by calling some friend in California) and gave Chris a card with the Goodman's number written on the back. Chris's holiday could finally get started.

An 8.50pm flight time meant they needed to be at the airport by seven; that left them time to drop Grey Mountain off at the park. Chris said he'd like to see how the quarter-finals had gone that afternoon.

Moran said he was prepared to handcuff Chris to his wrist if it meant not letting him out of his sight, but he agreed to the detour.

They arrived just as the last games were coming to an end. On the pitch nearest the point where Moran parked his grey Lexus, the yellow and black shirts of The Orchards were just celebrating having scored their fifth goal against the team from East Chicago, high-fiving and whooping with joy. Their supporters were clapping and cheering. The Chicago keeper shrugged at his team mates and fetched the ball from the net.

There was no sign of any blood-red shirts, but Chris was delighted to see the all-whites on the furthest pitch. He couldn't imagine how Lawrence had got through their first game, but there they were. It appeared that they were doing OK too, although Chris couldn't tell the score from where they were.

He looked over towards the noticeboards by the red building, intending to see what had happened in the morning games, but Grey Mountain was already on his way to the top pitch.

Chris and Detective Moran trailed in his wake. As they passed the other pitches, Chris felt eyes following him. He turned his head and saw Gary Lukas watching them pass. His face was unreadable, but there was no way he was pleased. Chris noticed that the two minders weren't there.

Leaning on his staff, Grey Mountain sailed past the angry glares all around him and marched through the small wood and along the trail until they came out near the top pitch. He hadn't so much as glanced at the spot where he had been ambushed that morning.

'We're winning,' said Grey Mountain.

'How does he do that?' Moran wondered out loud, scratching his chin.

Chris wasn't so impressed. The Iroquois were playing a team in red and white hoops, bewildered and exhausted young men who were struggling to keep up with the pace. If they had been protecting a lead, the red and whites would have been much more animated. Instead they looked spent; a beaten team.

The fact that the scoreboard said it was 2-0 to the Wabash Iroquois was an even better clue.

Moran saw that two uniformed officers were loitering over by the fence. 'What are they doing here?' he muttered. Chris took a quick look, but then went back to watching the game.

'If you move from this spot, I'll shoot you,' said Moran, and he started walking round the pitch to talk to the two uniforms. Chris stood as still as he could manage.

This was his first chance to watch the Iroquois properly, and he wasn't that dismayed. The two taller boys he had noticed earlier were very good on the ball; one was working the centre of midfield, the other played up front. The whole team worked hard and tackled like demons. They tended to cluster together, uncomfortable at being too far from the ball, but Chris saw that mistake repeated often enough back home.

The defence worried him a little too. The keeper seemed prone to leaving his area at the first excuse.

He even went up for corners, like Mark Crossley. Crossley only did it when Forest were in trouble; this guy did it as a matter of principle.

Chris could feel a familiar itch inside his head. Let me at them, his instincts were calling. Two-nil down? I could have the red and whites back level inside two minutes.

Not that the team in the hoops were much better at the back. Their problem appeared to be that they had been run off their feet by a fitter, more committed side. 'No, better still,' Chris said to himself, 'put me on for the Iroquois and we can be five-nil up by the finish.'

As he watched, the tall midfield player skipped a challenge from one of the red and white players and bounded upfield. His close control wasn't anything to write home about, but he was fast over the ground, and the red and whites were backing off.

Chris imagined him and Nicky in this situation. Nicky would be screaming up the right touchline, arm aloft, calling for the pass. Chris would put the ball up behind the labouring full back, then swerve left, aiming for the far post. Nicky wouldn't need to break stride to pick up the pass, nor look up to see where Chris had gone. The cross would be a low, fast arc; just high enough to beat the keeper but close enough to keep him interested. It would be a foot above Chris's head by the time it fell at the rear post. Take off from the right foot, cock the head and WHAP! The ball would be in the back of the net and he and Nicky would be banging heads. Thank you and goodnight.

Chris smiled. It would have been a great goal.

The Iroquois didn't manage to engineer anything quite so special. The tall midfielder was tackled and suddenly the red and whites were streaking back the other way, players finding their last reserves of strength. The Wabash defence was off balance, chasing the ball. As the ball went into the box, they had two chances to clear it, but the ball broke to an unmarked attacker and he thumped it along the floor and into the net.

2–1. The Native Americans would have an anxious last few minutes.

Chris turned away, unable to bear the sudden look of fear that had crept on to their faces. As he looked up, he saw someone in a white shirt coming out of the woods, having followed the same trail he had followed twice now At first he thought it might be CG, but he quickly recognised Jon, moving at his usual laid-back pace. Jon caught sight of him too and angled towards him.

'Hi,' Chris called. 'How's it going?'

'OK,' replied Jon. Chris had been hoping for something a little more precise, like the score, but he saw that Jon appeared to be quite flustered and anxious so he didn't push it.

'I've got a message for you,' Jon said. His eyes rolled up, as if he was trying to remember which cloud he had written the message on. It slowly came back to him. 'From CG,' he added at last. Chris waited patiently. 'After you got hauled away by the police this morning, CG went back to the hotel and rescued your bag. It's behind the desk in reception.'

Solid! Good old CG. Chris wondered how he had managed it, since there had still been a few minutes of the half to go, but he guessed that the confusion he and Grey Mountain had left behind must have continued for just long enough for CG to slip back to the hotel through the alley Lucky; he must just have caught the luggage before it was loaded on the bus.

'Great,' Chris said. 'Tell him thanks for me. I'm being taken out to the airport in a minute; I'd best go get it.'

Jon nodded, obviously relieved that he had managed to get the message right.

'How come you're not playing?' asked Chris.

Jon's face clouded over; he clearly wasn't happy about not playing. 'I got dropped after this morning's game.' Chris decided that this wasn't a subject to be pressed. 'So, how's it going?' he asked, then remembering that he hadn't got an answer the first time he'd asked this, he added: 'You guys winning?'

'One-one,' mumbled Jon, turning away. It appeared their chat was over.

'Thanks,' called Chris, but not too loudly.

He turned back towards the game, seeing that the red and whites were pressing forward now that there was a small chance their opponents were prepared to snatch defeat from the jaws of victory. Grey Mountain was watching the last few moments calmly, but there were plenty of other spectators screaming and calling advice of the 'hoof it up their end' variety.

Chris walked closer to the Chief. 'My bag's still at the hotel,' he said. Grey Mountain didn't respond. 'I'm going to go and get it. Will you let Detective Moran know where I am?'

'As you like,' said Grey Mountain. 'Although I don't understand why you want him to shoot you.'

Chris chuckled, 99 per cent sure that Moran wouldn't actually shoot him if he was gone for ten minutes fetching his bag. Then he remembered all the hardware he had seen in the boot of the police cruiser that had taken him and the Chief downtown. Chris wondered how many guns Moran had in the Lexus.

With that comforting thought in mind, he jogged towards the gate.

It took very little time to reach the front of the hotel, of course. Perhaps Moran wouldn't even have time to load his gun, Chris thought to himself.

He saw CG's mother as he entered the lobby. She was explaining something to a salesman in a faded brown suit, pointing to a map he had unfolded on top of the reception counter. Although she was smiling politely, there was a note in her voice that translated as, 'Look, stupid, I've told you twice, here's the place you're looking for . . .' Chris had thought of asking her what CG's second name was, so that he could win his bet (even if it was a little late to claim his free meal). One look at Mrs Amantani and he decided he didn't mind losing.

He waited patiently to one side, trying to think of more Italian names that began with G (Georgio? Graham-o? Gavin-o?) while she continued to explain the route the salesman needed to take to reach his destination. The more Chris looked at Mrs Amantani, the more he felt he was barking up the wrong tree.

She didn't really look Italian. Not that Chris was an expert or anything, but he did have the experience of having seen all eleven million members of the Fiorentini family. Mrs Amantani had dark hair, sure, but it had a kind of blue-grey steel in it, like Superman's. Could CG be from Krypton?

'Mr Stephens?'

The voice made him jump. The face he encountered when he looked round made him jump a little higher.

'Could we talk?' asked Mr Lukas.

There was a small lounge just off the lobby. It had four low, circular tables in the middle, and others in small alcoves around the wall. Chairs with soft blue seats were scattered all around. Only two of them were occupied.

The two goons grinned at Chris as he saw them. Great . . .

'I've got you a Pepsi,' Lukas said in a friendly voice, indicating one of the central tables which also had a tall, white coffee pot, a sugar bowl and a cup. Everything was neatly arranged. 'That is what you prefer, isn't it?' the businessman asked, unfastening the inside button on his jacket as he sat down. 'They always say that people who actually try both prefer Pepsi to Co—'

'Actually, I prefer Virgin cola,' Chris said quickly. It was good to see that this floored Lukas for a moment. He decided to add: 'They're the new sponsors for Oldcester United, so it's a loyalty thing mostly, but I think I actually do prefer the taste as well.'

As he hoped, Chris saw Lukas's face twist in a grimace that proved he hadn't got a clue what Chris was talking about. Perhaps, Chris thought, he ought to learn a few more fascinating facts like this, for the next time he was dragged off by a criminal mastermind.

'You have me all wrong, you know,' Lukas was saying, having recovered his wits. 'I'm not a crook.'

He was stirring some Sweet & Lo into his black coffee. Chris was still standing. He wondered if this put him at some kind of advantage, but then decided that it would just be more tiring, and sat down.

Lukas pushed the tall glass of iced cola closer to Chris. 'I have never engaged in any criminal activity; I have never used any criminal or illegal methods to get what I wanted.' He spread his hands wide, smiling broadly. 'I don't have to. I'm very good at what I do.'

Chris didn't reply. He did, however, allow himself the time to take a long lingering look in the direction of the two heavies sitting at the next table. What had Moran called them?

Fehnman and Spanish Johnny. It wasn't difficult to decide which was which. Johnny had long, slicked-back hair, a long, lean body and a gap between his front teeth you could drive a bus through; Fehnman had a military shave-cut, those bulging piggy eyes, a head shaped like a cube and arms the size of tree trunks.

Up close, and even though they were wearing The Orchards school track suits, it was hard for Chris to ignore what they really were.

'No, neither of the boys have criminal records either,' Lukas said smoothly, having seen where Chris was looking. 'As for this morning, they asked Chief Grey Mountain to come and speak with me and there was a genuine misunderstanding. There was no violence or threat of violence until you threw that drum at Spanish Johnny.'

Gap-Tooth was looking at Chris with something close to a snarl on his face. He rubbed the back of his head. Chris made a mental note not to leap to conclusions based on appearances.

'You shouldn't leap to conclusions based on appearances,' said Lukas. Chris froze for a moment, confused by a feeling rather like déjà vu. Lukas took a sip of coffee, then continued. 'For example,' he said. 'On the basis of an unfortunate mis-understanding and a few hours in the company of a confused old man, you have decided who is right and who is wrong about this business with the Indians' land at Bitter Lake. Tell me, Chris, have you studied much American history at school in England?'

'Some,' replied Chris, quietly.

Lukas continued in a way that suggested that he hadn't minded whether Chris answered yes or no. 'Grey Mountain's people were part of the Iroquois nation. The Iroquois and the Hurons ranged over what was called the NW Territory after the War of Independence – that was when we Americans kicked out the British.'

'We heard,' replied Chris.

'Over the next thirty, forty years, the population of the original thirteen States doubled. Those extra mouths needed more land. Settlers came this way in their millions, gradually taming the wilderness as far west as the Mississippi. And they took the land from the Indians; no one denies that.'

Chris thought about what Grey Mountain had said. The

Indians had never owned the land in the first place; the settlers weren't so much stealing the land from the Native Americans, they were taking for themselves something which could have been shared freely.

'You know how many Indians there were in the NW Territory in 1816? A few tens of thousands. Imagine that, Chris. Tens of thousands, keeping the land for themselves, when millions needed it.'

Lukas was idly picking off pieces of lint from his suit, smoothing out small imperfections in the way the cloth was lying. He was speaking the words almost without thinking, as if they were comfortably rehearsed in his mind.

'This state was founded in 1816. We've been here for over 175 years. You can't roll back over two hundred years of history just because of the survivors of those few tens of thousands. This land is part of the United States of America now. Nothing can change that.'

Who wanted to? Chris wondered. Why was Lukas waving the flag?

'It's easy to feel sympathy for the Indians and what they lost. It's much harder to realise what all those settlers would have lost without this land.'

He paused and took another sip of coffee, allowing Chris to think about what he had heard.

'What has any of this to do with what you're doing to Grey Mountain's people today?' Chris asked. 'You keep talking about history, but this is happening right now. You've got Indiana; why do you need every last piece?'

Lukas looked up at the ceiling. He had very clear blue eyes, Chris noticed. He wondered where Lukas's ancestors had been in 1816.

'There was a war between the Iroquois and the settlers. The Indians lost. General Wayne signed a treaty that guaranteed the Indians land south of here. It also ensured that their holy places would not be sold or built on so long as they kept to the treaty.'

That was an interesting way of putting it, Chris thought. 'You mean as long as they were living on the land at Bitter Lake,' he said.

Lukas smiled, his thin lips stretching. 'That was part of the treaty, yes. There were other provisions. Such as not taking

81

part in any further wars against the settlers, such as staying on the lands reserved for them. They broke those conditions within ten years. So, you see, that treaty they are hiding behind really doesn't mean that much, does it?'

Chris kept silent.

Lukas waited for a moment. He appeared disappointed that Chris hadn't responded in any way. He sipped at his coffee again, holding the tiny handle between his finger and thumb.

'In the 1950s, the Indians were always the bad guys in the movies.' He put the cup down and made a pretend gun from his fingers 'John Wayne, eh? You heard of John Wayne? He always led the cavalry to the rescue.'

Still Chris said nothing. He wondered how long it would be before Grey Mountain said anything to Moran and how long after that it would be before the detective came to get him. Then we'd see who led the cavalry . . .

'Now, it's all *Dances With Wolves* and *Pocahontas*. "The Indians were robbed"' Lukas shrugged. 'It's just fashion, kid. No one remembers who the real heroes were any more' The businessman smiled, but not with such a friendly expression as he had before The last of the coffee disappeared Lukas stood up, fastened his jacket and smoothed a hand through his long, blond hair.

A small lump jumped up into Chris's throat. The chat was at an end. He knew he'd failed the test. The question was, what would Lukas do, now that he could see Chris wasn't going to be persuaded round to his point of view? Chris caught Spanish Johnny shifting in his seat from the corner of his eye.

This would be a good time to be somewhere else.

Chris had no doubt at all that he was in grave danger Lukas was smooth, but there was a hard, determined man under that suit. Chris hadn't missed the practised way he had spoken; he would bet his last US dollar that Lukas had been in court before. It wasn't that he had lied, it was just the sneaky way he told the truth He hid behind words. 'I have never engaged in any criminal activity'; no, of course not. His hirelings did the dirty work for him 'Neither of the boys have criminal records'; a subtle difference It could easily be read as 'they've done all my criminal deeds for me and never been caught'.

So, there was no point sitting there waiting for Lukas to issue some kind of instruction to his minders. Nothing would be said. They would just deal with Chris the way their master wanted, with no words spoken.

The very thought of it made Chris's blood freeze.

Move, he told himself. Move fast.

Lukas was still smoothing out the creases in his jacket, having dropped a few notes on the table to cover the bill; Spanish Johnny was grinning, looking back at his partner. Only Fehnman was watching Chris, and he was too far away to do anything about what happened next.

Chris dipped forward, grabbed the Pepsi and flung it up at Lukas's face. In the same movement, he leapt out of his seat and started to run for his life.

In the instant in which he was turning, Chris saw the look of amazement and horror on Lukas's face as his suit was splattered with cola. The chair he had been sitting in was tipping back. One of the thugs was yelling 'Hey!' (Chris didn't try to guess which one of them it was), but by then Chris was already out of the lounge and skidding on the smooth floor of the lobby as he raced for the back of the hotel.

It had to be the back. Out front, there was just an open space, a straight road and the footpath. At the back of the hotel there were corridors, passageways, doors, lifts, stairs, rooms of all shapes and sizes. He just had to get out of sight and he'd lose them. Lukas wouldn't want any fuss.

Several guests were in the lobby, their attention attracted by the sudden uproar. Mrs Amantani was behind the desk, so she was out of the game, but the brown-suited salesman was there, blocking the straight route to the lifts. An elderly couple were walking in from the back of the hotel, where there were ground floor rooms. A mother and her daughter were fussing over by one of the other doors.

Chris sized up the space instinctively, as if he had just busted an offside trap. The best opening was to the left, where the woman and her kid were static. Chris's momentum, though, was all the other way. The salesman looked like he could be trouble; he'd tackle Chris just to find out what was going on. That left the old couple coming up the middle. The sweeper.

Chris dummied one way and went the other. It wasn't strictly necessary, but it felt right.

He went through the dining room doors and flashed between the tables, scattering a couple of chairs behind him.

He couldn't hear anyone close behind him, but there were loud voices from the lobby. He didn't look back.

The swing door into the kitchen was swaying. Chris hoped it would work as a distraction. He'd instantly seen the route he wanted to take. The wide window leading out into the yard, the one beside which he had been sitting that morning, was wide open, lace curtains fluttering in the breeze.

He dived through.

He hit the paved area just outside quite hard, but his hands took the worst of the shock, shedding skin as they scraped across the paving stones. He pulled his feet from underneath and continued running. The fence narrowed his options to left or right . . . or maybe over.

He gave jumping over the fence a lot of very rapid thought. On the other side were the two uniformed officers; maybe Moran would still be there. Plus a zillion witnesses. The only problem was that the fence was about seven feet high. Plus, there were bushes along the bottom at almost every point. This was going to have to be some jump.

One more shout from somewhere spurred him forward. He sprinted forward, gathered himself to leap, and threw his hands up to catch the top of the fence. That was the last thing he could recall clearly afterwards.

Except for the sounds. First there was a distant CRACK!!, like a Christmas cracker being pulled or a branch snapped. Then there was a WHAM!! and, the smallest fraction of a second later, WHAM!! again.

That's odd, Chris thought, and the idea came to him as if he was outside his brain and everything was moving very slowly. Two WHAMS!!! One was me hitting the fence. What was the other one?

He knew that he was falling. The ground rushed up to meet him. He felt wood snapping under his back.

There was a deep blackness after that, as if his mind shut down his eyes to spare him from seeing what a mess he'd made of the jump. He could still hear though. There was a voice. A woman's shrill voice. She was screaming.

'He's been shot!!!!'

Oh, oh, Chris thought, and he stopped listening as well.

Eleven

It was quite a bizarre dream.

Chris felt as if he was flying, as if he was an eagle, turning in slow circles, high above the world. Nothing below looked familiar, but then he was so high, even cities appeared like dots on a map.

He turned again, looking for something he could recognise. There were rivers, low hills and lakes. None of them reminded him of anything.

Another circle. The wind ruffled his hair (or should that be feathers?). It annoyed him, the way the wind deafened him to anything else. That is, it deafened him to everything but the sound of his own heart, pounding away as it pumped blood around his body.

And maybe, just maybe, there was a voice.

Still, what did that matter? He was an eagle. Eagles didn't have to listen. They had the best eyesight of all. All he had to do was keep looking, and he'd find his way back.

The more he looked, the more he thought that one of the hills looked familiar. Streams ran along its flanks. One of them trickled into a lake. That looked like a good place to be.

Chris could feel the bright light of the sun on his face. It was getting him down. The drumming of his heart, the bright light, the distant whisper. It was all irritating him.

Time to land, Chris thought, and he swooped down. Funny how the last thing he felt was the sensation of moving up . . .

Chris sat up. It wasn't a good idea. He lay back down again.

'Urgh,' he said, which was the best way he could find to describe how he felt. There was a strange, prickling sensation all over his body.

'He's awake!' came a voice.

'Let's get him inside,' said another.

'Is it all right to move him?' asked a third.

Chris forced his eyes open, expecting to find the sunlight dazzling. In fact, it was quite dark. That worried him for a moment, before he realised that the afternoon was getting late and some clouds left over from the storm were blotting out the last of the sun.

Which meant he'd been out for just a little while.

That wasn't good. However, being able to see was good for his morale in another way, in that he discovered the source of the prickling sensation. He was lying in the middle of one of the bushes at the foot of the fence. The branches were scraping at his hands and face, and there were several older scratches that were starting to sting now that they knew his brain was paying attention.

'What happened?' he began to ask. The memory of being chased pushed to the front of his mind, so he decided to check out who he was talking to.

More relief. The three people were CG, still wearing his dazzling white kit (slightly smudged with grass streaks and dirt, but still bright enough to be seen from outer space), Grey Mountain and Running Waters. The first and last of this trio looked relieved, though a little pale with shock. Grey Mountain's face was perfectly calm, as if he had known all along that Chris would be all right.

'We should get him to a hospital,' Running Waters said. Her voice sounded edgy and nervous. Chris wondered just how bad he looked.

'There's no need,' he said. 'It's just some scratches and a bit of a bang round the head . . .'

She wasn't convinced. 'You may have a concussion or something. A blow to the head can be very serious.'

Over the last eighteen months, Chris had become well aware of how little fun being struck on the skull could be, but his had proved remarkably thick. Dense, Nicky called it.

'Honestly, I'm all right. I must have landed a bit funny . . . or something. I remember jumping for the fence and then . . .' He tried to find the right words to recall what had happened, but things were still a little fuzzy. There were those two bangs, he recalled.

'What were you doing out here?' asked CG

That was an easier question. 'I got your message,' Chris began.

'What message?' cried CG, looking very flustered. Maybe this bit wasn't going to be so easy after all.

'Your mate Jon came over while I was watching the Iroquois playing. He said you'd rescued my bag from the pile this morning...'

'No, that's not right!' exclaimed CG. 'I thought of it, but there was no time We were right in the middle of our first game when you got taken off. So I told Jon to ask my mum to do it. He'd been substituted. I told the coach your idea, and he decided to switch our style of play for the second half, seeing as we were under such pressure It worked too! We managed to get a second goal in the last fifteen minutes and...'

Running Waters didn't seem to be quite so interested in the way the game had gone. 'I don't get it Why would your friend have got the message wrong?' CG shrugged 'Did your mother take Chris's bag off the pile?' she continued. CG shrugged again 'Perhaps we should go and ask her,' she concluded CG didn't move perhaps he'd exhausted all his gestures.

Running Waters stepped back, but remembered at the last moment that they had other pressing business back there in the bushes

'Are you OK to walk?' she asked.

Chris managed to sit up, which pulled his body out of the worst of the brambles CG reached in and gave him a hand to clamber out the rest of the way. Chris sat on the lawn and felt his chin It felt like he'd had quite a whack there.

He looked around him He was just under the part of the fence he had been diving for Although the light wasn't so great now, he could see that the panel was sagging back quite a bit, as if something had run into it pretty hard. The top bracket that held the panel to the fence post was snapped. Had it been broken when he jumped at it, Chris wondered? He didn't think so.

'When I came back to the hotel, Gary Lukas and his two thugs were waiting for me...' he said, pulling his mind back to the tale he had been telling.

Once again, Running Waters jumped in. 'He was here? In the hotel? With Fehrman and the other guy?' Chris could see this wasn't news she had been expecting. 'You're sure it was them?'

'He wanted to talk to me. I think he was trying to persuade me that you guys were in the wrong.'

Grey Mountain uttered a small, mocking grunt. Running Waters was still dealing with the earlier news.

'So he was in the hotel when you heard the shot?'

Now it was Chris's turn to be amazed. 'Shot?' he said, in a small, low voice.

CG's face was full of slightly frightened excitement as he blurted out the news. 'A cop got shot!'

Chris didn't know how to react. All he managed was a ragged 'What?!'

Grey Mountain's face was as unreadable as always, but Chris could see from Running Waters' expression that it was true. And there was worse to come.

'Chris . . . it was Detective Moran. He was standing on the other side of the fence when . . . someone shot him from the trees grandpa was taken from this morning.'

Oh, man! Could it be true? And how bad was it? Did shot mean . . . killed? He could see that he still hadn't had the full, awful truth.

Running Waters gave it to him right then.

'They've arrested Joseph Blackdeer for attempted murder.'

In the silence that followed, Chris had plenty to think about. That terrible double WHAM! made sense now. One was the sound of him hitting the fence.

The other . . .

The other must have been Moran being thrown back against the fence from the other side. Which meant the CRACK! he had heard had been the gun-shot. He had actually heard Moran being shot.

Just thinking about it made his head spin.

'Are you OK?' asked CG, his face twisted with concern.

'Yeah, sure . . .' said Chris quietly. Then he looked up sharply. 'You said attempted murder.'

Running Waters nodded, although she didn't look any more

relaxed. 'They think he'll be OK. It's a clean wound. He's at Community Hospital now, undergoing emergency treatment. We were just looking round the field for some clues the police might have missed when we heard CG call.'

'I guess the cops didn't think to look over the fence when they found Detective Moran,' said CG. 'I barely saw you myself. I was just wondering how the bush had been flattened when I realised it was your foot sticking out.'

'I must have blacked out,' muttered Chris, recalling the dream.

'We should take you to the hospital,' said Running Waters again.

'Honestly,' Chris replied, 'I'm fine.' That was actually true this time. The more he sat there, the better his head felt. After a while, he was even ready to stand up and walk stiffly towards the hotel dining room.

'I could do with something to drink,' said Chris as they went in. CG ran off to find something. While they waited, Chris gradually managed to latch on to the other part of Running Waters' news.

'You say they've arrested Joseph Blackdeer?' Running Waters nodded. 'Why?' Chris asked.

'The police found him in the trees with a rifle. He says he found it there, after the shot. He says he saw a tall man skulking around and became suspicious after what happened this morning. He followed the man into the wood. He didn't see anything before the shot was fired, but then he ran towards where it came from and found the rifle leaning against a trunk. He picked it up. The police arrived at the same moment and arrested him.'

Running Waters looked at her watch. 'I ought to get back to him. The police should have finished booking him by now. I just wish we'd found something useful.'

Chris managed not to feel offended.

'I guess you'd better come with me too,' Running Waters continued. 'The police may want to talk to you.'

'Me? Why? I didn't see anything.'

At that moment, Grey Mountain shuffled in his seat, speaking for the first time. 'He saw what he was meant to see,' the old man announced. Neither Chris nor Running Waters knew what he meant. 'You're the perfect witness,' the Chief said, still not explaining anything. Chris just looked back at him; Running Waters laid her hand on his shoulder and started to speak.

'Grandpa . he can't be a witness; he didn't see anything.'

'He is *the* witness,' the Chief explained. 'He saw Lukas just as he was supposed to' He turned to face Chris, peering at him from under his heavy, grey brows 'From the first moment I saw you, I knew you would play an important part in what is yet to come Several nights ago, I dreamed of a small eagle, dropping from the sky It saw many things as it fell to earth, before it took to the sky once more You are that eagle, and I believe it is your destiny to be a witness to our struggle to regain what is rightfully ours It is our duty to make sure that you have that chance'

He stood up

Chris wasn't following any of this Eagles? Falling from the sky? And what was all this about him being meant to be a witness?

Running Waters didn't seem to understand her grandfather any more than Chris did Her face was trapped in an ex pression that said she preferred the horrible legal problems that awaited her in the city to listening to Grey Mountain flying off on some strange journey to *The X Files*

'But you can't take Chris away if he's a witness,' she began

Grey Mountain looked at her as if he was annoyed that she couldn't see what was so obvious to him

'Don't you understand? Chris saw that Lukas was in the hotel when the shooting occurred, along with his two hire lings What he witnessed was that neither Lukas nor his henchmen could have shot Detective Moran'

'Of course,' Running Waters replied 'Chris can prove that they didn't do it'

'Which means,' said Grey Mountain, smiling, 'that they did'

90

Twelve

Chris lay on the bed, his eyes closed, feeling sleep creeping up around the edges of his mind. There was a small ache behind his eyes that suggested he was getting a headache. Maybe it was some kind of delayed reaction to crashing into the fence, maybe it was just because he'd eaten so late.

Or maybe it was because he didn't know what he was going to do.

He'd had plenty of advice in the last few hours, of course (probably another reason why he was getting a headache). When he called his father, there had been plenty.

'Great! You've finally got there,' Mr Stephens had said, his voice sounding so sharp on the clear line that Chris had turned round, half-expecting his father to be right there in the room.

'Not exactly,' Chris had admitted. His father had groaned.

Chris gave his father the edited highlights of the day's events. He left out a few items, partly because there was a lot to get through (and the call was costing about a pound a minute), partly because his father would worry unnecessarily. After all, what was there to tell, really? He'd been caught up in a shooting, an attempted kidnapping, a high-speed car chase (sort of) and he'd been arrested. Just an ordinary day, really.

The trouble was, leaving out some of the excitement made the story harder to follow.

'Let me get this straight. The police want you to stay because you were a witness to someone *not* committing a crime.'

Chris sighed. He'd managed to confuse his father really well this time . . .

'This guy who's trying to steal the land from the Native Americans . . .'

'The who?'

Another sigh. One step forward, two back.

'Native Americans – the Indians, dad.'

'Why didn't you say so?'

Never mind, thought Chris. 'Anyway, they think this guy is trying to rip them off, so when there was some trouble at the football tournament, they thought he might be involved. But he was talking to me at the time, so the police think he can't be involved.'

'Is any of this meant to make sense?' asked Mr Stephens.

Chris decided all he could do was repeat the shortest version of the day's events. 'I just have to give the police a statement in the morning. Then I'll catch the midday plane, honest. It's all arranged.'

'You'd better catch it this time, Chris. Mr Goodman has spent so long waiting at San Francisco airport, he's been given his own parking space.'

Chris knew. He'd already called Jace's father to confess that – yet again – he'd not made the flight he was supposed to be on. Before she left to go back to help Joseph Blackdeer, Running Waters had called the airline and managed to get the ticket changed. Chris had had the pleasure of informing Mr Goodman, who was actually on the freeway into the city when Chris called.

'Keep this up and by the time you get here it will be time to fly back to England,' Mr Goodman had said, and he sounded pretty teed off. Who could blame him?

Still, thought Chris, my part in this nonsense is over. After she'd left them at the hotel and gone into the city, Running Waters had called to say that she'd heard Detective Moran was out of surgery and out of danger. In fact, he was pretty healthy for a man who'd been shot. Chris wondered if he'd have time to see the policeman before he caught a cab to the airport, but decided maybe he'd write instead. It would be just his luck to get caught up in a major crisis at the hospital. *The doctor's fallen off his boat – there's no-one who can perform this life-saving operation on the President.* *It's OK, there's this kid in Ward B who plays football, perhaps he can do it instead.*

No-one was interested any more in what had happened in the morning. The local news programme briefly mentioned that there had been an earlier 'incident' at the park before the shooting. All the police cared about, though, was nailing the guy who had tried to kill Detective Moran.

And they had pretty much decided who that was.

Detective Enzio was interviewed on TV, managing to look even sweatier, fatter and less intelligent than he did in real life. Chris learnt that he had been the first one on the scene after the shot rang out. He'd caught Joseph Blackdeer red-handed, with the rifle in his hands. No-one else had been found in the area. Only Joseph's prints were on the gun.

Case solved.

No-one seemed that interested in why Joseph Blackdeer would have tried to kill Moran. Everyone assumed it was caught up in the Bitter Lake business somehow, though no-one knew how.

Chris found himself wondering if it was because of Running Waters' friendship with the cop. It annoyed him that he was able to think of Joseph being guilty so easily.

But what other explanation was there? The clincher came when Enzio revealed that the rifle the police had found was one of a batch of old firearms the Iroquois used for hunting.

Things looked bad for Joseph.

But, Chris told himself, that's not my business. Since all I have to offer is proof that it wasn't Lukas – not that anyone now thought it was – all I have to do is catch a plane and leave it all behind. It went against the grain, but what else was there he could do?

So, he had watched Running Waters and Grey Mountain leave to go and help Joseph, then he'd eaten a meal with CG and his family, and finally he had gone back to the room he had occupied the night before to get some sleep before setting off for the airport in the morning.

He didn't think he'd have much trouble sleeping. In fact, his eyes were closing even as he lay there in the darkness.

There was a knock at the door.

'Chris? It's me, CG. You awake?'

'No,' replied Chris. He remembered that the door was locked and that he'd have to get up if he was going to let CG in. He was just trying to decide if the effort was worth it when he heard a key turn in the lock.

'Hey,' his waiter/footballing pal said in greeting. He was holding up a key ring. 'I borrowed the pass keys.'

'I would have let you in, honest,' moaned Chris, squinting when CG switched on the room lights.

CG was grinning wildly, like Nicky did when he had good news. 'I've got great news,' CG said.

Chris sat up on the bed, running his hand through the tight mop of light hair that sat on top of his head.

'Really?' he asked, unenthusiastically.

CG was grinning so widely his face was threatening to break. 'The team from The Orchards are staying here.'

Chris wasn't that impressed. 'So?'

'So, they're downstairs in the lounge watching TV. A soccer training video, would you believe.'

Chris still didn't get the point. 'So?' he asked again.

The smile faded. CG was getting impatient. 'So, we could sneak into their rooms while they're not there.'

The nagging pain behind Chris's eyes got worse. He'd finally found a difference between Nicky and CG. Talking with CG made even less sense.

'Why would we want to do that?'

CG shrugged in a way that suggested he thought it would be fun even if they didn't have a good reason, then offered: 'We could see if their coach has left any secret plans about their strategy for the semi-finals.'

This was getting worse. CG clearly believed that soccer was coached like NFL football, with lots of complicated diagrams and plans. At the highest level, maybe it was. At school, 'Flea', the PE teacher, used a small, wonky blackboard, and even then it was just to pin the team list up on.

'What do you care, CG? You guys got knocked out this afternoon, didn't you?' The small pain in Chris's head throbbed again, as if to remind him what getting knocked out really meant.

'Not for me, you dope – for your Native American pals.'

Chris looked hard at CG, who was obviously buzzing with excitement at the prospect of a little spying. The American's face was glowing with pride at his own cleverness, even though Chris still failed to see the reason why.

'I thought the tournament had been abandoned?' Chris said, remembering what had been said earlier.

'Nah!' scoffed CG. 'That was just when they thought the cop was in danger. Now they're saying that they'll leave it tomorrow, but play the semi-finals and finals on Wednesday instead.'

So, thought Chris, the competition is still on and the $50,000 is still there to be won.

'I don't know, CG,' he said. 'Who's to say the Iroquois will want to take part after what's happened? Who's to say they won't get thrown out?'

'That's not what I read downstairs,' CG insisted. 'According to what I saw, the semi-finals on Wednesday are The Orchards vs Gary and the Wabash vs Peru.'

It took Chris a moment to remember that there was a place called Gary, as well as a crook.

So, Grey Mountain's people were up against the team that knocked CG's mob out, thought Chris. He considered that for a moment.

'What chance have Gary got against The Orchards?'

'None that I can see,' CG replied. 'Face it. Your boys are going to play The Orchards in the final.'

With just the small matter of the semis first, thought Chris. And that was assuming they played again. It wouldn't be easy, turning up to play in the same park where their coach was supposed to have shot a policeman.

'So?' asked CG, throwing it back at him.

'This is stupid . . .' muttered Chris, but he was swinging his legs off the bed anyway.

The Orchards team had been given rooms on the ground floor, in a separate part of the building. A passageway led from reception to the rooms. Chris and CG crept through the brightly lit lobby and through the doors, making sure that neither CG's mother nor anyone connected with Lukas or The Orchards team saw them.

As insurance, CG was carrying a load of towels he had taken from the linen cupboard.

'If we get caught, we'll say we're delivering these,' he explained.

Very believable, thought Chris. Laundry service at 10.30 in the evening, delivered by the owner's son and one of the guests.

CG waved aside any complaint. He was putting a key in the lock of the first door.

'This is their team coach's room. It's one of the best rooms along here, except for the one right at the end, which is where Lukas is st–'

Chris almost leapt out of his skin. Following that, he almost beat CG to death in frustration.

'Lukas is staying here?' he demanded in an urgent whisper.

'Yeah,' muttered CG, still making as if he was going to open the door they were standing outside. 'You'd think he'd want to stay somewhere posh, wouldn't you? Maybe this is a better hotel than we think!'

'But he is here?' Chris persisted. He actually had to put out his hand to stop CG turning the key.

'Sure,' shrugged the American. 'He's sharing with his son.'

Chris's heart was beating fast. The idea of what he was close to suggesting was almost too daring for words.

'Is he actually in the hotel right now?' he asked.

'I don't think so,' CG replied. 'His car's not out front. I think he went off someplace with those two gorillas who keep following him round.'

Chris pulled him bodily away from the door.

'We have to search his room,' Chris hissed.

Suddenly, CG wasn't smiling any more.

'I don't know,' he began.

'Think about it!' Chris insisted, dragging CG into the nearest thing to shadow he could find (as if anyone coming into the corridor could have missed them). 'We're not going to find anything useful in these other rooms. If they have any bits of paper that show how they're going to play the last two games, they'll have taken them with them to this session they're having now.' CG opened his mouth to speak but Chris was in full flow. 'But Lukas might have left something.' Something really useful. Chris could see it in his mind. 'He's the master-mind behind the team after all. So, if they have some trick up their sleeves, his room is the place to find it.'

CG looked extremely doubtful. Pinching some game plans from a player's room, that was one thing, the kind of thing kids got up to all the time. But sneaking into a rich man's hotel room (the kind of rich man who was followed around by two minders), that was something else.

Chris could see CG was wavering. He tried to think of something that would convince his American pal to go along with the scheme, but couldn't. He tried to think of some words that would make it sound like all they were doing was mucking around, but he couldn't do that either.

About the closest he got was a lame: 'Look, all you have to do is open up and keep watch. I'll do the sneaky bit.'

If Chris had been with Nicky, Fiorentini would have been offended at being asked to play second fiddle Keeping watch was for wimps. CG, on the other hand, seemed quietly relieved at the idea. There really was a lot of difference between them.

'OK,' CG whispered He showed Chris the pass key in his fist. 'This way,' he said.

There was a turn in the passage before they reached the room at the end, which gave them just a little more scope to pull this off, Chris had been wondering how they were going to hide if someone did come their way, but there was a fire exit and a set of stairs at the end of the hall, so that was OK.

CG unlocked the door.

'Go back to the corner,' Chris said. 'If they come back, get back here as quickly as you can without being heard We'll go out through the fire doors and upstairs to the other floor From there, we can play it by ear.'

CG nodded. Chris gave him an encouraging wink, then looked away before the gloomy, worried expression on CG's face got him any more scared He turned the handle gently and pushed the door ajar.

The lights were off, but lanterns in the car park outside threw in just enough illumination to see by. Chris allowed the door to swing closed behind him, letting his eyes adjust to the gloom.

The room was a lot bigger than Chris's, of course, with windows on two sides and a connecting door through to a luxurious bathroom There were two beds, both neatly made A large cupboard occupied the one windowless wall to the right, while a dressing table and chair stood to the left at the foot of the bed. Lukas and his son had put their luggage away out of sight.

Almost all of it, anyway.

Chris had had no idea what he was looking for before he entered the room. In fact, he had spent the last few moments of the walk along the hall wondering if he wasn't being a complete moron. After all, was it likely that Lukas would leave

97

some vital clue in his room? A nice, neat piece of evidence that would prove he was cheating Grey Mountain's people?

However, as soon as he saw the three identical briefcases lined up one beside the other, Chris felt a tingle run up his spine.

No-one needed three briefcases. Not even the busiest businessman in Indianapolis. He had a plush office downtown to keep his papers in. What could he possibly need to carry round in three identical cases?

Chris answered his own question. Money. Drugs. Weapons. Maybe all three.

He was almost shaking as he crossed towards the bed.

'Get real,' he told himself, pausing to take a close look at the three bags. He was sure he was letting his imagination run away with him. There would be a simple explanation . . . For all he knew, Lukas really was just a property developer, playing the game hard but fair, and the Iroquois were losing out as a result. OK, he kept some thugs on the payroll, but what did that prove?

Chris knew he had no right to be in this room, and certainly no right *at all* to look at the cases. But he did it anyway.

Although the three cases were exactly the same type and colour, a single detail did separate one from its two brothers. Attached to the side there was a yellow Post-It note, with a message written in neat handwriting. It was upside-down, so Chris had to turn his head to read it properly.

It said HE, T PK, 11.30PM.

Chris pulled his hand back from the case. Didn't HE stand for High Explosive? Was this a bomb?!

The very thought of it made him freeze. He had no idea how long he spent standing perfectly still, breathing so gently he almost passed out, his heart pounding in his chest. Slowly, though, he calmed down.

HE could be anything, he realised. T PK didn't make a lot more sense. However, 11.30PM was pretty clear. Chris sneaked a look at his watch — it was coming up for eleven now. Did the note refer to this evening? Once again, Chris found himself sweating over the idea that the case might contain a bomb, timed to go off in thirty minutes. Eventually, though, he reasoned that the average mad bomber didn't advertise on his luggage, except in Pink Panther cartoons. He was just being paranoid. Sometimes, even the baddest of bad guys could stop short of wanting to blow up anyone who got in their way.

'I've got to stop watching *Bugs*,' Chris muttered.

All the same, he decided that he would inspect one of the other cases more closely first. Summoning up his courage, he stretched out his hand towards one of the two unlabelled bags. As his fingers closed round the handle, he wondered if he'd actually hear the explosion before the bomb killed him.

'No, take a look at the one with the label first!'

CG's voice split the silence more loudly than any bomb could have done. It nearly killed Chris just as effectively too.

'What are you doing?' he cried.

'I just thought I'd take a peek too,' CG replied, apologetically.

'You're supposed to be on look-out!'

'That's boring,' said CG from the doorway, pouting. 'Besides, when I saw these cases, I couldn't resist taking a look. I bet there's something really interesting in here . . .'

He walked over to the bed and reached for the briefcase with the yellow label. Chris grabbed hold of CG's wrist and held him back.

'Go and watch the door!' he insisted.

'Hey, if it wasn't for me we wouldn't even have got in here!' CG cried sulkily, but he dropped his hand away from the case.

'All right,' sighed Chris, picking up the case he had been reaching for before CG spoke (he was just about starting to calm down from the shock). 'We'll take a quick butcher's together . . .'

CG stared at him as if he had no idea what Chris was talking about, but kept silent anyway.

Chris laid the case down flat on the bed. He felt for the catches.

Needless to say, after all the preceding fuss, it was locked.

'Nuts,' muttered CG. 'Try the others.'

Chris shot him an angry glare, fed up with the way a perfectly good plan was falling to pieces. All the same, he reached for the second of the unlabelled cases, even though he was certain it would be locked as well.

The catches sprang open.

He hesitated for a moment before he opened the lid, even

though he had just about forgotten the silly idea that it might be a bomb. Something told him that whatever he found, it might be even more explosive.

And it was.

Chris stared. CG gasped. Packed in two rows, in eight columns across the width of the case, were small bundles of American money. $20 bills. The face of some American President grinned at him in sixteen identical ways, as if to say, 'You've just found a lot of money here, son.'

'There must be thousands of dollars!' gasped CG.

Chris was already totting it up in his head. Two rows, eight columns. Sixteen stacks of bills. And in most of the stacks there were eight bundles of twenty crisp new notes, wrapped with a small paper band. Twenty times twenty times eight times sixteen. Allowing for the few stacks that only had seven bundles instead of eight, that was about $50,000.

No, there was no doubt about it, Chris knew. It was *exactly* $50,000.

The same amount as the prize money for the soccer tournament.

Chris believed in coincidence, but this felt altogether too neat to be true. After one last look, he closed the case, still checking the maths in his head.

'Fifty thousand dollars,' he said out loud. CG whistled.

'Fifty grand? Just sitting here? Is he out of his mind? Anyone could have broken in here!'

Instead, Chris was thinking, it was us.

They both looked at the third case, with its sticky label on the side.

'So . . .' CG whispered. They were both almost too stunned to touch it.

'Go and check the hall!' hissed Chris impatiently. He heard CG mutter something in reply, but the American moved off, opening the door. After a moment's delay, he stepped outside and the door swung closed once more.

Alone again, Chris stared at the third case. He started to pick it up, but almost at once he set it down again. It felt incredibly heavy, and the contents had shifted with a solid thump and a muffled rattle. Something about that sound made Chris feel uncomfortable.

He took the label in his hand to read it again. It came off the case, which made him feel even more exposed. Cold shivers were running up and down his spine.

He was still standing there, wondering if he was cracking up, when there was a rap on the door and some kind of hoarse whisper. Almost at once, there was a second thump. It took him a moment to work out what it was.

The fire door, slamming shut.

'CG?' he asked into the darkness. But when he heard the footsteps coming closer and the key turning in the door, he knew at once that it couldn't be CG outside.

Thirteen

'What do you think it was?' asked Spanish Johnny.

'How should I know?' Fehnman replied, sounding crabby.

'You should take a look,' Spanish Johnny insisted.

His partner made a sort of clicking noise with his mouth. 'Why me? You're the one sees ghosts.'

'I didn't see nothing, I just heard the fire door slam. Someone was out in the hall, I'm tellin' ya!'

'So? They ain't there now, are they?'

Faced with that kind of logic, Spanish Johnny fell silent for a moment. He crossed the room, his shoes squeaking as he paced over the carpet.

'Look here. Someone's been messin' with these cases.'

'What?'

'I'm sure they were neater than this when we went out.'

'Neater?'

'Yeah! Neater!!!'

The other man laughed.

'What? You think someone broke in here, found a case full of money, and just decided to mess things round a little?'

'Look,' Spanish Johnny said, his voice strained with bad temper. 'I'm telling you . . .'

Chris held his breath as the argument started a second lap. He was trying to edge himself a little bit more under the bed, but he was terrified of making a noise. In the split second between hearing the key in the lock and the door opening, Chris had dived over the corner of the bed with the cases on, falling into the space between it and the second bed. In the microsecond after that, before the light snapped on, he'd realised that he still had the sticky label in his hand. He'd sat up, smacked it on to the side of the case and laid flat again.

Since then, he'd been listening to the argument between

Lukas's hirelings, wriggled half his body under the bed with the cases, and thought up some terrible revenge he would inflict on CG when he caught up with him.

'Look, we don't have time for this!' Fehnman growled, obviously tired of Spanish Johnny getting the upper hand (Chris suddenly realised he had no way of telling that it was that way round; for all he knew, Spanish Johnny was the one being asked to go out and check the hallway).

'What'd you say?'

'I said it's gone eleven, and we gotta get out to Thunder Park to make the pay-off. So, let's go.'

Chris bit his lip. The two men were moving around briskly. Chris knew that if either of them moved into the centre of the room, they would be bound to see him. So far, all his wriggling had achieved was to get one leg, one arm and part of his body under the bed. He was starting to realise that he might not fit anyway.

One of the two goons was picking up a case from the bed.

'So, we just goin' to leave this case in here?' Chris wondered which one he meant.

'What do you want to do with it?'

'We should put it in the hotel safe. That's what GL would want. Just to be on the safe side while we go out.'

Fehnman/Spanish Johnny grunted disapprovingly. 'You want to get that crazy Jewish woman to open the safe at this time of night? Fine, you go ahead. Me, I vote we just stash the case in the wardrobe. We'll be back in less than an hour.'

Mrs Amantani was Jewish? thought Chris. No, that was never right.

Spanish Johnny/Fehnman had also been thinking, only he was still focused on the briefcase. Eventually, he decided to agree with his mate. Only one case was removed from the bed. The arguing was over.

'I'll drive,' said Spanish Johnny/Fehnman as he opened the door. The light went out.

'No, I'll drive,' came the reply, just before the door closed.

Chris let out a long breath. It seemed as if he hadn't taken in any air at all while the two minders had been in the room. Even now, he lay still, enjoying the darkness and the silence.

There was always a chance that they'd be back.

Then he heard a tap on the door, followed by the sound of it opening. Chris could imagine CG's face peering in.

'Chris?'

Chris sat up suddenly. CG almost jumped out of his skin.

'Man, I thought they'd caught you for sure!'

'Some look-out you are!' muttered Chris bitterly as he pulled himself to his feet. He badly wanted to get out of here.

'Hey – they were walking along the hall just as I got to the corner!' CG complained. 'I barely had time to knock on the door and skedaddle out of sight.'

Skedaddle?

Chris looked at the bed. There was just one case there now. He felt like lifting it to test which one it was.

'Did they take the money?' asked CG.

'I think so,' said Chris. 'They were talking about making a pay-off.'

'Hey, man! They must be paying some guy off to help Lukas over this Bitter Lake business. We should follow them.'

Chris sighed and looked CG straight in the eye. It had obviously been a lot easier on the nerves hiding outside than trying to crawl under the bed.

'How? We can't just borrow a car!'

CG opened his mouth as if to argue, but decided against it. Chris's face had a 'don't cross me' look about it that he didn't care to challenge.

'Where's the other case?' he asked instead.

'In the wardrobe. Who cares? Let's get out of here!'

CG glanced at his watch. 'Actually, I don't think we can.'

Chris was almost ready to scream. 'Why not?'

'Well, because The Orchards guys are coming back from their little conference . . . As I came in, I heard them coming down the hall.'

'What?!'

'Come on, we can hide in the closet,' CG suggested.

Chris was muttering dark threats under his breath as they stepped into the large wardrobe. He would happily have throttled CG at that point, not just for getting them into this mess, but for being so cheerful about it.

'There's a case on the floor in here,' the American whispered.

104

Chris remembered the conversation he had overheard. The two goons had been rattling on about putting something in the hotel safe, but had settled for leaving it in here. That must be the case CG was treading on.

Which one was it? Chris bent down, groping in the dark. He found the handle and lifted it, feeling the solid, heavy weight inside. Not the money, then, that had gone with the two men. Not the locked case. This was the one Chris had thought might be a bomb.

The one that had had the sticker on.

'Hang on,' he said, as much to himself as to the invisible figure beside him. 'That doesn't make sense.'

'What?' hissed CG.

'This is the case that had the sticker, the one that those two morons were supposed to take, the one they have to deliver at 11.30.'

'So?'

'So the money was in another case. Not this one. They said they were making a pay-off, but they were supposed to take this case, not the cash.'

Chris was having enough trouble keeping up with the three briefcases himself, so he was sure his explanation would lose CG. He was delighted when he realised the American had been able to keep up.

'Maybe there was money in two cases . . .' CG suggested.

'No, just try lifting this thing. It doesn't feel anything like the other case. It's like a solid lump of something inside. Whatever's in here, whatever they are supposed to be delivering at 11.30, it isn't money.'

He could almost hear CG thinking.

'So, what's in this case? Did you look? Is it locked?'

'I don't know.'

CG shifted alongside him. 'Want to take a peek now?'

'In a pitch-black cupboard?' Chris mocked. 'I don't think so. Just leave it for now.'

There were voices behind him, getting louder, and feet running quickly along the hall. Someone was close by – probably Lukas's son. Chris breathed a prayer that they weren't about to get caught.

'So, if they left this case behind, which one did they take?' asked CG.

Chris thought back to the moment when the door had last opened. He had realised that he still had the Post-It note in his hand and had slapped it on the nearest case. But because he had dived across the bed, that meant it was the one that had been furthest away. Or the one that had been in the middle, maybe.

The more he thought about it, the less sure he was that they had put the cases back in the right order after they had inspected them. He had no idea which case Fehnman and Spanish Johnny had taken, except that it wasn't the right one.

As soon as they realised they had the wrong bag, they'd know someone had been mucking around in the room. The more he thought about it, the more Chris wanted to get out.

CG was hissing him to be silent. Chris was closer to wanting to yell, 'You're telling *me* to be quiet?', but he managed to control it. He heard someone coming into the room.

He froze, once again trying not to breathe. At this rate, he was going to suffer from oxygen starvation. It was spooky, hiding in the complete darkness of the closet, not daring to shift an inch, even conscious of blinking too loudly. Meanwhile, he strained to catch every footfall from the room outside. If Lukas Junior was the only teenager in the universe who hung his clothes up at night, they were sunk.

There was a long period of silence. Then Chris heard the sound of water running.

'He's in the bathroom!' hissed CG. 'Let's go for it!'

Chris didn't argue. Ten minutes of skulking in a cupboard after five minutes trying to hide under a bed that was just three inches off the carpet and Chris was ready to do anything rather than stay here another second.

CG was already opening the wardrobe door. Chris almost fell over him in his eagerness to get out. The room seemed awfully bright, and he was dazzled for a second or two. Then he felt CG tugging at his sleeve, pulling him towards the door.

Moments later, they were out in the hall. There was no-one about, thank goodness, but they took no chances on being discovered at the last minute and went out through the fire door and beyond, outside into the car park.

CG was grinning from ear to ear.

Chris started to copy him, relieved to have escaped without detection. Then he realised that CG was laughing about something more than he was, and his face locked solid, frozen in a look of dismay and horror.

'My guess is that this is the bag with all the money,' CG chuckled, holding up the case for him to see.

Chris could scarcely believe it. While he had been adjusting to the light, CG had calmly walked over to the bed and taken the third case.

'I don't believe it!' he gasped.

CG looked at the case, frowning. 'Sure it is,' he said. 'We left the heavy one in the closet, the goons took the locked one, so this must be the cash.' He started to thumb the catches.

'No!' cried Chris, realising that CG had missed the point entirely. 'I mean I don't believe you took it! That's stealing!'

CG managed to grin and still look quite hurt and offended, which was quite a trick. 'I'm not going to keep it! I just thought, well, you were right about them knowing someone had been in the room. So, I figured it would look more natural if the money had gone. We could just dump the case somewhere they could find it.'

'With our prints all over it!' Chris yelled. He knew that a high-volume argument in the middle of the car park wasn't going to help them keep the secret, but he couldn't help himself.

'Oh, we'll wipe those clean,' said CG, matter of factly.

Chris couldn't think how to develop his argument from there. CG looked so pleased with himself . . .

'Or maybe . . .' he began.

'Don't even think about it!' Chris wailed.

'No, wait,' insisted CG. 'Fifty thousand dollars The same as the prize money your mates would get if they won the tournament. The money they need if they're going to beat off this land deal of Lukas's. It'd be kind of neat if they beat him with his own money, don't you think?'

Chris wasn't prepared to put into words what he was thinking right then. So it was just as well someone else was

'You can't win an honest game with dishonest cards,' the voice said, drifting in from out of the shadows. The two boys turned, surprised, but they both knew who they were expecting to see before he stepped into the open

107

'Grey Mountain!' Chris exclaimed. 'What are you doing here?'

'I want to show you something,' the old Chief explained. It was a typical Grey Mountain explanation, in that it didn't tell Chris anything.

'I can't –' he began.

'It's not far,' Grey Mountain said calmly, cutting off any objection. 'The rest of my people are waiting nearby. We can be there and home again in just a couple of hours.'

Chris's mouth flapped open like a landed fish. Grey Mountain reeled him in.

'We need your help,' he said.

Fourteen

⚽

'I'm going to die!!!'

Chris clenched his fists even more tightly, as if he could somehow hold on to the wooden floor of the flatbed truck. In fact, he was being held still solely by the closely pressed bodies packed around him. What they were holding on to, he couldn't tell in the darkness. Perhaps it was best he didn't know.

The truck was pushing south along a six-lane highway, similar to the one leading to the airport. They were following signs to a place called Franklin. Chris had no more idea of where they were going than that.

Grey Mountain was up in the cab. It had occurred to Chris about five miles back that with Joseph in jail, there wasn't another adult among the Iroquois squad. He realised he couldn't see the tall guy who played in midfield on the back of the trailer. That wasn't a comforting thought.

The wind whistled through his hair. Overhead, the night sky was full of stars. Chris quite liked being out at night, but right now he wished he was tucked up in bed and not on the back of a lorry hurtling through the night to who knew where.

They'd been going flat out for no more than about twenty minutes when Chris heard the gears crunch and the ancient flatbed truck started to slow down, steering towards the side of the road. Chris peered over the heads of the sleeping boys around him. A chain-link fence was running along the top of an embankment. Small bushes were growing along its foot. Beyond, just visible in the darkness, were several strangely shaped structures, large and small.

There were signs on the fence warning people to keep out. Chris had no doubt that this wasn't about to apply to them.

The lorry shuddered to a halt, crunching into the gravel at the side of the highway. The passenger door opened and Grey Mountain stepped out, his staff clattering against the side of the truck as he lowered himself to the ground.

'Are you awake, Chris?' the old man asked.

Like I could have fallen to sleep back here, thought Chris. He decided not to say that out loud, but poked his head up above the others who were managing to sleep quite soundly all round him.

'Where are we?' he asked.

'Come see for yourself,' said Grey Mountain. He was already stepping away from the truck, climbing the embankment towards the fence.

Chris muttered something unkind about old men who never managed to just come out and say what they meant. Then he tried to stand up, hauling himself out of the press of bodies. It took him several moments to find anywhere he could put his feet without treading on someone, but finally he reached the side of the flatbed and dropped down to the ground.

Grey Mountain was already at the top of the embankment. Chris scrambled up the slope to join him at the fence.

'What is this place?' Chris asked, irritably.

'An amusement park,' replied Grey Mountain, pronouncing the words carefully as if it hurt his mouth to say them. Chris was amazed – that was virtually a straight answer as far as Grey Mountain was concerned.

Chris looked through the links of the fence. Now that he knew what he was looking at, the strange shadows started to make sense. There was some kind of cable car ride, and a rollercoaster made of tubes of steel; a huge circle in the distance could only be a Ferris wheel. The biggest building appeared to be a viewing stand, like one whole side of a football stadium.

'So, uh, why are we here?' asked Chris.

'I thought you'd like to see it,' replied Grey Mountain. Chris sighed. Had the old man brought him all this way to visit an amusement park that had closed for the night?

Chris took another look. It really was just an amusement park. Most of it was completely dark and silent, but Chris could see that there were a few lights near the Ferris wheel.

Further along from where they had parked the truck, there was a gateway leading to a vast parking area. That too was brightly lit. It wasn't hard to work out why they were parked here at the darkest point.

'And?' Chris asked, struggling to understand.

'Lukas owns this place. He built it on land he acquired years ago for just a few thousand dollars. Now it's worth millions.'

Chris continued looking. There was nothing sinister about the place that he could make out. And, he realised, why should there be? It was just an amusement park built by a man who'd taken a bit of farmland and turned it into a vast funfair.

'I don't understand,' he confessed.

'This is what he has planned for Bitter Lake. He will take our land and build an amusement park on it. And make millions of dollars.'

Chris sympathised, but he still didn't get the point. He didn't need to see this place to know that Lukas didn't want Bitter Lake just because he liked the peace and quiet. The TV news had said that he was going to turn the area into a vacation resort. Maybe there would even be a funfair.

The Chief was inspecting a fence post. Chris felt very sorry for the old man – and for the rest of them. He wanted to help. But what good did it do to come here and look at the scene of another of Lukas's triumphs?

'I don't get it,' he said.

Grey Mountain was running his hand along the post. 'Don't you want to see what goes on in here?' the old man asked.

Chris thought he had a pretty good idea already, without needing to do or hear anything more. His father had taken him to Alton Towers a year or two ago and . . .

While Chris was still trying to figure things out, Grey Mountain was tugging on the fence. The panel swung back about a metre, just like it was some kind of door. Grey Mountain held it open for Chris to step inside ahead of him.

'How . . ?'

'Some of our people worked on building this place,' Grey Mountain explained. 'At the time I thought it was a bad idea, but it has its advantages.'

Chris still hadn't moved.

'We can't just sneak in!' he protested. 'What about guard dogs and things? What are we doing here anyway?'

Grey Mountain's eyebrows lowered fractionally. 'Do all English boys ask as many questions as you do? If you had been alive when your ancestors were getting ready to colonise America, I think my people would still be living in their ancient homes.'

Chris wasn't going to be deflected so easily.

'Look, this is getting out of control. I'm supposed to be catching a plane to San Francisco tomorrow. If I miss another flight, my father is going to have some kind of fit! And what about the police? I'm in enough trouble already – and so are you!'

Grey Mountain didn't react at all. Chris's protest ran out of steam.

'I'm not going in there, Grey Mountain,' he insisted. 'Forget it. What is this place, anyhow?'

'It's called Thunder Park,' said Grey Mountain stepping through the gap in the fence.

'How did you know they would be here?' Chris whispered.

'The same way you did,' replied Grey Mountain.

Chris turned his head and looked up. He was kneeling at the corner of the small confectionery stand while Grey Mountain stood over him. The darkness hid them from view, but it also made it hard for Chris to see the old man's face. Not that he could normally tell anything from Grey Mountain's unchanging expression anyhow.

'You can't have. I was listening in Lukas's room,' Chris insisted.

'There you are then,' Grey Mountain replied.

Chris shook his head, knowing that he would never get a straight answer from the Chief by asking a direct question. He faced the open space in front of the stand again, looking across to the entrance to the Ferris wheel ride.

'What are they doing?' he wondered out loud.

Fehnman and Spanish Johnny were standing by the pay booth, smoking cigarettes. Some time ago, Fehnman had taken a call on his cellphone, but apart from that they hadn't done anything in all the time since Chris and Grey Mountain arrived.

Chris couldn't see the briefcase either.

'This is where things get interesting,' Grey Mountain said quietly. Chris looked up at him again, about to ask what he meant, when he noticed some lights weaving towards the ride along the wide pathway. A car. Chris could hear the engine now, sounding rough and uneven.

'The pay-off,' said Chris.

'So I believe,' Grey Mountain agreed.

The car was coming close, in quite a hurry. Fehnman had noticed it now and dropped his cigarette to the floor. He tapped Spanish Johnny on the shoulder, who followed his partner's example. They stepped out on to the path as the car's headlamps flooded the area with a brighter light. Fehnman held up his hand and Chris heard the car's brakes squeal as it came to a stop on the dusty path. The engine roared once, then was silent. Moments later, the headlamps went out.

It took Chris a moment or two to adjust to the low light again. The small payment booth behind the two goons had a small bulb glowing inside, and there were lights in the control shed too. Even so, it was still pretty dark.

The car door opened, then closed. Chris heard someone walking along the far side of the vehicle, about to come into view.

He didn't expect to recognise the driver. After all, he had only been in the city for a few days. What did he know of the kinds of crooked politicians or city workers Lukas might have in his pocket? It wasn't as if he truly knew what he was witnessing, after all.

Which meant that when the heavy, scruffy man came into view, scuffing his feet along the floor as he walked, Chris was genuinely surprised.

'Enzio!' he gasped.

He felt Grey Mountain rest a hand on his shoulder to make sure his surprise didn't make him react any more visibly. Chris found himself staring at the detective as he approached Lukas's two hirelings. On the basis of their one meeting at the police station, Chris wasn't Detective Enzio's biggest fan, but he hadn't expected him to be tied into the story quite so firmly.

Enzio walked up close to the two suited goons. His face registered some suspicion and curiosity as he realised who had flagged him down.

'Where's your boss?' he asked.

'Couldn't make it,' replied Spanish Johnny with a big smile. 'He sent us. He wants you to give him a call.' He was showing Enzio the mobile phone.

'You got my money?' the detective asked.

'Sure!' said Fehnman, shrugging. 'It's right in here.'

Enzio looked at them both as if they had just crawled out from under a rock. Chris felt the same feeling. This didn't feel right at all.

'So, where is it?' Enzio asked.

'I'll get it,' said Fehnman. 'You call the boss.'

While Fehnman walked off to the booth, scratching at the back of his head where his slicked-back hair touched his collar, Enzio took the phone from Spanish Johnny, handling it delicately as if it were a trap. He flipped open the mouthpiece.

'Memory one,' Spanish Johnny instructed.

Enzio pressed the keys. 'You don't have a signal,' he reported a moment later, showing the thug the phone.

'Ah!' moaned Spanish Johnny, taking it back and shaking it (as if that would improve the reception). 'It's all the metal and electrics round here.' He looked around as if he was groping for an idea.

'You need to be higher up,' he said, handing the phone back. 'You want to take a ride on the big wheel?'

Enzio laughed once, a brutal grunt. 'Yeah, sure!' he said.

'What's the matter?' asked Spanish Johnny, who was managing to look quite offended. 'What? You think this is some kind of set-up?'

Enzio didn't reply. He just smiled at the other man, his eyes bright.

Chris was reminded again just how cruel and savage that smile could be. If this was a trick, he didn't fancy being Spanish Johnny if it wasn't a success.

'Look, up there you'll be able to talk to the boss real private. No snooping ears, eh? After all, who knows where that old Indian and the kid are?'

Chris instinctively ducked a little further back into the shadows.

Enzio snorted mockingly. 'You can forget about Grey Mountain and that Australian kid. After what happened this afternoon, they aren't going to show their faces in

Indianapolis for a while. I doubt they'll even be back for the rest of the tournament on Wednesday.' He paused, and Chris noticed his face take on a pained expression, as if what he was about to say left an unpleasant taste in his mouth. 'Joseph Blackdeer is going to take the fall for what happened to Moran. You can tell your boss that the whole situation is under control.'

Spanish Johnny was grinning back now. Did sharks eat other sharks, Chris wondered.

'He'll be glad to hear that,' Johnny replied. 'That's why we reached out to you, man, because we knew you'd get results.'

Enzio looked up at the Ferris wheel.

'Look, man, you're perfectly safe,' the goon said. 'We don't have any guns, see?' He pulled back the jacket of his suit.

'He's lying,' Grey Mountain whispered. 'See the crease in the back of his jacket? He has a gun in his belt there.'

Chris couldn't see anything of the kind, but he didn't doubt that Grey Mountain would be right. In the meantime, he concentrated on Spanish Johnny's continuing efforts to persuade Detective Enzio.

'What do you think we could do to you? This isn't *Bugs Bunny*, man, we can't make the wheel go round a hundred miles an hour. And Mr Lukas isn't gonna blow up his own amusement park just to save himself your fee.'

He laughed, as if to prove how silly Enzio was being. Chris knew that if it had been him out there, that laugh alone would have been enough to make him run a mile.

'Why don't I just call him from my car?' Enzio asked.

'On a police phone?' mocked Spanish Johnny. He stepped towards the booth, gesturing to Enzio to follow. Fehnman had reappeared and was standing at the entrance to the ride with the briefcase in his hand.

'This is stupid,' Enzio growled. 'What if you stop the wheel?'

'Hey, you can climb down the frame!' snapped Spanish Johnny impatiently. 'What's the matter, man? You scared of heights?'

Elementary school playground stuff, thought Chris. What do the bullies and the crazies always say when they want you to do something risky? 'What's the matter? You chicken? You afraid?' And nine times out of ten their victims go along with the stunt, just so they don't appear frightened. Chris had learnt a long time ago that it was better to just answer 'You bet I am' than follow whatever dumb scheme was waiting for him.

Enzio wouldn't have lasted ten minutes at Spirebrook Comprehensive.

'I'm not afraid of anything,' he insisted.

Except snakes, thought Chris. He was surprised at just how strongly that memory came back to him.

They had quite big snakes in America, didn't they? Big, heavy snakes.

Enzio was on his way towards the lowest car on the wheel. He had the phone in one hand and the other on the guard rail at the front of the car. Fehnman was holding the briefcase, ready to hand it to him as he sat down.

The car was swaying freely. Enzio couldn't find the lap belt.

It was suddenly all very clear in Chris's mind. Enzio was in Lukas's pocket, but now he was going to be cut loose. He knew too much.

More importantly, he'd shot Detective Moran. It chilled Chris to think of it. While Chris was being the perfect witness that Lukas hadn't been involved, Enzio had shot Moran. A cop had shot another cop. That was the kind of thing that Lukas made happen.

Enzio had shot Moran, partly because Moran was sniffing around, looking for proof that Enzio was on the take, partly because he saw the chance to frame Joseph Blackdeer for the crime. It was easier – or more effective, maybe – to shoot a fellow officer and shame Grey Mountain's people into defeat than it would have been to have shot Grey Mountain himself, or any of his people.

Enzio had been 'first on the scene'. He'd allowed Joseph Blackdeer to find the rifle, an old hunting gun like the ones Enzio said the Native Americans used. Maybe he'd stolen one from them, or found one in the police stores. The important thing was that the gun was genuine and that it had been found in Joseph Blackdeer's hands.

Had Lukas put Enzio up to it? Or had the detective come up with the idea all by himself? Only Enzio and his paymaster knew for sure. If Lukas wanted to make sure that no-one ever found out, he needed to ensure that Enzio kept quiet.

A cop had shot another cop. The thought wouldn't leave Chris's mind. In his book, whatever was about to happen to Enzio would be just reward.

Sadly, of course, he couldn't let it happen.

Fifteen

Fifteen

'Enzio! Look out, it's a trap!!!'

Chris roared the warning at the top of his voice, stepping out into the light so that the three men had a clear view of him. For a moment, none of them could move. Then Spanish Johnny reached under his jacket at the back and Chris had an instant's view of the gun he was pulling out.

'I knew it!' snarled Enzio, leaping up in the seat. He swung the briefcase in a wide arc, narrowly missing Fehnman but smacking Spanish Johnny firmly in the ribs. Chris heard air whoosh between the stricken goon's lips as he doubled up. The gun clattered to the floor.

Fehnman threw a fist in Enzio's direction which rocked the detective back. They were both trying to pull their guns, a race Fehnman looked to be winning until Enzio kicked his feet from under him. Fehnman fell off the boarding platform and rolled down beside the pay booth.

The two thugs were going to be out of the game for a while, Chris knew. That just left him and Enzio on the field. He hoped that the detective would be suitably grateful now that Chris had saved his life.

'Now would be a good time to start running,' came a voice from the darkness behind him.

Enzio had his gun out. His eyes were blazing with fury as he directed them at Chris.

All things considered, maybe Grey Mountain's advice was spot on.

Chris took off. He wasn't sure if Enzio would shoot at him, but this didn't seem like a good time to find out. This was a man who'd gunned down one of his own colleagues; it seemed unlikely that he'd be too shy about dealing with an Australian kid in the same way . . .

There was a slope just to Chris's left, with a path leading down towards some of the other rides. The only other choice was to jump back behind the sweet stand, but that would have just led Enzio straight to Grey Mountain. Chris doubted that the Chief would be much use in a foot race.

The slope looked good. Certainly it enabled Chris to take off like a sports car as he half ran, half fell down the incline. He was pretty sure Enzio would find it hard work keeping up with him – the detective's fat, heavy body didn't suggest much of the Linfords about him, either.

To his great relief there was no gun-shot. Bullets, he believed, were extremely quick.

Chris reached a crossroads at the bottom of the slope. Now things started to get difficult. He had no idea where he was going. A sign pointed to the exit, but that was too obvious. What he really needed to do was circle round somehow and find his way back to the opening in the fence.

From above somewhere, he heard a rough engine roar and tyres squeal. Enzio. It sounded like he was reversing back the way he'd come, which meant towards the main gates of the amusement park. That definitely put them out of play.

So, which way? To the left was some kind of kiddy play enclosure. To the right a tunnel leading further into the park. Nah. Straight ahead, that was the smart choice.

'At least I hope it is,' Chris muttered to himself as he chased along the path. He tried to tread as lightly as he could, to make sure that he would hear anyone pursuing him. Even so, he moved as quickly as he could, following the path as it curved round to the right and started to climb again. On both sides, he was hemmed in by arcades and attractions, all closed up for the night. The darkness was almost absolute. Only the stars shed any illumination at all.

At the top of the slight climb, the path branched left and right on to a wide access road. Chris wondered if it was the same road that led to the main entrance to the park. If so, he had made a big mistake coming this way. All the same, he didn't fancy turning back.

In front of him lay the entrance to the rollercoaster, charmingly called the DEATH CANYON! From what Chris could see, the ride's cars travelled along a track that twisted and turned through a canyon of fake rock and stone, sometimes

119

turning on their sides as the track took a sharp bend On the far side, he thought he could see a tunnel

The track soared up pretty high in places, supported by a forest of wooden posts and steel tubes. It would be easy to disappear in there for a moment, and wait for the search to get bored

Chris bit his lip and ran over the broad road. The loud note of the noisy car engine had gone silent All he could hear as he dodged across to the other side were his own footsteps and his heart beating faster.

He slipped under the barrier at the pay booth and crept along the side of the track, past the shed where the cars picked up their passengers. He picked his way carefully over half-buried cables and the huge bases of the wooden supports. After a few metres, he found a thick concrete post, on which was bolted a metal staircase climbing up to the trackway above This was obviously the way engineers got up to the top.

More importantly, the concrete post was thick enough to hide behind. Chris settled down on to his haunches and waited to see what might follow.

He didn't have long to wait After no more than 30 seconds, Spanish Johnny and Fehnman crept along the main road. Their effort to move as silently as possible was being ruined by the rumbling argument they were having.

'The boss ain't gonna like this . . .' sighed Spanish Johnny.

'Huh! It was a stupid plan anyway. If we wuz gonna get rid of the cop, why not just shoot him and dump him in a lake? Why all this nonsense about makin' it look like he fell?'

'You want I should tell GL that you said his plan was stupid?' Spanish Johnny tutted loudly. 'You know what he's gonna say to that?'

'No, what?' asked Fehnman, unhappily.

'He's gonna say it woulda worked just fine if that stupid Australian kid hadn't poked his nose in again; he'd say the kid shoulda been outta the way long ago. An' he woulda been too, if you hadn't let him get away back at the hotel.'

'Me?' howled Fehnman. 'What about you? You wuz there too!'

Spanish Johnny wasn't going to allow a fact like that to stop him. 'You wuz closer. You wuz closer to the cop too. Why'd you let him slug me?'

The two goons were on the road immediately outside the ride. Chris crouched even lower. He was pretty sure they wouldn't be able to see him in the darkness, but he didn't want to take any chances.

'Where you reckon Enzio is at?' muttered Spanish Johnny, not sounding so cocky any more. The two of them stopped. Chris wasn't sure, but he thought he could see something in Fehnman's hand.

'Who knows? If we're lucky, he'll open the case anyway!' They both laughed, then told each other to be quiet.

'This is crazy,' whinged Spanish Johnny. 'We got some torches in the car, right? Let's go back and get 'em.'

Fehnman obviously agreed with this plan, and the two of them turned away, moving back up the road the way they'd come.

Chris watched them carefully. This was his chance to slip back towards the gate. If the two goons had their car parked up somewhere behind the Ferris wheel, Chris could go back along the path he had followed, wait for them to go past again (it would be easy to see where they were once they had the torches on) and then head for the fence. The odds had to be that Enzio was over by the main gate.

He lost sight of the two heavies quickly. The jumbled, tangled web of the rollercoaster ride's supports hid them from him as easily as (he hoped) it hid him from them. He stepped out from behind the concrete post, trying to slip quietly back towards the entrance.

It was dumb luck that he tripped over a steel cable, although he'd tried to be careful picking his way along in the dark; it was even unluckier that someone heard when he sprawled on the ground. Even then, if it had been Lukas's two blockheads, he would still have fancied his chances of giving them the slip.

But his third unlucky break was that Enzio stepped out of the shadows of one of the booths opposite the rollercoaster, just as Chris hit the ground. He was less than fifteen metres away, separated by the fence but mighty close. Chris looked up into the detective's eyes. Enzio looked very glad to see him.

That wasn't good news.

Chris picked himself up and started to run again. Almost

straight away, he heard a crash as something hit the mesh fence. He looked back and was amazed to see Enzio hauling his large, flabby body up the fence, climbing up it at an unimaginable speed. The fence was shaking and rattling as if it might collapse, but it held on as Enzio reached the top, dragged himself over and fell down on the other side.

More than a little surprised at just how fit Enzio had proved to be, Chris tried to think quickly. There wasn't that much distance between them now and he didn't want to take a chance on Enzio being able to run as fast as he could climb. So, which way should he go? Back towards the entrance was suicide – Enzio would catch him up. If he ran towards the back of the ride, he'd just be hemmed in by the fence.

Chris took a long hard look at the concrete pillar.

It was another of Chris's strong beliefs, gained from years of watching TV, that it never made sense to start climbing anything when you were being chased. Almost every film or action show you ever watched it was the same; as soon as the bad guy ran away up the stairs to the roof, or started climbing up a ladder over a huge vat of bubbling liquid, it was certain he was going to fall. He and Nicky had talked about it after a particularly bad example in *Lois and Clark*. Even though Superman could fly, the bad guy had climbed up a tower at his state-of-the-art, conquer-the-world missile factory and had fallen off.

'The first thing I'd do if I was being chased,' Nicky had said, 'would be to run *down*stairs. It'd catch them by surprise if nothing else.'

But, thought Chris, trapped inside a fairground ride with hundreds of places to fall from, downstairs wasn't an option.

He raced over to the stairs, very aware of just how close Enzio was getting. The detective was puffing loudly. Chris thought he saw steam coming off his back. There was always a chance that he'd never be able to make the climb.

Chris was blowing a bit himself by the time he reached the top of the stairway. Five flights of stairs, maybe twelve or fourteen stairs to a flight. Just as he'd thought, the stairs led up to one of the slopes the track followed as it climbed. There were more wooden steps leading up beside the track. It seemed to go up a long, long way.

Enzio's feet were crashing up the stairs, almost shaking the tower. The burly detective was trying to shout something like 'Stop, kid!' but it came out as 'Hufffff! Stufffff!!!!!'

There was no way Enzio could follow him up, thought Chris. And with luck, there'd be another concrete tower somewhere round the track he could climb down again, once he'd left the cop gasping for air.

Maybe this wasn't such a bad idea after all.

The steps were pretty steep and hard-going. Chris had climbed about 40 when he heard Enzio reach the top of the metal staircase. That was the moment when he wondered if Enzio would actually use his gun. Chris's plan had allowed himself to be trapped in the open.

Bullets were not only quicker than young strikers but they didn't mind a few stairs.

At that moment, all the lights went on.

Chris hadn't really noticed before, but almost every part of the ride was covered in light bulbs. There had to be millions of them. They were all over the wooden supports, all over the sides of the track – everywhere. The parts of the ride that twisted and turned through the fake canyon walls were lit by blindingly white spotlights that twisted and swivelled automatically.

Over everything, there was a bright neon sign that read DEATH CANYON. Chris really didn't like that name any more.

The lights dazzled him; almost burnt him with their brilliance. He could feel the heat they gave off through his jacket. It was impossible to see out over the rest of the darkened park any more. There was just him, the rollercoaster and Enzio, equally dazzled. The cop had his gun arm up, shielding his eyes. Chris noticed he had the briefcase still firmly fixed in his hand.

A voice called from below, sounding small and lost over the hum of electricity that had sprung up from all sides.

'Hey, Enzio! What you doing up there?'

Enzio stepped across the track and looked over the outside safety rail.

'Fehnman? What ... game ... do you think ... you're playing ... now?' It took him a while to get the sentence finished, with all the breaks he had to take to breathe.

123

'No game, Enzio! Come down. The kid was lying, there's no trap.'

Enzio laughed bitterly. 'You mean . . . all there . . . is . . . in this case . . . is money?' he mocked.

'Sure!'

Enzio was still sneering as he turned to look up at Chris. 'What about it . . . kid?' he asked.

Faced with actually having to put his theory into words, Chris found himself feeling pretty stupid. He didn't have any proof at all, of course. Just a deep suspicion that the reason that no-one ever accused Lukas of being a crook was that no-one ever lived long enough to do it.

'I – uh!! – think it's a snake,' he said softly.

Enzio either didn't hear him over all the background noise, or was as stunned (and amused) by the idea as Chris was starting to feel.

'What?!'

'A snake. I guess they hoped you'd panic and fall off the wheel.'

At the very least it would have given Enzio a few sleepless nights in which he could think about not having any more bright ideas he didn't run past Lukas first.

Enzio lifted the case higher and gave it a suspicious look. His face had an expression that suggested he might shoot the case full of holes to be on the safe side. 'You seen . . . this snake?' He shivered as he said the word.

'No, but . . .'

'You get a lot of snake murders in Australia, right?' the detective mocked, shaking the case by its handle. 'This one must be pretty small. Doesn't weigh much.'

Oh, oh.

Enzio shook the case again. 'He must have had some car keys for breakfast too, by the sound of it.'

'Oh, man,' sighed Chris, remembering the mix-up in the bedroom.

Convinced by now that whatever he was holding in his hand wasn't stuffed full of boa constrictor, Enzio had become his usual objectionable self. 'Course,' he snarled, 'it don't feel much like my money, neither. So we'll not take any chances. You can open it.'

He watched Chris steadily with his beady eyes (quite

124

snake-like, in their own way, thought Chris). Chris didn't hurry back down the stairs.

'Enzio!' came another shout. The detective peered back over the rail.

'What?'

'You gonna come down so we can talk this over?'

Enzio uttered his short, yeah-that's-funny laugh. 'I'll be right down, Fehnman. Me and the kid need to have a talk first.'

'You don't wanta do that,' Chris heard the greasier of the two goons reply. 'All these lights on, people might come take a peek at what's going on.'

'Just wait, Fehnman. I'll be down in a minute.' Enzio paused, struck by a sudden thought. 'You tell Spanish Johnny not to get any cute ideas.'

Chris didn't think ideas were Johnny's strong point, but it did seem odd that he wasn't there to hold Fehnman's hand. Enzio was clearly thinking along the same lines, glancing towards the stairway, wondering if it could be climbed without making some noise.

'Don't you worry about climbing all the way back down here, Enzio,' yelled Fehnman from below. Chris could hear the laughter in his voice. 'Spanish Johnny's gonna get you a ride.'

Next second, there was a change in the humming and whining of the electrics all round, as if someone had just wound up the juice. Almost immediately afterwards, there was a grating, clattering noise from the centre of the track, where a heavy duty chain had started moving, driving a cogged arrangement in a small space between the rails.

Chris knew what that meant.

The lead car of the train leaving the station far below had bright lights on the front, like gleaming eyes. It clanged and crashed as it was caught by the whirling cogs at the bottom of the slope, and started to climb.

There was no great risk. There was plenty of space on the walkway beside the track to keep out of the train's way. All the same, it wouldn't be a lot of fun up here as it came by. And any one of the cars could have a passenger on board, gun in hand. And if he wasn't on the first train, he'd be on the one after that. Or the one after that.

Enzio growled and leant over the rail again.

'You better shut that thing off, Fehnman,' he yelled, but

there was no reply. He continued to look down, both over the rail and down the track towards the steadily rising train. Chris took the opportunity to put another few steps between them.

He had no idea how he was going to get out of this. His big hope was that the bad guys would concentrate on each other until Grey Mountain and his boys could come to the rescue. The idea appealed enormously to Chris's sense of balance (the Indians riding to the rescue) as well as his need to be rescued.

At least, in the current circumstances, he didn't see Enzio climbing up to get him while the train was passing. That had to be a good thing.

Wrong.

Enzio had always struck Chris as being pretty stupid, but even he knew a free ride when he saw it. As the train steadily came up alongside, he just grabbed hold of the side and stepped over the door and into the front seat.

Suddenly, the 40 or 50 steps between them didn't look a great distance any more.

Enzio was twisting rapidly back and forth in the seat, trying to keep an eye on the back of the train, in case Spanish Johnny popped out, and another eye on Chris, stuck on the trackside above him. It wasn't easy, but he was managing.

Chris remained quite still, aware that he wasn't going to get anywhere safe before Enzio's ride caught up to him.

The train clattered closer, the noise drowning out everything else. Enzio appeared to have satisfied himself that there was no-one else on the ride just yet; the goons' plan to force them off the trackway was about to backfire. Enzio was grinning widely, his eyes narrow and hostile. The front of the train was just a few feet from Chris now, blinding him with its lights. There wasn't enough space for Chris to let it pass him by without Enzio being able to reach out and grab him.

'Get in,' the detective growled as the train closed in on Chris. He was reaching out over the side of the first car, his hands stretched out like talons, ready to grab Chris and reel him in.

Chris was holding his breath, praying for a last-second rescue, but it wasn't going to happen. Enzio fixed his fingers in

Chris's jacket as the train pulled past. Frightened of being dragged under the wheels, Chris hopped on to the side of the train and allowed Enzio to pull him on board. He fell into the back seat of the first car.

Enzio was almost laughing now. Things were working out as well as he could have hoped. With Chris behind him, he could face the back of the train, keeping a watch just in case one of the goons was still hidden somewhere towards the back.

'You've got a lot of guts, kid,' Enzio snarled. He was standing in the front of the car, towering over Chris. The wind was blowing through his raincoat, making it flutter behind him like a corny comic book villain's cape. 'So, what was all this about a trap?'

Chris remained in the rear seat, unable to say anything. He was frightened, yes, but he was also aware that proving his theory about how Lukas had planned to get rid of Enzio wasn't going to be easy . . .

The detective held up the case. 'Somethin' to do with this, is it? Maybe there's a bomb in it after all?'

'Not exactly,' said Chris quietly. It was possible Enzio never even heard the reply over the crashing din of the climbing train.

Enzio dropped the case into Chris's lap and gestured with the gun he carried in his right hand. 'Open it.' Chris looked up at the cop's face, wondering what he might do if Chris refused.

'It's locked,' Chris said. Enzio didn't notice that Chris hadn't tried the catches first.

Enzio felt in his pocket and brought out a pocket knife.

'Force it,' he ordered.

Chris opened the blade and started to lever it under the first lock. He was amazed at how easy it was to snap it open. He got to work on the other side.

'Be careful,' said Enzio.

BE CAREFUL.

Chris's hands were still trembling, but finally the second catch snapped. He turned the case round so that it would open facing Enzio.

'Be real careful . . .'

KEEP YOUR HANDS INSIDE THE CAR.

127

Chris turned the case back round again so that it faced Enzio. He took his time, waiting for the right moment. At last, he very, very gently lifted the lid.

Enzio's eyes first narrowed as he tried to see what was inside, then widened as he worked out that there was no money in there and that Lukas had cheated him if nothing else. Finally, his eyes went kind of wonky and glazed before they closed.

In the split second before that last change, there had been a heavy THUNK as Enzio's head had whacked into the warning sign above the track. They weren't climbing that fast, but the sign which read DO NOT STAND had proved its point.

Enzio fell down in the front seat. The gun went over the side. Chris peered over the divide between the front and back seats hoping that Enzio wasn't too badly injured (although he wasn't sorry that the detective had been taken out of the game so neatly). The cop was lying on the floor, solidly wedged in front of the seat. He was moving, rubbing the back of his head with one hand. That was all Chris needed to know.

He could breathe a little easier now. All that left were the two heavies. They would be waiting for him at the end of the ride, but Chris knew that was two minutes away. The train continued the last few metres of its climb and prepared to enter DEATH CANYON.

After the events of the last few minutes, Chris thought it was the tamest ride he had ever been on.

To his surprise, when the train halted at the far end of the ride, there was no sign of Spanish Johnny or Fehnman, just the silent, unmoving figure of Grey Mountain flanked by several of the other Wabash Iroquois.

The two older boys were carrying bows. Chris saw a feathered arrow in the sign above the pay booth.

There was no need to ask if the two goons were still around, then. Chris imagined they had run back to their boss to tell him the good news.

'Detective Enzio's in the front seat here,' Chris indicated. 'I think he just realised his arrangement with Lukas is over.'

128

Grey Mountain smiled a little. His eyes lowered slightly, seeing that Chris was carrying a briefcase as he stepped out of the car.

'What's in there?' he asked.

'All kinds of fun stuff,' said Chris, grinning.

Sixteen

———— ⚽ ————

It was no more than a hopeful ball hit out of defence, but Chris latched on to it like a hunter, bursting across the halfway line, taking the ball on his chest and racing forward. The goalie appeared suddenly in front of him, having chased out of his area in a mad rush.

Chris chipped the ball over the bemused keeper and dodged to the side to avoid a collision. A couple of defenders continued to chase back, but after two or three bounces the ball slid into the makeshift goal at the far post.

'No, no, no!' Chris yelled.

Everyone stopped. Chris fixed his attention on the keeper.

'How many more times do I have to tell you? Stay in your area! Every time you come out like that, you can't handle the ball – or if you do, the ref has to send you off. And nine times out of ten you leave yourself open to getting lobbed like that.'

The Iroquois' goalkeeper nodded and smiled to show he understood. Chris sighed. The guy had nodded and smiled quite a few times already.

'Look, the way to beat a striker coming in on goal is to move steadily off your line, closing off the angle but not leaving room for him to chip the ball over you. Stand up tall and make yourself as big a target as you can. As soon as the striker brings the ball into the area, close him down fast, but stay on your feet. At the last minute, try to smother the ball by diving at his feet, but don't rush it.'

'I've got it this time,' the keeper said, grinning apologetically. 'It's not easy to get out of the habit of coming out of the area whenever I like.'

'My way works better, believe me,' Chris said.

The boy nodded again, and jogged back to his position in goal. Chris prepared to run the exercise again.

'Where's . . . what's the name of the guy playing sweeper again?'

'Jay Crowmask,' one of the nearest players said.

'Right. Which one is he?'

'Me,' the player said. It was Chris's turn to offer an apologetic grin. It was taking him time to get used to his new team, and the fact that there were several sets of brothers and cousins in the Iroquois line-up didn't make telling them apart any easier.

'OK. Now, you see what I mean about not leaving a big space behind if you move forward? Your primary job is defensive. If your lads are already pushing forward in numbers, your job is to drop back and provide someone who can rescue a situation like the one we've been practising.'

'I got you.'

'OK,' Chris said. Jay was the fastest runner on his team, comfortably quicker than Chris. Before Chris came along he had been playing in a central midfield role. 'Now, that time there was no way you could have caught me, so you should have run back towards the area to guard the goal; provide a bit of cover for the keeper. But if you think you can run me down, do it.'

Jay nodded. They set up the exercise again. Three attacking players knocked the ball around between them, trying to keep it away from the defence. As soon as they lost the ball, it was supposed to get thumped upfield so they could test Chris's new defensive plan.

Chris glanced at his watch. It was 10.30am, Tuesday morning. Since leaving Thunder Park they'd had seven hours' sleep, a hearty breakfast and now practice. Tonight they were going back to Indianapolis to be ready for the semi-final of the Indy Sports Challenge on Wednesday morning. Chris felt a little heavy legged, but not one of the Iroquois was even a little jaded.

The field was a gently sloping meadow just outside the small village in which the Iroquois lived. Chris had fallen asleep on the flatbed after they left Thunder Park, but he had been told they had driven along the main road to Bloomington, and had then followed the line of the White River until they reached the Iroquois village. Bitter Lake was about two hours away to the north-west, in a thickly wooded area. Chris had hoped to

131

get a look at the place all the fuss was about, but there wasn't going to be time.

Not unless he put his flight to San Francisco off for another day, of course.

'OK, go!' Chris called, and the exercise began again. This time, the defenders won the ball really quickly. The clearance was mis-hit, failing to get much beyond the halfway line. Chris still reached it first, but he had no clear run on goal. Turning quickly, he saw one of his 'team' moving up behind him. Chris knocked a pass back and took off upfield, calling for a firm return pass.

The lad actually overhit it, but Chris could see the defenders hadn't learnt the point of the exercise. Jay had been caught out by the mis-move and was drifting wide in support of one of the full backs who had gamely set off after Chris. Behind Jay, one of Chris's 'team mates' was free and clear.

If he had been able to reach the ball, Chris would have had an open man to pass to. He bit his lip. Jay was doing his best; getting bawled out by Chris wasn't going to help.

'Better!' he called, catching his breath. 'OK, let's take five and then we'll try something else.'

The Iroquois and their new 'coach' trooped to the sidelines, where there were some long tables set up on trestles, with benches on each side. Each table had a large platter of fruit and several jugs of cool lemonade on it. The weather had definitely improved since the weekend – the forecast was for 80 degree heat and no wind at all.

Chris munched a peach. It was so juicy it almost drowned him. He'd never tasted fruit like this back home.

'They're playing better already,' came a voice. Chris turned round on the bench.

It was Grey Mountain, although not as Chris had seen him before. Away from prying eyes, the staff, the drum, the leather clothes and the moccasins were all gone. Chris found it hard not to laugh. The Chief was wearing trainers, a Niagara Falls T-shirt and jeans.

'They – uh –' began Chris, gradually regaining control. 'They're doing all right.'

'This plan of yours, will it work, do you think?'

That was a good one. Would it work? Chris hadn't tried to think about that too much since he had arrived in the Iroquois'

132

home town. He had been caught up in the enthusiasm everyone had felt for getting back at Lukas, as if a little bit of coaching from their English guest was going to turn the Iroquois into World Cup contenders overnight.

It wasn't, Chris remembered, even his plan. It had been the Colts' manager, Iain Walsh, who'd had the idea to use a three-man defence against their American defence; a sweeper and two full backs, with a five-man midfield operating in front of them, taking turns at defensive duties. Chris remembered Rory Blackstone recommending the system to the guy from Parchmont School.

A five-man midfield made sense. Nearly all the American teams Chris had played against over the last few months had been good teams. But they had struggled against an English-style game, where they had no time and no room to play. They'd pull five men back, trying to play a controlled, thoughtful game, only to find the Colts all over them in midfield, winning the ball and dominating possession. Coming forward, the Americans were reduced to hitting long passes over the midfield.

That was why Walsh had thought of the sweeper system. One player, roving freely at the back, could watch out for fast breaks and hopeful passes, but also look to start attacks from the back, pushing well up into enemy territory.

The Colts had been able to score frequently by running at the opposition defences from all angles, never repeating attacking patterns. Chris was sure the Iroquois could do the same, using their natural pace. The only thing that worried him about the plan was the pressure it put on the back three to work well together – and the fact that Cody Snowbird liked to race all over the field.

'They look OK,' Chris replied. His red-shirted companions grinned.

Grey Mountain's expression didn't change at all. 'So, you are sure we can win?'

Chris held up his hands. 'I didn't exactly say that. I'm pretty sure we can give the Aztecs a good game, but those guys from The Orchards are pretty good players. Assuming they get through to the final –' something Chris would be prepared to have a bet on '– we'll have to be a lot sharper to beat them.'

'But we have their game plan,' said White Ash, one of the two older players.

'We have what *may* be their game plan,' sighed Chris. 'All we know for sure about the stuff we found in the briefcase is that The Orchards play a pretty orthodox four-four-two. Well, we've all seen that for ourselves already. The only extra thing we gain from reading the stuff from the case is knowing a few trick plays from free kicks and corners.'

He hadn't been able to persuade the Iroquois players that soccer wasn't a game you could plan in the same way as NFL football or basketball. The best you could hope for was a game plan that told players what they were supposed to be doing and where. Once the game kicked off, anything could happen.

'Now that Mr Lukas knows we have the plan, won't van Zale change the way they play?' asked Jay.

'Maybe, maybe not,' said Chris. It didn't matter that much. The sweeper formation ought to catch The Orchards on the hop whatever style they adopted. Or so he hoped. 'I suppose we have to assume he's worked out by now that Pinky and Perky brought the wrong briefcase to the meeting with Enzio.' The two goons would have reported back to their boss and it wouldn't have taken long for the truth to be discovered. It would be equally obvious that if the case had gone missing, Chris must have taken it after the encounter on the roller-coaster.

'Lukas might have other things on his mind,' Grey Mountain pointed out. There were a few delighted grins at that idea.

'Anyway,' said Chris to the players. 'Don't worry about what The Orchards might do. You've got to master your own game. And there's the little matter of getting past the Peru Aztecs first.'

No-one looked too worried. The Iroquois were bubbling with confidence about the semi-final. Everyone seemed to have forgotten that there was a real chance that it might not take place.

'Have you heard from Running Waters?' Chris asked Grey Mountain.

'She's with Joseph Blackdeer,' the Chief replied flatly.

'Oh,' said Chris. The Chief didn't volunteer any more information, so Chris decided to dig for it. 'Are the cops going to let him go?'

'Not right away,' Grey Mountain replied. Chris wasn't sure what that meant. Were the police going to hold Joseph for another hour? A day? Months?

'But surely there's no case any more? Running Waters did tell them about what Enzio said?' Chris could feel his temper rising. 'He's not denying what he told us?' Not after everything that had happened at Thunder Park.

'Detective Enzio has no desire to go to prison, Chris. Just because he is no longer in Lukas's employ, it doesn't follow that he's our best friend.'

Chris thought about that for a moment. 'But we heard Enzio! He confessed to –'

'It's called hearsay, Chris. It's not admissible in court. And besides, if you think about what we overheard, it wasn't exactly a confession.'

Chris ran as much of the conversation between Enzio and Lukas's goons through his mind as he could remember. Grey Mountain was right. Telling Spanish Johnny that things were 'under control' was hardly an admission that he'd shot Moran.

Grey Mountain reached out a hand and patted Chris on the shoulder.

'Leave the legal stuff to us, Chris. Just concentrate on the football. All you have to worry about is getting our boys into shape to beat The Orchards.'

'And Peru . . .' said Chris.

Grey Mountain shrugged. 'I don't think the Aztecs are going to be such a problem.'

Chris sighed. Obviously this overconfidence the Wabash team was feeling ran through the whole village. Grey Mountain moved off. Chris remembered one more question he wanted to ask.

'Where is Enzio now?'

The last time Chris had seen the bent detective, he had been loaded into the back of his car by the Iroquois players and the tall striker had got in behind the wheel. Quite apart from wondering where a fourteen-year-old boy learnt to drive, Chris was also deeply curious about where Enzio might have been taken.

Grey Mountain didn't turn back to face Chris, but kept walking away. Chris just about heard his voice, but it was quickly obvious that Grey Mountain wasn't going to give him an answer. He was talking on the phone. The mobile Spanish Johnny had been carrying.

'I guess that's fair enough,' muttered Chris. After all, it seemed only fair that the Chief was working on the next stage of their plan and running up Lukas's phone bill at the same time.

The morning passed quickly. The Iroquois were fast learners and Chris felt he'd got some of the worst kinks out of their defence by the time they broke for lunch.

He planned to use the afternoon to work with the strikers. The tall boy was good, but he tried to do everything himself. Chris wanted the midfield players to run through in support, and for Crazy Fox (no kidding!) to lay the ball off rather than try to turn. It was hard work. Crazy (as Chris liked to call him) was older than the other boys and – from what Chris could work out of the family connections – he was more closely related to Grey Mountain than any of the other players. That meant he didn't like sharing any of the 'glory' with them.

'You see, this is a team game,' Chris explained for the zillionth time. 'If you score a hat-trick but your team loses four-three, that's a bad thing.'

Crazy Fox asked what a hat-trick was.

There were quite a few other things Crazy Fox didn't know much about. He could dribble with the ball quite well, but he just ran forward, regardless of where the defenders were. His passes were all hit with the same ferocity as his shots. As for heading the ball, Crazy never bothered trying unless there really was no chance of a glamorous overhead kick.

'How many times have you played soccer?' asked Chris.

He watched as Crazy Fox counted off the two games they had played on Monday. 'I normally play basketball,' the young Iroquois explained. 'Did you know the Native Americans invented basketball?'

Not all of the others were as difficult to work with. Joseph Blackdeer's kid brother was a tidy midfield ball winner, a kind of darker version of David Batty. White Ash, the other older player, could pass a ball and didn't mind having a poke at goal in the right circumstances.

Then there was a ten-year-old headcase who worried Chris a lot. He had more scars on his face than a dog has fleas, but the lad could tackle like someone twice his age and ran round like a racing car for 90 minutes.

They weren't classy, but they were OK. Even so, Chris didn't really fancy their chances if they did get through to play The Orchards. The Peru Aztecs were going to be enough of a test.

Grey Mountain hung round the sports field all afternoon. He was using the phone nearly all the time. Just after three, though, he suddenly stopped talking, shook the cellphone once, then tossed it into a rubbish bin.

'Cut off,' he explained with a shrug.

Chris had the players playing six-a-side. He wanted to get them used to the idea of keeping on the move, closing down the other teams for space when they didn't have the ball and supporting the front players quickly when they did.

There was so little time, thought Chris. They were going to drive back to Indy Sports the following morning. He waved the players off for lunch, aware that he didn't dare ask too much of them in case he burnt them out before tomorrow.

'Have you heard anything?' It was the tenth time Chris had asked. Despite being told to leave the other stuff to Grey Mountain, he was still desperate to see how the different parts of the story would work out.

'You'll be glad to hear Detective Moran is much better.' said Grey Mountain. He was digging in a small leather bag at his feet.

Chris was pleased to hear it. One of Grey Mountain's daughters put a plate of food in front of Chris. There was a kind of split slice of bread, filled with meat, peppers and tomatoes, a paste of some kind, some beans and a tall glass of milk. Chris didn't think it was the kind of food English players ever trained on.

It was good, though. He devoured his meal in a few minutes. It only took him that long because it was so spicy.

'This is good,' he said with his mouth full. 'Is it Indian food?'

'Nah,' replied Grey Mountain. 'Mexican. Much better than our grub.'

His exploration of the bag had turned up yet another

cellular phone. Chris suspected this one didn't belong to the Chief either. Grey Mountain must have realised what he was thinking, because he looked at the phone, looked at Chris and then said: 'Detective Enzio's. He won't mind us borrowing it.'

'Isn't it the police department's phone really?' asked Chris. 'I mean, are you sure you should be using it?'

'I'm not going to!' insisted Grey Mountain, as if offended at the suggestion. 'Do you want to?'

'Me?' Chris uttered, gaping.

'You could call your father. When I spoke to Detective Moran, he told me that the police were out in force looking for you. They may even be coming here. It appears your father is getting a little worried about the number of times you have missed catching your flight to San Francisco.'

Chris groaned. He knew how much trouble he was in already. Did he really need to call home just to hear it first-hand?

By the end of the day, Chris was exhausted. He watched Grey Mountain wandering around the sports field, organising, talking and directing. How did the old man keep going?

Chris had called a halt to practice at 3pm. They had done as much good as they could do in one short day – and Chris didn't want them burnt out before their game next morning.

Running Waters arrived some time before the evening meal. She had a rapid conversation with her grandfather, then they both went over to join Chris.

'I need you to sign this,' she said, putting a piece of paper on the table in front of Chris. She glanced at Grey Mountain nervously as she did so.

Chris looked at the paper. It was some kind of legal document.

'What's this?' he asked.

'It's a little awkward to explain,' the lawyer said, and she certainly sounded awkward about it.

'It's to do with the help you're giving the team,' Grey Mountain said. 'Insurance.'

Chris nodded. 'OK,' he said, taking the pen Running Waters was holding. He signed the document where she indicated. He didn't really understand what Grey Mountain was plotting, but after all the effort they had gone through, he didn't want to raise any objections.

'OK,' said Grey Mountain 'Eat up. We have to get going.'

Chris looked up quickly. 'I thought we were going back to Indy Sports in the morning?' he said.

'The rest of the team are,' Grey Mountain said. 'You and I have to make a small detour.'

Chris felt a small twinge of warning run up the back of his neck. He didn't like the worried look on Running Waters' face either.

'Wait a minute. I can't go off on some mystery tour with you! If I don't leave Indianapolis soon, my father is going to have the FBI chasing after me! And what about the games tomorrow?' Chris asked.

'We'll be back in plenty of time for all that,' Grey Mountain insisted. 'I promise you; by tomorrow, you'll be on your way to San Francisco, your father will be a happy man and everything will be fine. Now, in the meantime, didn't you say you wanted to visit Bitter Lake?'

Seventeen

They drove up there in a battered old truck, following some dusty back road through the open countryside. Away from the Iroquois village, they were travelling through farmland which stretched as far as the eye could see in every direction. Fields of corn and tall barns lay on every side.

Indiana was one of the flattest places in the universe, but along the White River it managed to find the energy for a few low rolling hills. They crossed the river by means of a rickety wooden bridge. On the far side, it was more woodland than farm, and the track was even more rough and pitted.

Finally, after they had been driving for just over two hours, Grey Mountain stopped the jeep.

'Now, we walk,' he said.

The reasons for abandoning the vehicle became clear after just a few hundred metres. For one thing, the track pretty well disappeared. For another, there was a wooden rail fence and a gate directly across their path. The gate was fastened with a heavy chain and padlock.

Chris looked around. 'That fence is supposed to keep people out?' he asked in disbelief.

'Not really,' the Chief replied. 'But then, no fence would. It's more a way for Lukas to say "This is mine; stay away".'

They stepped over the fence, Chris helping Grey Mountain climb the rails. On the far side, they followed a narrow path through the trees, scrabbling over loose rocks and roots. Chris was worried that Grey Mountain would find the going too hard, but his guide never faltered for an instant.

They hiked for about 20 or 30 minutes before Grey Mountain walked even faster, as if he was keen to get to the next corner of the trail. When Chris caught up with him, he realised why.

At the corner of the trail, there was a gap in the trees, a fire break which led down a gentle slope to the bottom of the valley. Below them was a crystal-clear lake. The trees on the shoreline came down almost to the water's edge, save for one rocky outcrop off to their left, which stuck out into the water like a jetty.

It was wild country, barely tamed. It was also one of the most spectacular places Chris had ever seen.

'This is Bitter Lake,' said Grey Mountain, as if Chris hadn't guessed. 'The lake itself, these forests, and a few acres of the plains beyond are all that are left of a much, much larger area that was once an Iroquois holy place. After General Wayne defeated us and we signed that treaty, we had to move to the village where we live now to grow food. But we tried to make sure there was always someone staying here, to keep the land ours.

'The trouble is, so few of us live around here these days. The young people go to the cities to find work. No-one has stayed here for years.'

And Lukas, who knew about the treaty already, had discovered this and knew it meant the land could be developed. If he won, Bitter Lake would be taken away from the Iroquois for good.

And made into what? A holiday village? Another Thunder Park? Chris had nothing against either, but surely a place as beautiful as this just needed to be left alone.

'Come on,' said Grey Mountain, 'Running Waters is waiting.'

The old man led the way down the slope, along the side of the fire break. As they walked, Chris saw a deer on the other side of the break, watching them from the shelter of the tree line.

'There are all kinds of creatures in these woods,' Grey Mountain observed. Chris could believe it. All around, there were birds singing, and the bushes rustled as smaller animals scampered away from their noisy descent.

They finally reached the side of the lake. Grey Mountain showed Chris how the land curved round in a kind of 'C' shape, trapping the water inside. On the open side, a mudslide many hundreds of years before had blocked a small stream, and dammed up the lake behind it. The stream had broken through now, and tumbled off south east towards the White River.

'The story goes that two young Iroquois hunters were trapped up here by a storm the day the mountain fell. They were lost, and all they had to eat or drink was the water from the stream. There must have been an earthquake or something; anyway, a mudslide blocked the river. It threw a great plume of smoke into the air, and pushed huge rocks into the water.

'The rocks dammed up the stream and turned it into a lake. Only there must have been something in the mud, because where the stream's waters were sweet, the lake was very sour. That was a long time ago; the water is as pure as anything now, but the name sort of stuck.'

Grey Mountain looked out across the clear, blue waters. 'I bet Lukas even wants to change the name. Bitter Lake isn't a very good brand name.'

'You haven't lost yet,' said Chris.

For the first time, the old man looked tired. 'Perhaps not,' he said in a quiet voice, 'but it will not be easy. We have just twenty-four hours to raise the five hundred thousand bond, and so far we have just a fraction of what we need. Without the rest, we will lose before the fight has even begun.'

Once again, Chris found himself wondering how the Iroquois were ever going to turn the situation round. The prize money from the tournament would help, but it would still leave the Wabash massively short of their target.

Grey Mountain was pointing towards the spur of rock that jutted out into the lake near where the stream entered it. Chris could see a small cabin there. A tell-tale plume of smoke was rising from the chimney.

'I see Running Waters has the evening meal started,' said Grey Mountain. 'She's a good cook. You might want to mention that to Detective Moran, if you see him tomorrow.'

'He's out of hospital already?' gasped Chris.

'No,' the Chief replied. 'But he has been making such a nuisance of himself that I think they will be glad to see him leave. The bullet didn't make a hole in anything vital. Apart from shock and the loss of blood, he's fine.'

'I guess we're lucky Enzio is such a lousy shot,' said Chris.

'Or such a good one. I think Enzio may have tried to hit Moran in the shoulder. He may be a fat, slovenly, crooked, slimy piece of work, but I don't think he's a killer.'

Chris grinned at the character reference, then followed as Grey Mountain set off along the shore, aiming for the hut.

It wasn't far. Chris was thoroughly enjoying the walk anyway. Grey Mountain had been right – he needed to have seen the place at the centre of events before he finally left Indianapolis.

The sun was setting slowly in the west and Bitter Lake gradually became dark. They reached the hut just in time.

Chris was starving. From about 200 metres away, he had been able to smell something cooking. He couldn't wait to see what Running Waters had made.

However, there was actually a delay before dinner. Running Waters had the meal almost ready, but she wasn't the only occupant of the small hut up on the rock. Chris almost fell back through the door with surprise.

'Oh!' muttered Grey Mountain. 'Didn't I mention that your father would be here?'

After the initial shock had passed, and Chris was able to get his arms, legs and mouth working again (more or less in that order, too), he ran over to greet his father. John Stephens looked pretty pleased to see him too.

'How did you get here?' Chris gasped.

'Taxi, train, plane, bus and jeep,' his father replied, grinning. 'I've used them all.'

'No,' spluttered Chris, still flustered. 'I mean how, why . . .' Actually, he didn't know exactly what he meant.

'Even I only know half the story,' Mr Stephens (half) explained. 'It got to the point where I was wondering if you were ever going to leave Indianapolis, so I was tempted to come out here anyway.' He managed a stern glance at Chris, but couldn't keep it up. 'Then I got a call from the police, so I was *really* worried. This guy called Enzio made it seem like you were America's Most Wanted criminal.'

Chris thought about butting in to explain, but decided against it.

'Then I get another call, from this young woman here, who explains that far from being a gangster, you have been helping her people fight some kind of scam. I thought about it for a while. I thought, either the detective is telling the truth and my son is in big trouble with the law, or this lawyer is right and Chris is just sticking his nose in. I mean, who was I supposed to believe?'

Chris grinned awkwardly. 'Actually, I didn't mean to get involved at all. You see, I saw Grey Mountain playing a drum and –'

'You can save your side of the story for later,' his father said quickly. 'What persuaded me that Running Waters was telling the truth was that she offered to arrange for a plane ticket so I could come out here and catch up with you myself.'

'You paid for my dad's air fare?' asked Chris.

'Grandfather's idea,' said Running Waters, nervously.

Grey Mountain shrugged. 'A small price to pay, after all the help you have given us. Besides, I'm sick of having to keep an eye out for you all the time.'

'But the money . . .'

'A small withdrawal from the war chest. We're so far short of the $500,000 we need, another $2,000 isn't going to make much difference.'

Chris decided not to argue. It was pretty good to see his father again, even if it did mean he had an awful lot to explain.

'So, here I am,' said Mr Stephens. He looked a bit washed out with jet lag, but otherwise fine. Chris crossed his fingers and prayed that this meant he wasn't in too much trouble.

His father reached into his pocket and drew out a slender envelope. Chris knew at once what it contained.

'I bet you know what these are,' his father said, sternly. 'And tomorrow, we're going to use them. That's what you do with plane tickets, I've discovered. You get on aeroplanes and fly places with them.'

Chris offered a sick smile. 'Uh – what time . . .'

'I know all about this football tournament tomorrow,' his father said instantly. 'And the court case. Well, I'm sorry, but our plane leaves for home tomorrow morning.' He handed Chris the tickets.

'Tomorrow morning? Home?'

'Home. What did you think? Haven't you driven Jace Goodman's father mad enough already? He's spent three days waiting for you to reach San Francisco! If we went now, it would almost be time to come home again anyway.'

So much for a holiday in California. Chris knew better than to argue, though. Well, almost . . .

'Wait! What about my stuff? What about —'

'Taken care of. Hey, I've had all day to sort things out. The airline sent back your passport and other stuff; I picked them up when I arrived. Then I went with Running Waters to meet Detective Moran. He explained what had been going on in more detail.' Chris gulped. 'Oh, yes,' his father continued. 'I've met all your friends, except for this Lukas character, and I'm not going to be sorry if I miss him. Believe me, Chris, I'm not letting you get any more involved in all this craziness.'

Chris flicked through the ticket book. He wondered if he was missing something and looked again. No, he had been right the first time.

'Um . . . dad. This ticket is one way.'

It was Mr Stephens' turn to be surprised. 'What?' he gasped, snatching the booklet back.

'Ah,' said Grey Mountain. 'I've been meaning to mention that.'

Chris's father was completely gobsmacked.

Grey Mountain didn't so much as twitch a muscle as he watched Mr Stephens try to deal with what he was being told. Finally, though, he held up a hand. 'Please, Mr Stephens, don't be alarmed, we do have the rest of your travel arrangements in hand. We just have a few details to sort out first.'

'Details?'

'Really, yes. You see, we need Chris to stay around for one more day, if you'll agree to let him. And we need you to stay too.'

Chris was just as amazed as his father now.

'Me?' Mr Stephens gasped.

'Yes,' Grey Mountain said, and he took a deep breath. 'Running Waters, would you mind dishing up some dinner while I tell Mr Stephens the real reason why he's here?'

Chris could see his father didn't like what he was hearing. He was close to demanding the whole truth right there and then when Grey Mountain started to give it to him anyway.

Dinner was a little late.

Eighteen

●

Wednesday morning. A warm, bright day. The last of the storm's wind and rain had long departed and the ground was crisp and firm underfoot. There was barely a breath of air to stir the trees.

From early that morning, files of people started to work their way towards Indy Sports. The local news station had been talking about little else. People were coming from all over Indiana to see the final drama of the Indy Sports Challenge.

It had everything. A bitter rivalry, cut-throat business operations, one shooting and a reported ruckus at a funfair, an attempted abduction, allegations of fraud and double-dealing ... nothing showing at any of Indianapolis's cinemas could compare. In fact, there were rumours that one of the thousands of people trying to get into the park was a Hollywood TV producer, who wanted to make a real-life docudrama out of the events of the last few days.

Few of the spectators knew exactly what had been going on, of course, although there were plenty of rumours to fill in the gaps. However, most people had the gist of the story. The Wabash Iroquois had to win the tournament to stand any chance of getting the $500,000 they needed to hold off Gary Lukas's development of their land; Lukas was trying to get them thrown out of the tournament over the shooting of Detective Moran. Even if they stayed in the competition, the Iroquois still had to get past the Peru Aztecs before they could face their likely opponents in the final, opponents who just happened to include Gary Lukas's son.

Better than soap opera.

The teams from Peru and Gary were left completely bemused by all the activity around them when they arrived.

There was a vast sea of people around the pitches to be used for the semi-finals.

Chris was pretty bowled over by the spectacle himself. He'd played in front of decent-sized crowds before, but he'd never seen anything quite like this. There was talk of 20,000 people crowding into the park.

The Iroquois arrived shortly after, perched on the back of the flatbed truck. They stared back at the thousands of faces staring up at them. Some of the crowd were hissing; plenty of others gawped and stared and pointed, as if the Wabash were freaks in a circus sideshow.

The Iroquois remained impassive, their faces relaxed. Chris could only pray that they were as calm as they looked.

Chris, his father, Grey Mountain and Running Waters waited by the red-walled changing rooms. The police had cordoned off the area in front of it so that the teams could find somewhere to park and prepare for the games. As before, the Iroquois were already wearing their blood-red kit. Chris watched them get frisked by the uniformed police.

No-one was taking any chances, it seemed.

Jay, Cody, White Ash, Crazy Fox, Tommy Blackdeer and the others walked over towards Chris and Grey Mountain. The Chief honoured them with a short nod. Chris tried to find an encouraging word for each one of them.

'Is there any news of Joseph Blackdeer?' asked White Ash, solemnly. Grey Mountain shook his head. He'd already told Chris that the police were still holding Tommy's brother.

'You have to forget about that for now,' Chris told them

'What about the Challenge? Has anyone said if we'll be allowed to take part?' Chris almost told them not to worry about that as well, but realised he was being ridiculous.

'They're still thinking about it,' he said. When they had first arrived, the white-haired man from the local school board had told them that the tournament organisers were debating what to do. All that they had decided was that the Iroquois should play their semi-final anyway, while they sorted themselves out.

'Probably hoping we'll get knocked out,' said Grey Mountain, with a secret wink at Chris.

Chris could hear quite an argument going on nearby, and he looked over half-expecting to see Gary Lukas demanding that the officials change their minds. In fact, although The Orchards had arrived and changed into their wasp-striped kit, there was no sign of the millionaire developer. The argument was between the white haired man and the smarmy guy who had bounced up to the podium on the first day (representing the *other* millionaire, the one offering the $50,000 prize money). Today, instead of his blue suit, the guy was wearing an even less tasteful lime green jacket over snow-white trousers.

The competition organisers listened to his angry bleating, but then told him firmly that their decision to make no decision was a firm one. They scampered off to their room in the red building, supposedly to continue their meeting, but mostly to hide from Green Jacket and the media outside.

'Why would he want you guys thrown out?' Chris wondered out loud, watching Green Jacket reach inside his coat for a mobile phone

'Why indeed?' echoed Grey Mountain, with a superior smile on his face

Chris thought about trying to eavesdrop on Green Jacket's call, but by the look of it he didn't get through In any case, for the last few minutes a pack of sirens had been blaring up along the main road Chris would have had to be standing in the guy's pocket to hear anything.

The press were interviewing everyone and anyone who looked remotely connected with the championships or any of the teams. The two referees tried to get started on time, but it was impossible Apart from anything else, hundreds of people were milling around on the pitches, some waiting to watch football, others wondering about the sirens, the rest curious about who might get shot today.

It took 30 minutes for the police to clear the area enough for the games to get started By the time the two matches kicked off, the atmosphere at Indy Sports was like an FA Cup Final.

One thing about the two matches being played at the same time and on two nearby pitches was that it was easy to keep tabs on what was happening in both A few spectators tried to find spaces on the middle of the three lower pitches from where they could keep an eye on both the end ones, where

the games were being played. It was such a good idea that a couple of thousand people tried the same trick, after which no-one could see much of anything.

However, during those first twenty minutes, when he had a clear view across to the other game, Chris knew it had already started to go The Orchards' way. They'd scored once already, and the team from Gary (who called themselves the Giants, but who were all about half a metre tall) were giving away some risky free kicks around the edge of the area that threatened to make the situation worse.

The Iroquois, meanwhile, had started tamely against the Aztecs. White Ash was trying to get the five-man midfield to work as a unit, but there were times when all of them went forward or all of them went back. As Chris had planned, they were stifling the Aztecs in the middle of the park, but they were showing little creativity of their own.

At the back, Jay looked ill at ease, unnerved by playing out of position on a big occasion. Peru had yet to put him under much pressure, but it was only a matter of time.

Chris called a few instructions from the sidelines, particularly to Crazy Fox who was clearly determined to score one glorious goal to win the game, without bothering to wonder if his antics might not have led to two or three simpler chances. Some of the spectators were pointing at Chris, wondering who he was. It made him feel very self-conscious.

'Keep your mind on the game,' whispered John Stephens from beside Chris on the bench.

'I wish Joseph was here,' sighed Chris.

'Well, he's not, so this is your team now. You have to help them get the most out of themselves.'

Chris watched the next few minutes in silence, trying to judge the tempo of the game. It was odd, seeing it all from the sidelines and not being out there in the thick of things.

'How do you think it's going?' he asked his father. 'Did I do the right thing, do you think, switching them to this sweeper system?'

'It worked for the Colts, didn't it?' his father replied. He had clearly heard all about the week before (which seemed like a lifetime ago to Chris). 'Jay just needs to settle down. His trouble is, he expects everything to happen quickly. A sweeper needs to use his eyes and his brains much more than his feet.'

Chris wondered what Grey Mountain thought of the way things had started. The Chief had disappeared just before kick-off. Chris assumed that he had gone to talk to the organisers, but in fact he seemed to be holding a conversation with a man Chris hadn't seen before.

As Grey Mountain went back to the bench, the crowd parted to let him through, as if they were frightened he might touch them. Some of them were making that peculiar hissing noise. Chris grinned as he saw the Iroquois Chief shake his staff behind someone who was a bit slow to move. The snake rattles clattered in the man's ear and he scampered away.

Clearly Grey Mountain wasn't going to let public opinion get to him.

'What's the news?' asked Chris.

Grey Mountain appeared puzzled (one eyebrow moved up slightly). 'I thought you'd tell me,' he said, looking out on to the pitch. 'How are we doing?'

Just at that moment, not too well. The Aztecs had a corner, which Cody Snowbird chased out to meet, missing by a metre. The ball fell to an Aztec defender who had come up to the edge of the box, but he slammed his shot over the bar.

'I meant, is there any news from the organisers?' Chris continued.

'I've no idea. Before the kick-off, the chairman told me they were of the opinion that this game had to go ahead, since they have to find a way to ensure that Peru, Gary and The Orchards all have an even chance of winning if we are thrown out.'

Chris could see what they were trying to do. They could hardly just give the Aztecs a bye before the semi-finals had even started. By playing this match, they kept things the same for all the other teams. If the Aztecs knocked the Wabash Iroquois out, all well and good. If not, well, they could either play the final as planned or throw the Iroquois out and award the tournament to the winner of the other semi-final.

'I don't get it,' cried Chris. 'Why are you guys still in any danger of being thrown out? Why is Joseph Blackdeer still in jail?'

'Running Waters is with him now. I'm sure everything will be sorted out soon.'

Chris wasn't so confident. Wishing didn't make things so. Chris was wishing for a goal for the Iroquois, but the only score of the next few minutes was on the other pitch. Judging from the cries of 'Orchards! Orchards!' from the spectators, Lukas's pet team were 2–0 up.

An interesting thought came into Chris's mind. 'Can't you use some kind of magic?' he whispered.

The corner of Grey Mountain's mouth twitched a little. 'Magic? Whatever do you mean?'

'Come on!' scoffed Chris. 'What was all that about on Sunday night? You banging on that drum of yours, rattling that staff, and Joseph Blackdeer dancing around on the football pitch lines.'

Grey Mountain peered out on to the pitch. Scar-faced Tommy Talltrees had just scythed down the Aztec's right winger and was being given a stern warning by the ref. 'That wasn't magic,' Grey Mountain explained. 'That was ritual.'

Chris failed to see the difference.

'I told you before. Once, all this land was the home of the Native American peoples. The Iroquois roamed from the Ohio River to Lake Erie; from the Allegheny Mountains to the Mississippi.' Chris wasn't sure what all that meant in terms of geography, but he got the point – it was a large chunk of land.

'When the Europeans came, the first thing they did was stake out the land. They put up fences, built walls and ditches. They took all that great stretch of country and broke it into tiny pieces. They took much of the land from us, but even what was left was changed. It had boundaries, edges – lines.'

Chris struggled to understand what the chief was driving at.

'Lines on a map, lines on the ground. They're the magic, Chris. They are what robbed us of what was rightfully ours.'

'So . . .' Chris ventured, beginning to see the point. 'You were – what? Taking away the magic? Removing the spell?' He just about stopped himself from laughing. 'By dancing on the lines of a football pitch?'

Grey Mountain frowned. Chris hoped he hadn't been offended.

'Like I said, we don't do magic. These days, few Native Americans believe in the old ways any more. Half of my own people are baptised Christians. But a little ritual never did any harm. It focuses us on what we lost, and what we need to regain.'

Chris apologised for having been so rude as to find the situation funny. After all he had been through with Grey Mountain, he still didn't understand the old man at all.

'Don't worry about it, Chris.'

Chris wasn't worried – not about that, at least. 'Anyway,' he said, 'we won't be using the top pitch again anyway. If we get through this, they'll use one of the pitches down here for the final, won't they?'

Grey Mountain didn't reply.

Chris looked at his watch. Half-time was getting closer. He made sure all their supplies were close at hand – oranges, bananas and high-energy sports drinks. The game was still stuck in the pattern that had been established early on; the Iroquois were stifling play in midfield and the Aztecs were struggling to come up with an answer. Many of the spectators were drifting away. Chris caught the whisper that many of them believed that this was an irrelevant game anyway, that the Iroquois would be thrown out of the Indy Sports Challenge just as soon as the organisers got off the fence. People were drifting over to the other game, where the half-time score was 3–1 to The Orchards. The crowd over there was already three times the size of the one watching the Iroquois/Aztecs tie.

In the last minute before the break, Chris almost howled with frustration when Tommy Blackdeer split the Aztec defence with a great through ball, which Crazy Fox chased after. He was forced wide, but there was plenty of support coming up. Crazy Fox, though, didn't even look up. Ignoring everything around him, he tried to turn the full back, then hit a wild shot at goal from an impossible angle. The Aztecs' keeper beat it out for a corner which was never taken – the half-time whistle blew.

A chance like that was all it would take to split the game wide open, Chris knew. He wanted to scream at Crazy Fox for his selfishness, but he held back. He had to get them working as a unit, as a team, not pick out individuals for blame or praise.

Whatever it took, he had to use this half-time period to get things right.

Nineteen

'How long?' Chris asked. He knew he had asked the same thing just a few moments before.

'Eight minutes,' his father replied. 'What are the rules in this thing if scores are level after sixty minutes?'

'It's like Euro 96,' said Chris. 'They play 30 minutes extra time under the Golden Goal rule. The first one to score wins. If that doesn't settle it, after thirty minutes they have a penalty shoot-out.'

He sat on the bench, watching the game with his chin propped on his fists. If anything, the Iroquois were playing slightly worse in the second half than they had in the first. Crazy Fox had picked up a knock and was struggling to keep up with the pace (Chris would have taken him off, but Grey Mountain asked that he be allowed to get to the end of the game; a matter of honour, he was told!). The defence was in a muddle. If the Aztecs had been just a slightly better team, they would have scored a couple of goals no bother.

Instead it was 0–0. Some of the people watching the game – even a few supporters of the Iroquois (not that there were many) or Peru – were yawning.

In contrast, things had been really cooking on the other pitch. Gary had made a real fight of it, getting the game back to 3–2. Only in the last few minutes had the superior talent, skill and fitness of The Orchards team finally told. The word was it was now 5–2 and Gary Lukas Jr had a hat-trick.

There were now probably five people watching that game for every one watching the stalemate in front of Chris.

'They were a better team before I got hold of them,' sighed Chris.

'No, they just looked a better team,' came the unexpected reply. 'They wouldn't have stood a chance in this game if it wasn't for what you've done with them.'

'CG!!'

'Hi!'

Chris whacked the American on the back, pleased to see him. He turned to his father, intending to introduce them, but Mr Stephens looked as if he'd seen a ghost.

'This is my dad,' he said, hesitantly.

'Pleased to meet you, sir,' said CG politely, putting out his hand. Chris's father shook it as if he didn't quite believe it was real.

'He knows this Nicky guy, right?' asked the American.

'You can say that again,' laughed Chris. He allowed his father another moment to get over the shock. 'Dad, this is CG. His parents own the hotel back there, the one I was staying at on Sunday.'

Mr Stephens muttered something.

'What was that?' asked Chris.

'I said it's quite a likeness, isn't it?'

Chris turned to face CG again. Over the last few days, he had gotten used to the differences. The slightly brighter sheen to CG's hair, for example. The marginally darker skin.

CG squeezed in between Chris and the Iroquois substitutes. Looking along the line of faces, something else was dawning on Chris too.

'So, what are you doing here?' he asked.

'I thought I'd come and check out the game,' CG replied, but there was a huge smile on his face that showed there was more to it than that. 'All right,' he added, without being prompted, 'I was also hoping you'd be here. Have I got some stuff to tell you . . .'

Chris was intrigued. 'Like what?' he asked.

'I can't tell you,' CG replied. 'I've been sworn to secrecy.'

Chris was determined that wouldn't last too long.

'How goes the game?' CG asked, trying to deflect Chris's attention.

'Last five minutes coming up,' said Chris. 'It looks destined for extra time.' He wondered how his lads were bearing up. Late night and early morning journeys to and from the village were hardly ideal preparation for two hard games in a day, especially after all they had been through.

CG's face was bright with excitement. Anyone looking at

him would know that it had nothing to do with the game.

'Come on, CG, spill it,' said Chris, determinedly.

CG's willpower collapsed, setting a new world record for the shortest secret ever kept. 'OK, OK,' he said, grinning. 'Come back here and I'll tell you.'

Chris didn't think he should leave the game at such a vital juncture, but he was busting to know what was going on. Fortunately, CG was only suggesting they take a few steps away from the touchline.

'Guess who's been locked in his room all morning, unable to get out?'

Chris didn't have the faintest idea.

'Gary Lukas!' laughed CG, trying to stifle the words so that only Chris would hear, but nearly blurting it out to 2,000 people.

'What?'

'Go on, ask me how.'

Chris fought down a moment's irritation. 'OK,' he said. 'How?'

'A snake,' chortled CG. 'He was trapped in his closet by a snake!'

Chris felt his face open in amazement.

'I know!' CG cried. 'Isn't it wild?'

'Where – where did it come from?' asked Chris, although he was sure he knew. Had he been right after all?

'I don't know for sure,' said CG. 'All I know is what my mum told me. Lukas was out all night, apparently. Then, when he got back this morning, he wishes Lukas Jnr good luck and goes to their room. An hour or so ago, there's a call to reception, and the next thing I know there's all kinds of a ruckus going on. We've had the police, paramedics – and some guys from the zoo with this noose thing on a long pole. They finally catch the snake and let Lukas out – and guess who is in the room with him?'

'Just tell me,' sighed Chris, anxious to know quickly.

'Detective Enzio!'

'Enzio!!?' choked Chris, who was finding it as hard as CG to keep his voice down.

CG was almost cracking up with laughter. 'Isn't that the craziest thing? The two of them, trapped in a closet by some kind of rattlesnake! Apparently, every time Lucas' mobile phone rang, it got really aggressive!'

Chris was still too stunned to find it funny Enzio? What was he doing with Lukas? The last Chris had seen, the fat detective was some way off being Lukas's biggest admirer; more than that, he had been lying brained in the back seat of his car, driven away from Thunder Park by White Ash.

How did he get back here?

Why?

Chris looked at Grey Mountain, who was still watching the game impassively If anyone knew the answers, Chris realised, it would be the Iroquois' leader. Which meant Chris might never find out . . .

At that moment, Grey Mountain turned and looked back at Chris There was something close to a smile on his face.

'It looks like it's nearly all over,' said CG. 'Your guys are bushed. They really could do with a miracle right now . . .'

There was little chance of that. Peru were on the attack, and their winger was pushing up along the flank, trying to turn the back. Plenty of players were up in support; the Aztecs were as tired as the Iroquois, but even keener to avoid extra-time.

The cross went over, a looping arc dropping just behind the penalty spot. Cody Snowbird came off his line like he was spring loaded and took off, clawing one handed at the air. Chris almost closed his eyes, sure the keeper was going to miss the ball, but Cody managed to stretch out a little further and tipped the ball down in front of him.

Everyone else was caught standing still or turning, but the momentum of that giant leap carried Cody out of the area He was quickest to the ball, taking it on his chest, sprinting forward another twenty metres and then hitting a fast, flat pass out to Crazy Fox.

After that, everything happened so quickly, Chris almost didn't draw breath Crazy Fox didn't try to do anything flash, he just laid the ball back like a born target man The first player out of the box was Jay Crowmask, running flat out He hit the ball first time as well, a long lob into the other half that had Chris wondering if he'd missed something. The ball was well wide of Crazy Fox; no other Iroquois striker was up in support – who was that a pass to?

That was when he realised Cody was still running.

'What the –?' choked CG.

The pass was much too deep, but still Cody kept going. He ran through the line of defenders. Only one centre back and the Aztec keeper were any further upfield.

'He's gone mad,' sighed Chris.

The Aztec defender was running backwards, head up, eyes fixed on the ball, which seemed to be hanging in the air. At the last moment, the lad half-stumbled, half-jumped, and headed the ball tamely back the way it had come.

Right to Cody's feet.

Chris drew in a sharp intake of breath. Never mind that his injured striker and sweeper were setting up a chance for his goalkeeper, this was the miracle he had been about to pray for. Cody had just a stumbling defender and the (other) keeper between him and goal. This was it, Chris thought, a real chance to settle it. Just run in, and chip the keeper like I showed the others . . .

The crowd sucked in a collective breath. Then, in the same instant, Chris and all 2,000 of them together realised that Cody – still 30 metres out from goal – had looked up and was going to shoot.

'No, you idio–' Chris began.

Some of the others in the crowd were beginning their own cries of disbelief or ridicule in that same moment. None of them had time to finish the sentence they were speaking before Cody drew back his foot and lashed the ball past the Aztec's keeper and into the net.

There was an instant of silence, and then a roar like a volcano.

'–oallll!!!!' screamed Chris. One small part of his mind told him what he had just said – 'No, you idioallll!' – but the rest of him was shouting deliriously. A goal! The goal! The goal of the century!!!

The Iroquois celebrated with wild whoops of joy and a massive scrum in the middle of the field. The subs were jumping up and down on the bench like crazed animals. Chris and CG hugged and pounded on each other. Even Grey Mountain was moved to nod his head and smile a little.

Chris saw that hundreds of people were turning back from the other game, rushing to see what all the fuss was about.

'Too late; too late!!' he laughed.

The Iroquois were in the final.

Twenty

———— ⚽ ————

'Having spoken with the sponsor's representative, and in the light of some public pressure, it is the decision of the organisers of the Indy Sports Challenge that the Wabash Iroquois team be disqualified from the Challenge under Rule 18b, sub-section B. As a consequence of this decision, and in the light of the results of the two semi-finals, it has been agreed to award the Indy Sports Challenge Trophy to the team from The Orchards School, Indianapolis!'

The cheerful, upbeat way that the chairman of the school board announced the decision showed that he thought he was making the right decision, one everybody would support.

But it was met with just a tiny ripple of applause and cheers from just one part of the crowd, all very clearly dressed in yellow and black.

'What a rip-off!!!!' cried CG. A few other people were shouting too.

Chris was too angry to say anything. The weasly guy in the green jacket was slinking away, but he clearly had been a major part of all this. The organisers were shuffling their feet in an embarrassed way, looking at each other as if to say, 'What's wrong with everyone; we thought they wanted the Iroquois thrown out?'

Twenty minutes before, maybe they did. But that one crazy goal had changed everything. Chris was discovering that although it seemed that Americans always thought in straight lines – black and white, left and right – they had a strong sense of natural justice. They didn't like to see anyone get ripped off.

Chris pushed through to Grey Mountain's side. 'You have to do something. Appeal or something.'

Grey Mountain was watching the organisers as they tried to manage a prize-giving no-one was ready for.

'That would not be appropriate,' the Chief replied.

Chris couldn't believe his ears. 'Appropriate? What does that mean? They're taking away your chance to win the competition; your chance to get the money you need.'

Grey Mountain grunted. 'Fifty thousand dollars,' he said. 'Chicken feed.' With that he turned away and walked off through the crowd.

Chris remained where he was, in the middle of the Iroquois team, a tight knot in their blood-red shirts. He could read the disappointment in their faces. A win like that, a goal like that, deserved better than to be thrown in the bin by an unfair disqualification. All around, the neutrals in the crowd were coming to the same conclusion. Chris heard that the team from Peru were planning an appeal – not for themselves, but on behalf of the Iroquois.

No-one minded The Orchards retaining their title – everyone recognised that they were the best team in the Challenge. But they didn't deserve to win like this.

Up on the podium, there was some confusion. The organisers knew that Gary Lukas was the honorary manager of the winning team, but he was still absent. Did that mean that his son, the team captain, should step forward? Or van Zale, the coach? Or should they wait a little longer for Lukas Senior – after all, they were finishing much earlier than anyone had expected.

'They'll be lucky if they see him for a while,' said CG, quietly.

'How's that?' asked Chris.

'Well, when I left the hotel to come see if you were here, there was still plenty of action going on up there. Enzio was pretty freaked out. He was blabbing about all kinds of stuff to the police who were there.'

'What? What kind of stuff???'

'How should I know? They didn't let me that close. All I know is that the cops were talking to Enzio, Lukas and my mum, and that Enzio wa–'

'Your mum? What's she got to do with it?' asked Chris.

CG's mouth curved in a lopsided smirk. 'She was the one who heard Lukas and Enzio calling for help. I don't know what she was doing down there; she must have been listening at the door or something.'

Had she heard something the cops could use to nail Enzio and/or Lukas? Was Lukas spilling the truth to the police. Chris could but hope . . .

Up on the platform, the decision had been made to call Gary Lukas Junior forward to receive the trophy. Then there was another delay. They needed Green Jacket to come forward with the cheque – but there was no sign of him.

That led to another bout of frantic shuffling and whispered conversation. It wasn't proving to be the officials' day. It was possible to argue that it really hadn't been their week.

Another decision. They'd present the trophy and worry about the money afterwards. Some comedian in the crowd shouted that it wasn't as if The Orchards school was short of the odd $50,000 . . .

Gary Lukas Junior stepped up to take the winner's trophy for the second year, holding it aloft. There was some applause, but not too much wild cheering. Everyone thought it was a bit of an anti-climax finishing the tournament this way.

People were starting to drift away. It looked as if the Indy Sports Challenge was all over.

But there were still a few surprises in store.

Twenty-one

'Who's this?' asked CG.

Chris looked up. There did appear to be some movement in the crowd on the other side. He caught sight of a couple of uniformed policemen opening up a lane through the massed spectators, aiming towards the podium. A murmur of excitement was racing through the crowd, reaching Chris and the small group round him long before the cops reached the platform.

'It's Gary Lukas!'

Sure enough, moments later, Gary Lukas climbed the steps on to the small stage. There was a splattering of applause, a few cheers, even one or two catcalls. Mostly, though, people watched his arrival in silence.

'Come for his share of the glory, has he?' asked Chris's father. Chris grinned. His dad had put himself in the spotlight after one of Chris's triumphs.

'The cops must have finished with him,' said CG.

There wasn't time to find out why. Lukas was holding up his hands to get a little quiet. He clearly was about to make some kind of announcement.

'Ladies and gentlemen, if I could just have your attention for a moment. I have something important I wish to share with you.'

A gradual hush spread through the masses in front of the podium. A few cameras whirred and clicked, but no-one moved or looked away. No-one else dared say a word.

'I've just heard that the organisers of the Indy Sports Challenge have disqualified the Wabash Iroquois because of the incident here on Monday in which a detective of the Indianapolis police force was wounded. In doing so, the organisers have awarded the trophy and the prize money to the team from The Orchards school, which includes my own son, Gary Lukas Junior.'

'While all this was going on, I was unavoidably detained ...'

CG made a hissing noise between his teeth. Chris covered his laughter behind his hand.

'... so I may have missed the exact nature of the offence the Iroquois team is accused of. All the same, I have just come into possession of some information which the organisers of the competition did not have, and which must – I feel – influence the decision.'

'Doesn't he go on?' muttered CG.

Fortunately, Lukas was about to get to the point. 'A few moments ago, another detective of the Indianapolis police confessed to the shooting. This means that Joseph Blackdeer is completely innocent of the crime.'

The uproar in the crowd was immediate. Journalists who had been creeping through towards the front suddenly sprinted forward, pushing up microphones and yelling questions. The WISH news team leapt up, trying to get even closer. All around them, ordinary people were turning to each other, trying to share what they had heard so that they could make sense of it.

One small island of people remained calm, though the announcement had caught them by surprise. The Iroquois and their English and American friends already knew the truth, of course. For them, the only issue was what all this meant.

Once again, Lukas supplied the answer. Shouting over the ruckus at his feet, he added one last, obvious fact.

'What this means, of course, is that the organisers – in complete innocence – have disqualified a team for no reason. As I understand the rules, it's not easy for them to change that decision, but if the Wabash Iroquois were to make a formal appeal, I'm sure everyone here would agree that they deserve to take their place in the final.'

More shouting, cheering and wild pandemonium followed. Suddenly, huge numbers of the spectators were looking for the Iroquois, standing on their toes, looking around to try and find them. Those nearest where the Iroquois were actually standing pointed them out, shouting out for Grey Mountain to step forward. Up on the platform, the organisers were holding a very hasty discussion. Chris had no doubt that they would be happy to change their minds.

He was standing near the front of the group, on the fringe of the small huddle made by the Iroquois team. From where he was, he had a clear view of Gary Lukas, who was still up on the platform, looking down. What was he playing at? Chris wondered. The Wabash were down and buried; the $50,000 was out of their reach. Surely he didn't need to do this.

Did he?

Chris knew from what CG had said that Detective Enzio had been blabbing about all kinds of things; it was obvious from what Lukas had just said that Enzio had now confessed to shooting Moran. But how had he done that and not implicated Lukas? How could Lukas have wriggled away from trouble?

It didn't make sense.

Chris could see that Lukas was looking past him, further back into the Iroquois group. Most of the heads around him were turned the same way. They were all staring at Grey Mountain, waiting for him to step forward. The journalists and camera operators at the front were all poised, aiming their attention towards him; even one or two of the Iroquois team were turning in his direction. Slowly, the noise around the old man ebbed away; only those further away were still talking or calling out to find out what was going on.

At the same time, equally slowly, a small gap was opening through the press of people between the Chief and the platform.

Grey Mountain's face was a mask. He said nothing and moved not a centimetre. He was breathing so shallowly that it was hard to believe that he hadn't frozen to the spot.

Finally, when all was silent except for some of the most distant voices. Grey Mountain spoke.

'We will make no appeal,' he said.

A stunned 'Ah!' ran through the crowd.

Gary Lukas was leaning forward, his hand to his ear as if he hoped that all he had done was mishear. 'What?!' he cried.

'We will make no appeal,' Grey Mountain said again. 'The Challenge is over.'

'Wait a minute!' spluttered Lukas. 'What do you mean? You can't walk away from this!'

Grey Mountain hadn't moved. He was still facing the platform, surrounded by a small bubble of space in the middle of the crowd. The TV people were tracking their camera back and forward between Lukas and the Chief, trying to record everything.

Chris was just a few metres away from the old man. He knew Grey Mountain would always be a mystery to him. The way the Chief's mind worked was unlike anything Chris had ever encountered before. Sometimes, he knew, Grey Mountain did things just because they were unexpected; he liked to throw people off-balance.

But this; this made no sense at all.

'Grey Mountain,' whispered White Ash, who was obviously no wiser than Chris. The Chief stilled the midfielder with just a tiny flick of his hand.

Chris wasn't so easy to dismiss.

'You *have* to appeal,' he said, stepping closer. 'After everything that's happened ... how can you not want the final to happen?'

Grey Mountain didn't even look at him, but there was an instant when Chris thought he saw the corner of the Chief's mouth lift, as if he was smiling at some great joke inside. Then he raised his staff and started to walk towards the platform. The last few people in his path quickly stepped aside.

Grey Mountain climbed the steps of the platform slowly. The news teams quickly positioned themselves so that they could catch him and Lukas together for the first time. The property developer was watching Grey Mountain, his face twisted as if he was completely lost. The Iroquois leader didn't glance at his opponent even once.

It was deathly silent. If a pin had been dropped anywhere in the whole state of Indiana, they would have heard it.

'There will be no appeal,' Grey Mountain said for the third time. Finally, he added an explanation. 'The Wabash Iroquois will not ask for any favours. We were disqualified because of what people believed. We will not accept crumbs of comfort just because that belief has been proved false.'

'Crumbs of comfort?' spluttered Lukas, standing just behind and to the side of the Chief. 'This isn't just some compensation you're being offered! You're getting your chance to win the Challenge! It's no different to how things were before the shooting.'

'Isn't it?' the Chief replied, without so much as a glance back.

There was a puzzled, excited whisper running through the crowd. No-one knew what to make of it. Chris felt the same way. From just in front of him, the WISH woman was shouting questions up at the platform, lifting her microphone high to see if she could get some kind of explanation.

Grey Mountain said nothing.

For some reason, Lukas was almost beside himself with frustration about the Chief's attitude. Chris couldn't get over how weird this was – all this time, Grey Mountain had been trying to win the Challenge and Lukas had been trying to stop him. Now, suddenly, Grey Mountain was walking away from a shot at the title and it was Gary Lukas who wanted him in!

'How can you just turn tail?' Lukas shouted, his face red. 'Is it that you know we'd beat you?'

Grey Mountain actually did turn very slightly in the millionaire's direction, his lip curling in mockery. 'We would win,' he said.

'Then prove it! Let's finish this whole thing here and now! Put your boys on the field against my boys, and let's see who is the better team!'

There were small beads of sweat on Lukas's smooth features. Grey Mountain allowed his smile to become a little wider.

'Is that a new challenge, Mr Lukas?'

'Hell, yes!' his rival shouted.

'And if we win, you will abandon your claim to Bitter Lake, and let us buy back the land?'

In that moment, Chris knew what this was all about at last. There was even a moment when he thought it might have worked. But Gary Lukas wasn't the kind of guy who got tricked that easily.

'Oh, no!!' he sneered. 'No way. You want to win that game, you'll do it in court. No, this is purely about the Indy Sports Challenge. I'm offering you a chance to play for the title. Take it or leave it.'

Grey Mountain didn't even hesitate. 'We leave it,' he replied.

Lukas threw up his hands as if to say, 'What more can I do?' He was on the point of stomping off the stage when Grey Mountain spoke again.

'You asked if we were afraid to lose. You said you wanted to prove which was the better team.'

'Yes, but you just said –' Lukas replied, off-balance again.

'I said we would not play merely to decide the fate of the Indy Challenge. Nor will you play to decide the fate of Bitter Lake. But will you play for a different stake?'

Lukas turned back, intrigued. 'Like what?'

'The prize money for winning the championship. Fifty thousand dollars. If you lose, that money is ours. If you win, we will pay you two hundred and fifty thousand dollars.'

A gasp went through the crowd. Chris thought he must be hearing things. It seemed Lukas was struck by the same thought.

'*You* are offering *us* odds?'

'It's only fair,' said Grey Mountain evenly, 'since we are going to win.'

Lukas was both shocked and amused by what he was hearing. His mouth opened and closed like a stranded fish while he searched for a suitable answer. Finally he found one.

'Do you have that much money, old man?'

'It is what we have raised towards the five hundred thousand dollar bond,' Grey Mountain explained.

Lukas laughed. 'Well, I'll happily take that money away from you, you old fool. You're on!!!' He laughed even louder, throwing back his head. 'You must be crazy! I'd have taken that bet if the odds were even! But this way, I get to see my boys prove who are the best, I get to make a tidy profit and I get to walk out of court this afternoon with the Bitter Lake deal all sewn up!!!'

'Only if you win.'

Lukas was too busy laughing to respond to that. 'Give us an hour and a half to get over this morning's game, then we'll be ready for you. Grey Mountain, you just threw everything away. The Orchards are going to wipe the floor with those kids of yours, and then I'm going to drive downtown and wipe the floor with you in court!!!'

Twenty-two

●

'I just don't get it, Grey Mountain,' Chris said. 'I can't see what possessed you to do something like that!'

The Chief looked past him at the swelling crowd milling around on the three lower pitches. They were sitting on the steps of the platform, eating hot dogs Chris's father had purchased from the happiest man in Indianapolis – a guy who'd turned up with a small truckload of fast food and found that half the city was camped out in Indy Sports.

Actually, Chris thought, there was probably one man in Indianapolis who was even happier with the way the day was going. Gary Lukas. As far as Chris could see, the millionaire would be laughing fit to burst.

'I thought eagles had good eyesight,' Grey Mountain said.

Chris sighed and looked down at the floor while he collected his thoughts. The last thing he wanted right now was for the Chief to go all mystical on him; for the first time it was making him quite angry. He waited a moment until the feeling had passed, then looked up at the Chief again.

'We had a chance to beat The Orchards . . .' he began.

'We still do,' replied Grey Mountain, calmly.

'We could have won the Challenge and the fifty thousand you need . . .' Chris continued.

'We still can,' Grey Mountain said, his voice quite light and calm.

Chris took a deep breath. 'Yes, but now, if we lose, everything you have will be gone. Two hundred and fifty thousand! I didn't think you even had that much.'

'I'm sure we do,' said Grey Mountain, his eyes narrowing slightly as if he was trying to count up in his mind. 'Anyway, that doesn't matter. All you have to do is make sure we win.'

'Me?' gasped Chris, still struggling to understand how the

Iroquois Chief could be so calm. They were 30 minutes away from a game that could quite easily wipe out every cent the Wabash had. Yes, they had heard that Running Waters was on the way to the park with Joseph Blackdeer; yes, they had a *chance* to beat The Orchards and get a small part of the money they needed. But Grey Mountain had gambled everything they had on a game The Orchards were surely good enough to win.

And the Chief was still talking as if Chris was responsible.

'Wait a minute!' Chris cried. 'What do you mean, "me"? Joseph will be here in ten minutes. Surely he can coach the last game?'

'Of course,' said Grey Mountain. He finished his food and mopped at his lips with the edge of a paper napkin. 'Come with me,' he said.

'What next?' wondered Chris as he stuffed the last of his hot dog into his mouth and set off after the Chief. Grey Mountain paused to talk quickly with White Ash and Jay, taking a plain carrier bag from the sweeper. As Chris caught up, he turned and walked on, heading over to where the black and yellow hooped shirts of The Orchards were clustered around their coach, listening to some last-minute advice. As Grey Mountain got close, van Zale saw him and clammed up, as if he'd been in the middle of revealing some game-winning tactic to his team. The Iroquois leader ignored him, walking on to where Gary Lukas was huddled in conversation with Green Jacket. They both looked quite disturbed when Grey Mountain appeared silently at their shoulder.

'May I have a word?' the Chief asked.

The WISH journalist spotted the conversation and tried to creep closer.

'What do you want?' asked Lukas. Green Jacket tried to move further away as the camera operator came closer.

'I thought we needed to sort out a couple of details.'

Lukas looked back at him suspiciously. 'Details? What details?'

'Well, for one, which pitch we should play on.' He gestured towards the vast crowd on the three pitches by the red building. 'I think if we try to play down here, it will take us all day to move everyone off the field.'

'So? What do you suggest?'

'Shall we play on the top pitch? The one at the back of the hotel?'

Lukas was clearly trying to think what trick the Iroquois might be playing, but there was nothing in what Grey Mountain was saying but good sense.

'You played up there before, didn't you?' the millionaire asked. 'What, do you think that gives you home field advantage? Ha! Fine, have it your way.'

Grey Mountain nodded, satisfied that this had been sorted out.

'The other matter concerns the exact nature of this "new" challenge . . .'

This time Lukas wasn't so trusting. 'What are you trying to pull, Grey Mountain? The bet has been made. This is a new ball game, totally separate from the Indy Sports Challenge. Don't even think about going back on the arrangements! The trophy is mine — all we're playing for here is the money.'

'A whole new ball game,' whispered Grey Mountain. He paused, then threw the bag to Chris. 'This is yours,' he said.

Chris caught the bag and started to open it. Grey Mountain meanwhile was continuing to talk, his voice a little louder now, as if he was making sure the cameras caught it all.

'Very well, I understand. May I ask what your line-up will be for the game?' he asked.

Lukas was obviously convinced that there had to be a trap in there somewhere. Chris was just discovering that he couldn't make sense of it either.

'Uh —' he began.

'One moment, Chris,' the Chief said, holding up one hand to still the young Englishman. 'Well?' he asked Lukas.

'Are you going to tell me yours?'

'Of course.'

'Very well. Van Zale has just told me that we'll have the same team as finished the semi-final, which means that Thomas Clarke starts the game in midfield, and Billy-Ray Rogers is on the bench. I take it we'll have three substitutes, just like before?'

Grey Mountain shrugged in agreement.

'So,' said Lukas. 'What about your team?' Out of the corner of his eye, he had just noticed that Chris was pulling something out of the bag. Something blood red.

'Well,' Grey Mountain began, 'I really should wait for Joseph Blackdeer to arrive, but I'm sure he'll agree with me. We're going to rest Crazy Fox, and move White Ash up front. Jay Crowmask will play midfield. And in place of Jay at the back . . .'

Chris dropped the bag. He was holding a brand new Wabash Iroquois shirt in both hands, staring at it as if a football jersey was the only thing in the entire universe that he'd never seen before.

Grey Mountain completed his announcement. '. . . we'll have Chris Stephens playing sweeper.'

Everyone was talking at once. Everyone but Grey Mountain, that was.

'Now, wait a minute!' roared Lukas.

'Grey Mountain, I – I –' stuttered Chris.

'Chief Grey Mountain!' called the woman journalist from WISH.

There were quite a few other voices too. Grey Mountain had caught them all by surprise.

'You can't do that!' Lukas roared. 'He's not a registered player!'

'Registered for what?' the Chief asked, looking completely innocent.

'For your team,' roared Lukas angrily. 'The rules say you can only have registered players in your team.'

'*What* rules?' said Grey Mountain. There was now a mischievous sparkle in his eyes. Though he was much older than Lukas, he appeared to be much more energetic in that moment, twirling his rattlesnake staff in his hand.

'This is ridiculous!' Lukas shouted, looking directly at the cameras, as if he was trying to get the audience on his side. 'Look, I agreed to play the Wabash Iroquois – not some team you just threw together. What's to stop me picking anyone I like?'

'I'm not breaking our agreement,' insisted Grey Mountain. 'This is The Orchards vs the Wabash Iroquois. You can pick any of your students; so I can pick any of my people.'

'But . . .' spluttered Lukas, his hand trembling as he pointed at Chris.

'Yes, Chris Stephens is a Wabash Iroquois. Adopted by the tribe. It's all official.'

At least that last speech meant Chris was able to catch up. Now he was starting to see what Grey Mountain was up to, his face split in a broad smile. He took off his street shirt and pulled on the blood-red Iroquois jersey. He was going to have to find a pair of shorts and some boots from somewhere, but after all the magic the Chief had pulled off so far, he had no doubt a few items of kit would be no problem at all.

Chris let his mind slip back to the night before, when he and Grey Mountain had met Running Waters and Chris's father at Bitter Lake. After all the explanations about what had happened to Chris, Grey Mountain had told Mr Stephens how he could help the Wabash win their fight against the development at Bitter Lake. They had gone down to the water's edge and Grey Mountain had performed some kind of ceremonial dance and had painted John Stephens in the war paint of the Wabash Iroquois.

'This makes me a member of your tribe?' Chris's father had asked.

'No, we have all kinds of legal papers for that,' Grey Mountain had explained. 'Running Waters will show you where to sign.'

And then he had leant over and whispered for Chris. 'We just have to do this kind of thing for the tourists . . .'

At the time, Chris had thought this was just Grey Mountain's funny way of saying thanks – of showing how he appreciated everything Chris had done for them already.

'What does being a Wabash Iroquois mean?' Chris had asked. 'Do I get another passport?'

'No,' Grey Mountain had said. 'You only need passports when you have lines on a map; remember, to my people, the land is whole. Now that you are one of us, you have a claim on the whole of America.'

'We can wait for my daughter,' said Grey Mountain to a very unhappy Gary Lukas. 'She has the official papers, adopting Chris into the tribe. I promise you it is all in order. And the boy's own father – an adult – is here if you need any more confirmation. Do you want to speak to him?'

'No!' cried Lukas. 'No, I'm sure you've got it all sorted out. Fine, you can have the British brat in your team. You can have whoever you like!'

He realised what he had said the second after it escaped his lips. His face went quite pale, as if he was worried that Grey Mountain might produce the Brazilian World Cup team from behind the flatbed truck . . .

'That would not be fair,' said Grey Mountain, quite calm and with his normal expression firmly in place. 'We only have one other change to make.'

'Who's that?' growled Lukas, preparing for the worst. Chris was fascinated about who it might be too.

'His name is Amantani. I would have had him in the team for the Indy Sports Challenge, but he goes to another school, here in Lawrence.'

'He's Iroquois too?' muttered Lukas, scornfully.

'Half-Italian,' explained Grey Mountain. 'His mother is my niece.'

Chris laughed so loud he thought he might burst. Of course. He'd noticed that strange colouring in Mrs Amantani's hair and skin. Not Italian at all; Native American. And that meant CG Amantani was – what? His cousin?

Yes, it all made sense now, thought Chris. He was even sure that another little mystery had just been solved for him.

Lukas wasn't enjoying this half so much. 'Is that it?' he growled.

'That's it!' said Grey Mountain.

'Fine. Well, I have to say that I'm less than terrified, old man. If you think some Limey troublemaker and a reject from another team are going to help you beat us, you have another think coming! We are going to whip you, Grey Mountain. We are going to whip you bad!'

With that he turned his back and stormed off. Van Zale, who had watched all the action with the rest of The Orchards team, shook his head and smiled at Grey Mountain.

'Good luck, Chief,' he said. 'May the best team win.'

'I hope so too,' Grey Mountain replied, with a courteous nod in the coach's direction. As soon as the wasp-shirted players had all passed into the distance, he leant over to Chris and whispered: 'I wonder if he has any Native American blood in him?'

Chris was still laughing. He was sure that, by the time Grey Mountain was finished, he could have had everyone in the Indy Sports park adopted into the tribe.

With the possible exception of Gary Lukas, of course.

It was time. They walked over to the rest of the Iroquois team, preparing to transfer their few belongings up to the top pitch. Crazy Fox came over and handed Chris his boots and shorts. He didn't say a word, but just placed them in Chris's hand, then went off to lend a hand carrying their drinks bottles.

Chris looked around at his new team mates. They were all smiling. He wondered how long some of them had known of this plan.

He also noticed something. The others all had plain shirts on, but someone had embroidered a small eagle on the breast of Chris's jersey. It was coloured with dozens of different, tiny threads.

'Your father told me about your superstitions,' Grey Mountain explained. 'Always last on to the pitch; always touch your badge before you run on.' He rattled his staff. 'Honestly, Chris; how old are you? And you still believe in all that superstitious mumbo-jumbo?'

They walked up to the top pitch. As they rounded the lake, Chris saw CG heading towards them, lugging his kit bag. It looked remarkably heavy . . .

'Chief,' Chris started.

'Call me grandfather,' said Grey Mountain, straight-faced. Chris decided to let that one go.

'I know why you've done what you've done,' he said, 'but what's all this about putting me in defence? I've never played sweeper before.'

'Nor has Jay Crowmask.'

'Well, no, but . . .'

Grey Mountain didn't let him protest.

'Chris, what you've tried to do for the team is right, but it is not easy for us to play that way. Perhaps you were thinking so much about how to beat The Orchards that you forgot to look for the strengths and weaknesses of our team. Jay doesn't have your patience; he doesn't have your eye for the game. If this sweeper idea is going to work, you have to play there.'

'But if I play up front, I'll get goals,' Chris insisted. 'I'm good at that.'

'So is White Ash. You'll see; he has been dying to prove to Crazy Fox who is the better striker. All you have to do is keep The Orchards from scoring at the other end.'

A whirl of thoughts stormed through Chris's mind. He tried to shut them out, to focus on the game, but some of them just wouldn't go away.

'Have you had this planned all along?'

Grey Mountain made a small clicking noise with his tongue. 'A plan is something complete; it guides you along the road of life like a map. I like to think that I have looked at each junction as we came to it, and made the right choices.'

Chris thought about the money. He still couldn't see how taking the $50,000 off Lukas was going to save the day as far as Bitter Lake was concerned. All he could think about was how disastrous it would be if they lost.

'I'm not going to let that happen,' he told himself. He was forcing himself to believe it was true.

They arrived at the top pitch. Chris looked across at the buckled fence panel, where Moran had been wounded. Somewhere above it, he could see the window of the room from where he had looked out on Monday morning to see Grey Mountain and Joseph Blackdeer performing their strange ritual. Chris found himself wondering how much Grey Mountain had known back then. Had he been 'preparing' the pitch for that first game, or for this last one?

Twenty-three

'Take him, CG!!'

Chris was sprinting back, trying to keep goalside of the central striker while CG pounded after the winger. Out of the corner of his eye, Chris saw Gary Lukas Junior fade off towards the far post, and he changed his own run to cover the threat.

Their luck was in. CG was just quick enough to reach the through pass a fraction before the winger, knocking it into touch.

Chris slowed, looking around quickly to see where the others were. The Iroquois were coming back into position, getting plenty of bodies back in defence before the ball was retrieved for the throw-in.

'Ash, you take Lukas; Tommy, pick up their number six.'

The Iroquois followed Chris's instructions quickly. The wasp-shirted winger found few openings by the time he returned with the ball.

This was tough, Chris thought as his team mates picked up their marking assignments or moved off after the ball.

From the kick-off, The Orchards had been attacking non-stop. Although the Iroquois were packing midfield, they weren't choking the life out of the other team as easily as they had with Peru. Instead, The Orchards were playing a patient, passing game, opening up their opponents with some good moves up both flanks. Chris was being kept very busy at the back.

The sidelines were crowded with people who had walked up past the lake to come and see the final game of the day. Behind the distant Orchards goal, a band of supporters in yellow and black scarves were roaring on their team; they even had a squad of cheerleaders in the same yellow and black colours, waving pom-poms (or whatever they were called) and singing weird songs. From where Chris was standing (and he hadn't managed to stand very close to the other goal yet), no-one supporting The Orchards needed any encouragement to cheer. They were winning the opening rounds hands down.

Most of The Orchards guys could play a bit, Chris had learnt, but the stars of the team were the goalkeeper (not that he had had much chance to show off in this game), a play-maker named Macafee and – of course – Gary Lukas Junior. He'd tried one dipping long-range shot already that had caused Chris heart failure before Cody clawed it away.

Things did not look good.

In fact, there was only one gratifying thing from Chris's point of view – the neutrals in the crowd seemed to be siding solidly with the Iroquois.

Chris hadn't been sure at first, but now he was. People cheered whenever one of the Wabash made a tackle or tried to push upfield. Just a few hours ago, some of them had been hissing and booing at Grey Mountain, when they thought Joseph Blackdeer had been responsible for what happened to Detective Moran. Now, suddenly, the Chief was at the centre of a mass of admirers and supporters, over on one of the touchlines.

The Iroquois might be getting pummelled on the field, but their fans were making much more noise.

While Chris watched the action and listened to the din coming from every side, Lee Diamondback lost the ball just inside The Orchards' half and the Iroquois were thrown back into defence again.

'Here we go again,' sighed Chris.

It didn't get any better before half-time. Chris worked harder than he had ever had to work before, covering the man going for the tackle, closing off space in the middle, using his superior heading skills to shut down any threat from crosses.

Even so, Lukas was getting the better of Muskrat, who had been trying to mark him. Twice he almost got into a shooting position, but the first time Chris managed to block the shot and the second time Lukas fired it high and wide.

'Damn!' the boy roared as he saw the second effort go to waste.

Chris picked himself off the floor, having fallen making a desperate lunge for the ball. Lukas looked at him, and offered his hand to help Chris up.

He pulled Chris to his feet and the two of them stood shoulder to shoulder for an instant. This guy's nothing like his old man, Chris thought.

'Your luck has to run out, Indian lover,' hissed Lukas.

Chris was left gawping in amazement as Lukas trotted back to the halfway line. So much for that. It appeared that his father's genes had been passed on to Junior after all.

Still, that was no concern of Chris's. His job was to win the game. And that meant making sure the threat from Lukas was neutralised somehow . . .

'Tommy!' called Chris, signalling to the scar-faced, pint-sized midfielder. The boy ran over.

'I want you to swap places with Muskrat,' Chris said quickly. Tommy didn't argue, or even hesitate, although Chris was moving both players out of their best positions.

'Stay tight to him,' Chris instructed. 'And talk to him.'

Now that did get the youngster's attention. 'What was that?'

'Talk to him. Any chance you get. Sing him an Iroquois song or two. It wants to be just loud enough for him to hear, OK?'

Tommy nodded, even though his eyes betrayed the fact that he thought Chris was going mad.

'Oh, and one thing more,' said Chris. 'You know I told you to calm down when you went in to tackle someone? Well, as far as Gary Lukas is concerned, forget everything I said.'

The Iroquois survived. That was about all anyone could say about what was happening on the pitch. They were hanging on by their fingernails.

White Ash was flattened by a very suspicious challenge in midfield that the ref let go. Once again, The Orchards were pouring forward. Macafee called for the ball, then hit a pass first time through to Lukas.

WHAM!!

For the tackle that he committed, Tommy might have been sent off in England. Chris had noted that the refs were a little bit more lenient in the States, but even he was surprised when the tackle cost the short, explosive-tempered Iroquois no more than a booking.

'At least it wasn't a late challenge, ref,' Chris said, as he watched the official write Tommy's name in his book.

'No, in fact I'd say he was about five seconds early,' the ref replied.

Chris had to admit that Tommy had been very keen to get stuck in.

He called the boy over while the wall was forming to face the free kick. 'Take the near post,' he said. 'After the free kick, I want you to go back out on the left.' They both looked over to where Lukas was picking himself up painfully. As he got to his feet, the striker looked to see where Tommy was standing.

'Did you sing to him like I told you?' Chris asked.

'All the time,' said Tommy. 'An old Iroquois war song.'

'Good,' said Chris. 'Tell Muskrat which one it was. Tell him to start singing it from now on.'

This time the young boy couldn't stop himself from asking what was on Chris's mind.

'Muskrat isn't strong enough to worry Lukas,' Chris explained, 'but he didn't like it half so much when he had you snapping away at him. Now, when he hears that song, he might hesitate for a moment, wondering just who is coming up behind him . . .'

The half-time whistle blew. It was the most welcome sound Chris had ever heard. He wondered how he might be feeling after another 30 minutes of this kind of tension.

The Iroquois team trooped off, looking weary. It worried Chris the way a few of their heads were down. The Orchards players were blowing hard too – they had attacked solidly throughout the half – but they looked fresher than their opponents. It wasn't physical, it was mental, Chris knew. The Orchards believed they were going to win.

'You have done well, so far,' Grey Mountain said as they came off. Chris sat down on the bench and took a long pull from a bottle of glucose drink. He needed a moment to recover his breath.

'This isn't going to work,' said Chris. 'We can't win if we can't score; and so far we haven't been into their penalty area more than twice.'

'They haven't scored either, Chris,' the Chief commented.

'We've been lucky.' More than that, Chris knew, they were living on the edge. Asking them to hang on for another 30 minutes was going to be too much. He had to find a way to turn the tide.

'Listen, guys,' he said, making sure they were all paying attention as they took on liquid and chomped through their bananas. 'What's wrong? We've kept them out for half an hour, but you all look like we've come in eight-nil behind!'

'They're running all over us . . .' sighed Crane, one of the tallest of the younger players and one of the slowest. He had been through a rough half.

'It's not that bad,' Chris insisted. 'They must be feeling pretty frustrated after all they threw at us. Pretty soon, they'll start making mistakes . . .'

'But we haven't even been into their half,' moaned Cody (which made Chris worry that Cody might be the first one to try).

'We have to get a goal,' agreed Crazy Fox, standing just behind the goalkeeper. Chris wondered if that was some kind of plea to be brought into the game. Crazy Fox had still been limping ten minutes ago; Chris knew that the tall striker didn't have much left in him. But should he risk it?

'A draw is no good for us,' White Ash concluded. 'We have to win. For ourselves, but also for the tribe.'

The others all agreed, nodding their heads. He knew what was on their minds, though. If they lost, all that money would be gone – every last cent the Iroquois had saved and more. But even if they won, they could still end up losers. $50,000 didn't get them close enough to the target they needed for the court appearance.

Grey Mountain coughed quietly, and all the others fell silent. 'Trust me,' he said, 'we will win.'

But how? Chris wondered.

At that moment, there was quite a stir in the crowd just along from their bench. Chris stood up and peered over the heads of his team mates. People were stepping back to make way for some new arrivals.

Moments later, they appeared. Leading the way was Running Waters, clutching her bag to her chest and smiling triumphantly. People all around her were applauding loudly, cheering and whooping as if the President of the United States was right behind.

In fact, it was someone even more important than Bill.

Chris saw the wheelchair first, then the man in it, then the man pushing it across the grass.

Detective Moran looked pale and a little hollow-eyed, but other than that there was little sign of what he had been through just a couple of days before. His left arm was in a sling, clutched tight to the breast of his jacket, but he was OK, it seemed. Or at least he would be as soon as Joseph Blackdeer finally pushed the wheelchair to the end of the bench.

Grey Mountain was the only one not smiling. However, he looked about ten feet tall and there was a spring in his step as he walked over to greet them.

'You're late, granddaughter,' he scolded.

Running Waters lowered her eyes, but she couldn't hide the silly grin on her face.

'We made a slight detour, grandfather,' she explained gesturing at Moran. 'He was making such a fuss at the hospital they were glad to let him discharge himself.'

'Nurses are even bigger nags than lawyers,' complained Moran. It was clear that he was glad to be out of the hospital, even if it meant coming to a crowded field on the edge of the city.

'Some crowd,' he said, impressed. 'How's the game going?'

'Nil-nil,' said Chris. Moran looked at him blankly.

'What are you still doing here?' he asked. 'Aren't you supposed to be in San Francisco?'

'Chris is playing for the Iroquois,' Grey Mountain explained. 'He's going to help us win the money we need for the bond.'

Running Waters looked up, her smile disappearing. She said nothing.

In fact, everyone was silent for a moment, wondering what to say. It was good to see that Moran was OK, but there was so much still in the balance that it was hard to celebrate.

Grey Mountain was staring at the wheelchair.

'Did you lose the use of your legs when Enzio shot you in the shoulder?'

180

Moran made a grumpy face. He considered standing up for a minute, but Running Waters put her slender hand on his shoulder and pressed him down. Chris could see that she was going to be a much bossier nurse than anyone at the hospital.

'I just have to rest and avoid too much excitement,' Moran said, sighing. 'Sounds like I picked the ideal game.'

As he finished speaking, his eyes flicked up and the smile disappeared to be replaced by a harder, more determined expression. Chris turned round to see what the detective had noticed.

Gary Lukas was on his way over from the other bench.

The crowd were murmuring; the woman from WISH was whispering to her colleague to get closer. Once again, things were coming to the boil.

'Detective Moran,' Lukas cried, as if he had only just seen him. 'What a surprise! I'm delighted to see you looking so well!' He put out his hand. After a moment, Moran shook it quickly. Lukas grunted with satisfaction and looked up to Joseph. 'And I'm equally pleased to see you, Joseph Blackdeer. Justice has been done, eh?'

He offered his hand to the Iroquois manager. Joseph didn't take it.

Lukas hesitated for a moment, then put his hand into the pocket of his coat. 'All's well that ends well, eh?'

'For us, maybe,' muttered Running Waters. 'We'll have to see how things turn out for you.'

'Whatever do you mean?' Lukas asked.

'We know Enzio admitted to shooting Detective Moran,' the lawyer said. 'But didn't he also implicate you?'

After a quick glance at the TV camera, Lukas managed to appear shocked and offended. 'Ms Waters!' he exclaimed. 'Please be careful. I would hate to have to take you to court for slander. Let me take this opportunity to explain something; Detective Enzio may have convinced himself that he was doing me a favour, but my lawyers have already explained to the police that I never gave him any instruction to act in any way whatsoever; nor did I ever pay him money for services.' He uttered a dismissive laugh. 'Anything Detective Enzio says to the contrary is just a figment of his unbalanced imagination.'

'Enzio says you offered him fifty thousand dollars to frame the Iroquois,' Running Waters continued.

Lukas held up his hands as if to say 'See what I mean?', and then replied: 'He's never had any money from me, my dear. Nor would he have. I suppose it's no secret that the Bitter Lake project has caused some ... problems between the Iroquois and myself, but I'm not responsible for Enzio taking matters outside of the law.'

His face hardened. 'And anyone who says otherwise will be proved wrong in court.'

The confident smile returned, though no-one else was laughing. 'Speaking of court cases ... Grey Mountain, why don't you tell everyone just how much you have raised towards the bond you have to post in court in ...' He checked his watch. '... ninety minutes time?'

'My granddaughter has the figure,' Grey Mountain replied.

She did. And she didn't look happy about it. 'As of this morning, we had a hundred and seventy-nine thousand, nine hundred and forty-five.'

Lukas was almost bursting with glee as he repeated the figure. 'So, even if you win our little wager, that means you have just two hundred and thirty thousand. So, even if you win; you lose! No wonder your boys are playing so badly!' He laughed triumphantly. 'And tell me, just how do you intend to pay me a quarter of a million dollars if you lose?'

Running Waters' face fell open with shock.

'Grandfather!'

Grey Mountain held up his hand to silence her. 'We have the money,' he said.

'Oh really!' scoffed Lukas. 'And how's that?'

'I already had a little bet,' Grey Mountain explained. Along with everyone else, Chris narrowed his eyes and listened hard. Just what stunt was the old man going to pull now?

'Another bet?'

'Yes. On the Indy Sports Challenge.'

'On the Indy Sports Challenge?' spluttered Lukas, who was getting very good at repeating what he'd already heard. 'But you didn't win.'

'I know,' said Grey Mountain. 'The Orchards did.'

The truth dawned on Chris just before he heard the words. He pictured the stranger Grey Mountain had been talking to after the semi-final. Something had changed hands, Chris realised. And now he knew what it was.

'I bet on The Orchards to win. One hundred and fifty thousand at two to one. With our original stake that means we now have just under four hundred and eighty thousand.'

There was uproar all around as people heard the news. All through the Challenge, Chris had heard of small, personal wagers on this game or that; $10 here, $20 there. Americans loved gambling. But $150,000 on school soccer? It was hard for anyone to believe.

'But that's illegal! Betting against your own team is against the rules of the Challenge.'

'I know,' said Grey Mountain. 'But we've been disqualified.'

The truth was plain to everyone at last. Lukas flapped his mouth like a stranded fish while the spectators in the crowd gasped and started to do the maths. From further back, people who hadn't heard the story first hand were demanding to know what was going on.

Chris started to laugh. When he got back home and told all this to Nicky and the other guys at school, they'd think he'd lost his marbles.

'So all we have to do now is win!' he cried, crashing his right fist into the palm of his other hand. The rest of the team looked up at him. 'You hear that, guys? All we have to do is win!!'

As the facts slowly sank in, Chris watched their faces brighten. White Ash stood up tall and punched the air. Cody and Tommy grinned stupidly and slapped hands. They had $480,000 in the kitty; they'd get $50,000 for winning. They really could save Bitter Lake.

Gary Lukas was almost bright red with rage. His voice came out as a low, thunderous growl as he spoke. 'This isn't over yet. You have to deposit the money with the judge by 4.30pm. Every last cent. Suppose the money from our bet didn't get handed over before tomorrow? Think the judge would take an IOU?'

'Actually,' came a new voice, 'I don't think that will be a problem.'

Once again, everyone fell silent, seeking out who was about to spring the last surprise.

'Could you pass me my kit bag?' said CG. He waited for White Ash to pass it along. 'Thanks. I just remembered something, Mr Lukas. You left a case at the hotel? I don't mean the one with the snake; we all know what happened to that. I don't mean the one with all your papers in, either: the one Fehnman and Spanish Johnny took with them by mistake. I mean the other one.'

No-one had a clue what CG was talking about. Except CG himself, of course. And Chris. And, slowly, Lukas.

'I found it, Mr Lukas. The third case. And it had fifty thousand dollars in it.'

He reached into the bag and pulled out one of the bundles of cash. 'I guess that means you were the mysterious millionaire all along, huh? I mean, why else would you have had fifty thousand in cash?'

Lukas was shaking with rage. The red in his face had turned to ash white. His hand reached out, as if he hoped he could spirit CG's bag away. Moran beat him to it. Rising from the wheelchair, the detective took the bag from CG's lap and put it on his own.

'Why don't I look after this?' he said.

Lukas let his hand fall. It really did look as if the dream was starting to come true.

'My mum was listening outside the window when Fehnman and Spanish Johnny were talking,' CG explained quietly to Chris, pulling him closer so that they could whisper. 'She called Grey Mountain. Did you know she was part Iroquois?'

'I did, Carlo,' Chris said, grinning. 'Or should I say Carlo Geronimo?'

CG shook his head in disbelief. 'Now, how did you do that?' he asked.

'It's the only Native American name I know,' Chris said. 'Or the only one I knew before Sunday, anyhow.'

'You're a freaky guy, Chris Stephens,' CG said, slapping his team mate on the back.

'You're pretty cool yourself,' replied Chris. 'Seeing as it's too late for lunch, you can spring for tea before we head off for the airport.'

No-one else had moved while the two of them were talking. Lukas was still frozen in place like a statue. Chris straightened and looked him in the eye.

'Like I said,' Chris said for the third time. 'All we have to do is win.'

Lukas was about ready to explode. He knew he was beaten;

he knew that the Iroquois had their destiny in their own hands. There was only one thing he just didn't understand.

'What is all this to do with you anyway?' he wailed.

'Me? Nothing. I'm just here to play football.'

And that was all that was left. There were no more tricks to play, no more surprises. It all came down to what happened in the next 30 minutes.

Last man on to the field, Chris touched the embroidered badge on his shirt and followed the others out. The crowd was roaring. Everyone knew what was at stake.

Lukas was right, of course. This wasn't really anything to do with Chris, even if he had been 'adopted' into the tribe. But for his new friends, this was going to be the last part of the most important game of their lives. And that meant Chris knew it was the most important game he had ever played.

'Make it happen,' he whispered to himself as he took up position. And then, more quietly still: 'We can do this . . .'

Twenty-four

The Orchards came out pretty fired up. They were baffled by what they had heard from the other bench, but Gary Lukas had gone back and had demanded that they give it their best shot. They were the best team; they were still the Challenge champions. For the sake of their pride, if nothing else, they had to win.

Pride is a strong motivator. Chris remembered the end of the 1995/96 season, when Alex Ferguson had wondered if some teams were playing harder against Manchester United than they were playing against other teams, particularly their rivals for the Premiership, Newcastle United.

Along with thousands of fans up and down the country, Chris had read that and had cried out, 'Well, of course they do, Alex!' Manchester United were the best team in the League; no matter who they supported, almost any football fan knew that. But did that mean everyone should love them? Of course it didn't. The fact is that everyone in the country who wasn't a Reds fan wanted their team to beat Manchester United more than any other team (barring a few local derby rivalries, maybe!).

So what was Ferguson doing? The answer had come a few nights later. Nottingham Forest had already lost 5–0 to United at Old Trafford; then Ian Woan hit a screamer that tied the game with Newcastle 1–1. Two points that Newcastle couldn't afford to lose.

Forest's season was over – they had nothing to play for, but their pride had been hurt. Ferguson got what he wanted.

Of course, whether that meant Manchester United were any more popular when they won the title the week after, no-one could say. Chris was certainly hoping that Oldcester

United would give them a good hiding now that they were back in the top flight.

So, Chris knew, playing for pride alone didn't mean The Orchards were going to be pushovers. But the Iroquois came out on to the field with a lot more to lose – and a lot more to gain. After everything they had heard at half-time, they were a changed team.

From the restart, The Orchards went forward in numbers as they had before. Macafee took a pass from another midfield player and looked up, searching for the best passing option. All he saw was Tommy racing towards him, flat out.

Macafee hit a hurried, panicky pass. It went straight to Jay.

Now it was the Iroquois' turn to attack.

They played a short passing game, just as Chris had drilled them. Players ran into space, looking to provide outlets all the time. The wasp shirts buzzed all round them, trying to find the ball but never quite reaching it.

Finally, White Ash saw an opening and drove a low shot towards the near post from just inside the angle of the penalty area. At long last The Orchards' keeper had to earn his keep, taking the ball in his middle as he sprawled on the ground.

Among the spectators, the noise level picked up even more.

That scare caused The Orchards to rethink. They had to keep a few more defensive options open, which meant they could no longer run over midfield in numbers. In the next few minutes, the pattern of the game altered slightly.

The Orchards were still dangerous in attack, but by no means the same threat as in the first half. Twice, as he drifted past, Chris heard snatches of song from just behind Lukas Junior. Twice, as the ball came at him, Lukas looked up at the vital moment and lost his first touch. Chris grinned.

Sixteen minutes gone. White Ash was flagged offside as he broke through the opposition defence.

Eighteen minutes gone. Lukas sliced a half-chance over the bar. Almost immediately, The Orchards were thrown into confusion after a break by Jay and Tommy, and White Ash headed on target, only to see it saved.

Twenty-three minutes. A deflected shot ended up safely in Cody's arms. He gave Chris the thumbs up.

Chris looked around. The Orchards players didn't look

fresher than the Iroquois any more; they looked winded and confused. He could see it clearly in their faces, they couldn't understand how a team they had been swarming all over before the break could be turning the game against them. A couple of them had argued bitterly over some mistaken calling.

They were cracking, but they were still dangerous. Macafee collected the ball in midfield and looked up, checking out his options. Only two strikers were forward of him; Lukas and a ginger-haired kid moving crossways to the left, arm aloft. Both were marked, but not that tightly. Chris was more or less halfway between them both, covering the space between the pair and the goal.

Macafee hesitated – and Chris knew at once that this meant he was going to pass to the ginger kid. If he'd still had any confidence in Lukas, he would have hit the pass early. He knew it was a gamble, but as Macafee drew his foot back to hit the pass, Chris was already sprinting forward. Macafee's face opened in alarm as he saw Chris appear where there had only been empty space, but it was too late.

Chris intercepted the ball at full stretch, then brought it under control with a second touch. He was wide to the right, in the clear. Just a little wider, and twenty metres upfield, CG was moving into the space behind the opposition midfield Nicky territory, thought Chris.

He hit the pass with perfect weight, letting CG run on to it without checking his stride. The full back was already turning, knowing that CG was going to go round him Along the rest of the line of defenders, there was panic.

Chris pushed up, knowing that this was a chance to kill the game, knowing that from any half decent cross he could make it happen. He was running at full pelt, arm aloft and calling. It was a long, hard run, but Chris's speed carried him across the grass like lightning, through midfield. He had almost made up the twenty-metre start CG had before he reached the box.

If it had been Nicky out there, Chris would have known instinctively where the ball would fall. It was like they were telepathically linked or something. In this situation, the near post was favourite; Chris could get up there and squeeze the ball down between the keeper and the post But would CG know this was where to deliver the cross?

Amantani hadn't looked up. Chris was racing into position. He also knew that he was racing *out* of position; if this attack broke down, they'd be really stretched at the back.

But Chris knew this was the best chance they'd get. He could see how badly out of shape The Orchards' defence lay. The Iroquois might never have a better moment than this.

Go for it, Chris decided. And a small voice in the back of his head said: 'Near post.'

Nicky would have hit the pass flatter but with a wicked late dip. CG lofted it a bit more, but the defence were clustered in the middle, watching White Ash and Jay, so there was no-one there but Chris as the ball came down.

He met it with a practised flick of his head, perfectly balanced. He was four metres in front of the near post, unchallenged. It was going to be a goal from the moment it left his head.

Only it wasn't. He'd directed the ball down, aiming at the goal-line. One second it was an inviting hole, the next a boot appeared and the ball cannoned up off it.

The Orchards' keeper had just pulled off a brilliant save. Chris had never been robbed by a better one.

Unbelievable.

The ball squirted out, hitting Chris on the thigh as he landed. He was almost on the goal-line himself now; almost treading on the fallen keeper. The ball was underneath his foot.

I can still do this! Chris thought, but he knew it wasn't going to work. He was off-balance; the keeper's body blocked the ground and two defenders were streaking towards him.

He felt a moment of desperation deep in his guts, like this was the only chance there would be, like he was the only one who could make it happen. In that moment he wanted to shoot, even if he would have to shovel the keeper out of the way first.

In the next instant, though, he flicked the ball sideways off his right instep, the ball actually passing behind his left ankle as it flew across the goal.

Heads turned like cracking whips, trying to see what this sudden change of direction meant. Almost all the defenders were frozen, or had committed themselves to throwing their bodies in Chris's path.

Alone on the penalty spot, White Ash met the ball as it bobbled over the grass. It occurred to Chris like a flash of lightning that this was the very same penalty spot on which Joseph Blackdeer had been dancing three nights before. And he remembered the rest of the dance. A dash along the right wing, a funny little jink on the edge of the six-yard box.

Had Blackdeer been 'rehearsing' the goal? Chris wondered. He knew he would never find out for sure.

And who cared anyway? Chris watched as White Ash lashed the ball into the back of the net and leapt high up into the air, punching at the sky.

Ten minutes later, the fat lady started singing. The ref's final blast was greeted by a roar from the onlookers which must have made people in England turn round to see where the noise was coming from. Hundreds of baseball caps went sailing into the air. The Iroquois fell on top of each other in a heap. The most recent member of the tribe wasn't sure how far down the pile he was and he just didn't care.

The next twenty minutes were just a blur to Chris. After the mountain made by the Wabash players had slowly untangled, they made their way to the sidelines. Chris didn't see any of The Orchards' players and by the time he looked for him, Lukas was gone. Only Tony van Zale went over to shake his hand.

'You played a great game,' the former NFL player said.

'Thanks,' Chris gasped. 'Your guys are a great team. You should be proud of them.'

Van Zale twitched his mouth as if he might offer a different opinion, but didn't. Instead he said: 'I guess I should get some videos of this Oldcester United bunch, huh? That's who you play for, right?'

Chris touched his hand to the embroidered badge on his shirt. He took a moment to savour what he had just done.

'That's right,' he replied.

Van Zale smiled. 'I'll watch for your name in the papers.'

Chris thanked him again. Then he found himself asking for a favour. 'Could I get some baseball caps like yours? Some friends of mine would think they were really neat.'

Van Zale took his cap off and looked at it. 'You got friends who support the Indianapolis Colts?' he said, clearly disbelieving it.

'Kind of,' Chris said. But he knew that when they got their gift, his former team mates at Riverside would be knocked out.

Van Zale put his own cap on Chris's head. 'I'll have some more sent over,' he said. He slapped Chris on the shoulder again and went off after his team.

The Iroquois were singing. Chris had no idea what they were singing about. He went over and taught them 'Ee-aye-addio, we won the cup.'

'Ee-aye-addio?' asked Grey Mountain. 'That's Iroquois!'

'What?' cried Chris.

'Sure . . .' said Grey Mountain. 'It means the eagle has landed!' And his face split into a wide grin.

The celebrations had to be cut short, of course. Grey Mountain and Running Waters had an appointment across town.

'Before we go,' the Chief said, 'I have to give you this.'

He handed Chris's father two airline ticket envelopes. Two first-class tickets from Indianapolis to San Francisco; two undated first-class tickets from San Francisco to London.

'You deserve it,' the Chief said. 'And we have a little money left over, even after we give the judge the five hundred thousand bond.'

Running Waters broke in. 'I've spoken to your boss, John. Told him how important it is that you both stay in the USA for another ten days while we get all the legal formalities sorted. He's pretty cool about the idea.'

'She's even managed to persuade Bob Goodman to meet you at the airport . . .' Grey Mountain added.

'I don't know what to say,' said Mr Stephens. 'Good luck with everything in court.'

'It'll be fine!' laughed Running Waters. 'I think we'll get the money back pretty soon too. After what happened today, I bet Lukas gives up on the Bitter Lake idea altogether.'

'You'll be able to buy the land yourself!' cried Chris.

'That's if I can stop grandfather gambling it all away on a horse race,' the lawyer observed.

They had to go. Chris and Grey Mountain hugged.

'Keep the shirt,' said the Chief.

'You were never going to get it back anyway,' Chris replied.

'So long, Tall Eagle,' the Chief said.

'So long, Chief,' said Chris. 'Listen, why don't you come to England one day. We'll get you adopted by our tribe.'

'Or at least you can join the Oldcester United Supporters Club,' his father said.

They said another round of goodbyes. Finally, Running Waters prised her grandfather away and they set off to find her jeep.

CG wandered over. Chris was watching the Chief depart, a solid lump in his throat.

'Want to come and claim your free dinner?' CG asked.

'Sure . . .' whispered Chris. Then he gestured at the celebrating Iroquois, who were now dancing on the back of the flatbed.

'Can I bring a few friends?'

Twenty-five

Hours later, Chris was still laughing when three men walked into the hotel dining room.

'Now this is completely unbelievable,' said Chris.

'There he is!' said Alan Shearer. He wandered over, watching all the celebrations at the tables on either side and beaming with glee. Behind him, Uri Geller's face was quite sombre.

'I bet him a fiver it would be you,' Shearer explained. 'We just arrived to film the next part of the video in Indianapolis tomorrow, and I heard people talking about this English kid who'd helped a Red Indian tribe beat a posh school. They were talking about it as if it was the game of the century, and I bet Uri that it would be you.'

Uri was frowning, partly because he didn't like coming second to a footballer (even an England striker) in a looking-into-the-future contest, but mostly because the Iroquois were taking it in turns to bend spoons in their hands.

'Don't ever take up magic,' he said, looking back at Chris, 'or I may have to get you arrested.' Then his face cracked into a wide smile. 'Hey, do you think this lot would agree to appear in our training video?'

'Sure,' said Chris. 'But watch out for their lawyer – she's really tough.'

Bringing up the rear, John Motson was looking around at the continuing celebrations.

'I take it we missed a good game,' he said.

'You bet,' said Chris. 'It was quite remarkable.'

The stories so far. Other books in the Team Mates series (in order):

WE NEED YOUR HELP . . .

to ensure that we bring you the books you want –

– and no stamp required!

All you have to do is complete the attached questionnaire and return it to us. The information you provide will help us to keep publishing the books you want to read. The completed form will also give us a better picture of who reads the Team Mates books and will help us continue marketing these books successfully.

TEAM MATES QUESTIONNAIRE

*Please **circle** the answer that applies to you and add more information where necessary.*

SECTION ONE: ABOUT YOU

1.1   Are you?

         Male / Female

1.2   How old are you? .... years

1.3   Which other Team Mates books have you read?

         Overlap
         The Keeper
         Foul!
         Giant Killers
         Offside

1 4 What do you spend most of your pocket money on?
     (Please give details.)

     Books _____

     _____

     Magazines _____

     _____

     Toys _____

     _____

     Computer games _____

     _____

     Other _____

     _____

1 5 Do you play football?
     Yes / No

1.6 Which football team do you support, if any?

     _____

1.7 Who is your favourite football player, if you have one?

     _____

SECTION TWO: ABOUT THE BOOKS

2.1 Where do you buy your Team Mates book/s from?
     W H Smith
     John Menzies
     Waterstones
     Dillons
     Books Etc
     A supermarket (say which one) _____
     A newsagent (say which one) _____
     Other _____

2.2   Which is your favourite Team Mates story and what do
      you like most about it?

      _____
      _____
      _____

2.3   How did you find out about Team Mates books?
              Friends
              Magazine
              Store display
              Gift
              Other _____

2.4   Would you like to know more about the Team Mates
      series of books?
              Yes / No

      If yes, would you like to receive more information
      direct from Virgin Publishing?
              Yes / No

      If yes, please fill in your name and address below:

      _____
      _____
      _____
      _____

2.5   What do you find exciting and interesting about the
      Team Mates stories?

      _____
      _____
      _____

SECTION THREE: ADDITIONAL INFORMATION

3.1   Are there any other comments about Team Mates you
       would like to make?

_____

_____

_____

_____

---

*Thank you for completing this questionnaire. Now tear it out of
the book – carefully! – put it in an envelope and send it to:*

Team Mates
FREEPOST LON 3453
London
W10 5BR

No stamp is required if you are resident in the UK.